MISS MAPP

MISS MAPP

E. F. BENSON

WILDSIDE PRESS

MISS MAPP

Published in 2008 by Wildside Press.
www.wildsidepress.com

PREFACE

I lingered at the window of the garden-room from which Miss Mapp so often and so ominously looked forth. To the left was the front of her house, straight ahead the steep cobbled way, with a glimpse of the High Street at the end, to the right the crooked chimney and the church.

The street was populous with passengers, but search as I might, I could see none who ever so remotely resembled the objects of her vigilance.

E. F. Benson.
Lamb House, Rye.

CHAPTER I

Miss Elizabeth Mapp might have been forty, and she had taken advantage of this opportunity by being just a year or two older. Her face was of high vivid colour and was corrugated by chronic rage and curiosity; but these vivifying emotions had preserved to her an astonishing activity of mind and body, which fully accounted for the comparative adolescence with which she would have been credited anywhere except in the charming little town which she had inhabited so long. Anger and the gravest suspicions about everybody had kept her young and on the boil.

She sat, on this hot July morning, like a large bird of prey at the very convenient window of her garden-room, the ample bow of which formed a strategical point of high value. This garden-room, solid and spacious, was built at right angles to the front of her house, and looked straight down the very interesting street which debouched at its lower end into the High Street of Tilling. Exactly opposite her front door the road turned sharply, so that as she looked out from this projecting window, her own house was at right angles on her left, the street in question plunged steeply downwards in front of her, and to her right she commanded an uninterrupted view of its further course which terminated in the disused graveyard surrounding the big Norman church. Anything of interest about the church, however, could be gleaned from a guide-book, and Miss Mapp did not occupy herself much with such coldly venerable topics. Far more to her mind was the fact that between the church and her strategic window was the cottage in which her gardener lived, and she could thus see, when not otherwise engaged, whether he went home before twelve, or failed to get back to her garden again by one, for he had to cross the street in front of her very eyes. Similarly she could observe whether any of his abandoned family ever came out from her garden door weighted with suspicious baskets, which might contain smuggled vegetables. Only yesterday morning she had hurried forth with a dangerous smile to intercept a laden urchin, with inquiries as to what was in "that nice basket." On that occasion that nice basket had proved to contain a strawberry net which was being sent for repair to the gardener's wife; so there was nothing more to be done except verify its return. This she did from a side window of the garden-room which commanded the strawberry beds; she could sit quite close to that, for it was screened by the large-leaved branches of a fig-tree and she could spy unseen.

Otherwise this road to the right leading up to the church was of no great importance (except on Sunday morning, when she could get a practically complete list of those who attended Divine Service), for no one of real interest lived in the humble dwellings which lined it. To the left was the front of her own house at right angles to the strategic window, and with regard to that a good many useful observations might be, and were, made. She could, from behind a curtain negligently half-drawn across the side of the window nearest the house, have an eye on her housemaid at work, and notice if she leaned out of a window, or made remarks to a friend passing in the street, or waved salutations with a duster. Swift upon such discoveries, she would execute a flank march across the few steps of garden and steal into the house, noiselessly ascend the stairs, and catch the offender red-handed at this public dalliance. But all such domestic espionage to right and left was flavourless and insipid compared to the tremendous discoveries which daily and hourly awaited the trained observer of the street that lay directly in front of her window.

There was little that concerned the social movements of Tilling that could not be proved, or at least reasonably conjectured, from Miss Mapp's eyrie. Just below her house on the left stood Major Flint's residence, of Georgian red brick like her own, and opposite was that of Captain Puffin. They were both bachelors, though Major Flint was generally supposed to have been the hero of some amazingly amorous adventures in early life, and always turned the subject with great abruptness when anything connected with duelling was mentioned. It was not, therefore, unreasonable to infer that he had had experiences of a bloody sort, and colour was added to this romantic conjecture by the fact that in damp, rheumatic weather his left arm was very stiff, and he had been known to say that his wound troubled him. What wound that was no one exactly knew (it might have been anything from a vaccination mark to a sabre-cut), for having said that his wound troubled him, he would invariably add: "Pshaw! that's enough about an old campaigner"; and though he might subsequently talk of nothing else except the old campaigner, he drew a veil over his old campaigns. That he had seen service in India was, indeed, probable by his referring to lunch as tiffin, and calling to his parlour-maid with the ejaculation of "Qui-hi." As her name was Sarah, this was clearly a reminiscence of days in bungalows. When not in a rage, his manner to his own sex was bluff and hearty; but whether in a rage or not, his manner to the fairies, or lovely woman, was gallant and pompous in the extreme. He certainly had a lock of hair in a small gold specimen case on his watch-chain, and had been seen to kiss it when, rather carelessly, he thought that he was unobserved.

Miss Mapp's eye, as she took her seat in her window on this sunny July morning, lingered for a moment on the Major's house, before she proceeded to give a disgusted glance at the pictures on the back page of her morning illustrated paper, which chiefly represented young women dancing in rings in the surf, or lying on the beach in attitudes which Miss Mapp would have scorned to adjust herself to. Neither the Major nor Captain Puffin were very early risers, but it was about time that the first signals of animation might be expected. Indeed, at this moment, she quite distinctly heard that muffled roar which to her experienced ear was easily interpreted to be "Qui-hi!"

"So the Major has just come down to breakfast," she mechanically inferred, "and it's close on ten o'clock. Let me see: Tuesday, Thursday, Saturday — Porridge morning."

Her penetrating glance shifted to the house exactly opposite to that in which it was porridge morning, and even as she looked a hand was thrust out of a small upper window and deposited a sponge on the sill. Then from the inside the lower sash was thrust firmly down, so as to prevent the sponge from blowing away and falling into the street. Captain Puffin, it was therefore clear, was a little later than the Major that morning. But he always shaved and brushed his teeth before his bath, so that there was but a few minutes between them.

General manœuvres in Tilling, the gradual burstings of fluttering life from the chrysalis of the night, the emergence of the ladies of the town with their wicker-baskets in their hands for housekeeping purchases, the exodus of men to catch the 11.20 a.m. steam-tram out to the golf links, and other first steps in the duties and diversions of the day, did not get into full swing till half-past ten, and Miss Mapp had ample time to skim the headlines of her paper and indulge in chaste meditations about the occupants of these two houses, before she need really make herself alert to miss nothing. Of the two, Major Flint, without doubt, was the more attractive to the feminine sense; for years Miss Mapp had tried to cajole him into marrying her, and had not nearly finished yet. With his record of adventure, with the romantic reek of India (and camphor) in the tiger-skin of the rugs that strewed his hall and surged like a rising tide up the wall, with his haughty and gallant manner, with his loud pshawings and sniffs at "nonsense and balderdash," his thumpings on the table to emphasize an argument, with his wound and his prodigious swipes at golf, his intolerance of any who believed in ghosts, microbes or vegetarianism, there was something dashing and risky about him; you felt that you were in the presence of some hot coal straight from the furnace of creation. Captain Puffin, on the other hand, was of clay so different that he could hardly be considered to be made of clay at all. He was lame and short and meagre, with strings of peaceful beads and Papuan aprons in his hall instead of wild tiger-skins, and had a jerky, inattentive manner and a high pitched voice. Yet to Miss Mapp's mind there was something behind his unimpressiveness that had a mysterious quality — all the more so, because nothing of it appeared on the surface. Nobody could call Major Flint, with his bawlings and his sniffings, the least mysterious. He laid all his loud cards on the table, great hulking kings and aces. But Miss Mapp felt far from sure that Captain Puffin did not hold a joker which would some time come to light. The idea of being Mrs. Puffin was not so attractive as the other, but she occasionally gave it her remote consideration.

Yet there was mystery about them both, in spite of the fact that most of their movements were so amply accounted for. As a rule, they played golf together in the morning, reposed in the afternoon, as could easily be verified by anyone standing on a still day in the road between their houses and listening to the loud and rhythmical breathings that fanned the tranquil air, certainly went out to tea-parties afterwards and played bridge till dinner-time; or if no such entertainment was proffered them, occupied arm-chairs at the county club, or laboriously amassed a hundred at billiards. Though tea-parties were profuse, dining out was very rare at Tilling; Patience or a jig-saw puzzle occupied the hour or two that intervened between domestic supper and bed-time; but again and again, Miss Mapp had seen lights burning in the sitting-room of those two neighbours at an hour when such lights as were still in evidence at Tilling were strictly confined to bedrooms, and should, indeed, have been extinguished there. And only last week, being plucked from slumber by some unaccountable indigestion (for which she blamed a small green apple), she had seen at no less than twelve-thirty in the morning the lights in Captain Puffin's sitting-room still shining through the blind. This had excited her so much that at risk of toppling into the street, she had craned her neck from her window, and observed a similar illumination in the house of Major Flint. They were not together then, for in that case any prudent householder (and God knew that they both of them scraped and saved enough, or, if He didn't know, Miss Mapp did) would have quenched his own lights, if he were talking to his friend in his friend's house. The next night, the pangs of indigestion having completely vanished, she set her alarum clock at the same timeless hour, and had observed exactly the same phenomenon. Such late hours, of course, amply accounted for these late breakfasts; but why, so Miss Mapp pithily asked herself, why these late hours? Of course they both kept summer-time, whereas most of Tilling utterly refused (except when going by train) to alter their watches because Mr. Lloyd George told them to; but even allowing for that . . . then she perceived that summer-time made it later than ever for its adherents, so that was no excuse.

Miss Mapp had a mind that was incapable of believing the improbable, and the current explanation of these late hours was very improbable, indeed. Major Flint often told the world in general that he was revising his diaries, and that the only uninterrupted time which he could find in this pleasant whirl of life at Tilling was when he was alone in the evening. Captain Puffin, on his part, confessed to a student's curiosity about the ancient history of Tilling, with regard to which he was preparing a monograph. He could talk, when permitted, by the hour about the reclamation from the sea of the marsh land south of the town, and about the old Roman road which was built on a raised causeway, of which traces remained; but it argued, so thought Miss Mapp, an unprecedented egoism on the part of Major Flint, and an equally unprecedented love of antiquities on the part of Captain Puffin, that they should prosecute their studies (with gas at the present price) till such hours. No; Miss Mapp knew better than that, but she had not made up her mind exactly what it was that she knew. She mentally rejected the idea that egoism (even in these days of diaries and autobiographies) and antiquities accounted for so much study, with the same healthy intolerance with which a vigorous stomach rejects unwholesome food, and did not allow herself to be insidiously poisoned by its retention. But as she took up her light aluminium opera-glasses to make sure whether it was Isabel Poppit or not who was now stepping with that high, prancing tread into the stationer's in the High Street, she exclaimed to herself, for the three hundred and sixty-fifth time after breakfast: "It's very baffling"; for it was precisely a year to-day since she had first seen those mysterious midnight squares of illuminated blind. "Baffling," in fact, was a word that constantly made short appearances in Miss Mapp's vocabulary, though its retention for a whole year over one subject was unprecedented. But never yet had "baffled" sullied her wells of pure undefiled English.

Movement had begun; Mrs. Plaistow, carrying her wicker basket, came round the corner by the church, in the direction of

Miss Mapp's window, and as there was a temporary coolness between them (following violent heat) with regard to some worsted of brilliant rose-madder hue, which a forgetful draper had sold to Mrs. Plaistow, having definitely promised it to Miss Mapp . . . but Miss Mapp's large-mindedness scorned to recall the sordid details of this paltry appropriation. The heat had quite subsided, and Miss Mapp was, for her part, quite prepared to let the coolness regain the normal temperature of cordiality the moment that Mrs. Plaistow returned that worsted. Outwardly and publicly friendly relationships had been resumed, and as the coolness had lasted six weeks or so, it was probable that the worsted had already been incorporated into the ornamental border of Mrs. Plaistow's jumper or winter scarf, and a proper expression of regret would have to do instead. So the nearer Mrs. Plaistow approached, the more invisible she became to Miss Mapp's eye, and when she was within saluting distance had vanished altogether. Simultaneously Miss Poppit came out of the stationer's in the High Street.

Mrs. Plaistow turned the corner below Miss Mapp's window, and went bobbing along down the steep hill. She walked with the motion of those mechanical dolls sold in the street, which have three legs set as spokes to a circle, so that their feet emerge from their dress with Dutch and rigid regularity, and her figure had a certain squat rotundity that suited her gait. She distinctly looked into Captain Puffin's dining-room window as she passed, and with the misplaced juvenility so characteristic of her waggled her plump little hand at it. At the corner beyond Major Flint's house she hesitated a moment, and turned off down the entry into the side street where Mr. Wyse lived. The dentist lived there, too, and as Mr. Wyse was away on the continent of Europe, Mrs. Plaistow was almost certain to be visiting the other. Rapidly Miss Mapp remembered that at Mrs. Bartlett's bridge party yesterday Mrs. Plaistow had selected soft chocolates for consumption instead of those stuffed with nougat or almonds. That furnished additional evidence for the dentist, for generally you could not get a nougat chocolate at all if Godiva Plaistow had been in the room for more than a minute or two . . . As she crossed the narrow cobbled roadway, with the grass growing luxuriantly between the rounded pebbles, she stumbled and recovered herself with a swift little forward run, and the circular feet twinkled with the rapidity of those of a thrush scudding over the lawn.

By this time Isabel Poppit had advanced as far as the fish shop three doors below the turning down which Mrs. Plaistow had vanished. Her prancing progress paused there for a moment, and she waited with one knee highly elevated, like a statue of a curveting horse, before she finally decided to pass on. But she passed no further than the fruit shop next door, and took the three steps that elevated it from the street in a single prance, with her Roman nose high in the air. Presently she emerged, but with no obvious rotundity like that of a melon projecting from her basket, so that Miss Mapp could see exactly what she had purchased, and went back to the fish shop again. Surely she would not put fish on the top of fruit, and even as Miss Mapp's lucid intelligence rejected this supposition, the true solution struck her. "Ice," she said to herself, and, sure enough, projecting from the top of Miss Poppit's basket when she came out was an angular peak, wrapped up in paper already wet.

Miss Poppit came up the street and Miss Mapp put up her illustrated paper again, with the revolting picture of the Brighton sea-nymphs turned towards the window. Peeping out behind it, she observed that Miss Poppit's basket was apparently oozing with bright venous blood, and felt certain that she had bought red currants. That, coupled with the ice, made conjecture complete. She had bought red currants slightly damaged (or they would not have oozed so speedily), in order to make that iced red-currant fool of which she had so freely partaken at Miss Mapp's last bridge party. That was a very scurvy trick, for iced red-currant fool was an invention of Miss Mapp's, who, when it was praised, said that she inherited the recipe from her grandmother. But Miss Poppit had evidently entered the lists against Grandmamma Mapp, and she had as evidently guessed that quite inferior fruit — fruit that was distinctly "off," was undetectable when severely iced. Miss Mapp could only hope that the fruit in the basket now bobbing past her window was so much "off" that it had begun to ferment. Fermented red-currant fool was nasty to the taste, and, if persevered in, disastrous in its effects. General unpopularity might be needed to teach Miss Poppit not to trespass on Grandmamma Mapp's preserves.

Isabel Poppit lived with a flashy and condescending mother just round the corner beyond the gardener's cottage, and opposite the west end of the church. They were comparatively new inhabitants of Tilling, having settled here only two or three years ago, and Tilling had not yet quite ceased to regard them as rather suspicious characters. Suspicion smouldered, though it blazed no longer. They were certainly rich, and Miss Mapp suspected them of being profiteers. They kept a butler, of whom they were both in considerable awe, who used almost to shrug his shoulders when Mrs. Poppit gave him an order: they kept a motor-car to which Mrs. Poppit was apt to allude more frequently than would have been natural if she had always been accustomed to one, and they went to Switzerland for a month every winter and to Scotland "for the shooting-season," as Mrs. Poppit terribly remarked, every summer. This all looked very black, and though Isabel conformed to the manners of Tilling in doing household shopping every morning with her wicker basket, and buying damaged fruit for fool, and in dressing in the original home-made manner indicated by good breeding and narrow incomes, Miss Mapp was sadly afraid that these habits were not the outcome of chaste and instinctive simplicity, but of the ambition to be received by the old families of Tilling as one of them. But what did a true Tillingite want with a butler and a motor-car? And if these were not sufficient to cast grave doubts on the sincerity of the inhabitants of "Ye Smalle House," there was still very vivid in Miss Mapp's mind that dreadful moment, undimmed by the years that had passed over it, when Mrs. Poppit broke the silence at an altogether too sumptuous lunch by asking Mrs. Plaistow if she did not find the super-tax a grievous burden on "our little incomes." . . . Miss Mapp had drawn in her breath sharply, as if in pain, and after a few gasps turned the conversation . . . Worst of all, perhaps, because more recent, was the fact that Mrs. Poppit had just received the dignity of the M.B.E., or Member of the Order of the British Empire, and put it on her cards too, as if to keep the scandal alive. Her services in connection with the Tilling hospital had been entirely confined to putting her motor-car at its disposal when she did not want it herself, and not a single member of the Tilling Working Club, which had knitted its fingers to the bone and made enough seven-tailed bandages to reach to the moon, had been offered a similar decoration. If anyone had she would have known what to do: a stinging letter to the Prime Minister saying that she worked not with hope of distinction, but from pure patriotism, would have certainly been Miss Mapp's rejoinder. She actually drafted the letter, when Mrs. Poppit's name appeared, and diligently waded through column after column of subsequent lists, to make sure that she, the originator of the Tilling Working Club, had not been the victim of a similar insult.

Mrs. Poppit was a climber: that was what she was, and Miss Mapp was obliged to confess that very nimble she had been. The butler and the motor-car (so frequently at the disposal of Mrs. Poppit's friends) and the incessant lunches and teas had done their work; she had fed rather than starved Tilling into submission, and Miss Mapp felt that she alone upheld the dignity of the old families. She was positively the only old family (and a solitary spinster at that) who had not surrendered to the Poppits. Naturally she did not carry her staunchness to the extent, so to speak, of a hunger-strike, for that would be singular conduct, only worthy of suffragettes, and she partook of the Poppits' hospitality to the fullest extent possible, but (here her principles came in) she never returned the hospitality of the Member of the British Empire, though she occasionally asked Isabel to her house, and abused her soundly on all possible occasions . . .

This spiteful retrospect passed swiftly and smoothly through Miss Mapp's mind, and did not in the least take off from the acuteness with which she observed the tide in the affairs of Tilling which, after the ebb of the night, was now flowing again, nor did it, a few minutes after Isabel's disappearance round the corner, prevent her from hearing the faint tinkle of the telephone in her own house. At that she started to her feet, but paused again at the door. She had shrewd suspicions about her servants with regard to the telephone: she was convinced (though at present she had not been able to get any evidence on the point) that both her cook and her parlour-maid used it for their own base purposes at her expense, and that their friends habitually employed it for conversation with them. And perhaps — who knows? — her housemaid was the worst of the lot, for she affected an almost incredible stupidity with regard to the instrument, and pretended not to be able either to speak through it or to understand its cacklings. All that might very well be assumed in order to divert suspicion, so Miss Mapp paused by the door to let any of these delinquents get deep in conversation with her friend: a soft and stealthy advance towards the room called the morning-room (a small apartment opening out of the hall, and used chiefly for the bestowal of hats and cloaks and umbrellas) would then enable her to catch one of them red-mouthed, or at any rate to over-hear fragments of conversation which would supply equally direct evidence.

She had got no further than the garden-door into her house when Withers, her parlour-maid, came out. Miss Mapp thereupon began to smile and hum a tune. Then the smile widened and the tune stopped.

"Yes, Withers?" she said. "Were you looking for me?"

"Yes, Miss," said Withers. "Miss Poppit has just rung you up —"

Miss Mapp looked much surprised.

"And to think that the telephone should have rung without my hearing it," she said. "I must be growing deaf, Withers, in my old age. What does Miss Poppit want?"

"She hopes you will be able to go to tea this afternoon and play bridge. She expects that a few friends may look in at a quarter to four."

A flood of lurid light poured into Miss Mapp's mind. To expect that a few friends may look in was the orthodox way of announcing a regular party to which she had not been asked, and Miss Mapp knew as if by a special revelation that if she went, she would find that she made the eighth to complete two tables of bridge. When the butler opened the door, he would undoubtedly have in his hand a half sheet of paper on which were written the names of the expected friends, and if the caller's name was not on that list, he would tell her with brazen impudence that neither Mrs. Poppit nor Miss Poppit were at home, while, before the baffled visitor had turned her back, he would admit another caller who duly appeared on his reference paper . . . So then the Poppits were giving a bridge-party to which she had only been bidden at the last moment, clearly to take the place of some expected friend who had developed influenza, lost an aunt or been obliged to go to London: here, too, was the explanation of why (as she had overheard yesterday) Major Flint and Captain Puffin were only intending to play one round of golf to-day, and to come back by the 2.20 train. And why seek any further for the explanation of the lump of ice and the red currants (probably damaged) which she had observed Isabel purchase? And anyone could see (at least Miss Mapp could) why she had gone to the stationer's in the High Street just before. Packs of cards.

Who the expected friend was who had disappointed Mrs. Poppit could be thought out later: at present, as Miss Mapp smiled at Withers and hummed her tune again, she had to settle whether she was going to be delighted to accept, or obliged to decline. The argument in favour of being obliged to decline was obvious: Mrs. Poppit deserved to be "served out" for not including her among the original guests, and if she declined it was quite probable that at this late hour her hostess might not be able to get anyone else, and so one of her tables would be completely spoiled. In favour of accepting was the fact that she would get a rubber of bridge and a good tea, and would be able to say something disagreeable about the red-currant fool, which would serve Miss Poppit out for attempting to crib her ancestral dishes . . .

A bright, a joyous, a diabolical idea struck her, and she went herself to the telephone, and genteelly wiped the place where Withers had probably breathed on it.

"So kind of you, Isabel," she said, "but I am very busy to-day, and you didn't give me much notice, did you? So I'll try to look in if I can, shall I? I might be able to squeeze it in."

There was a pause, and Miss Mapp knew that she had put

Isabel in a hole. If she successfully tried to get somebody else, Miss Mapp might find she could squeeze it in, and there would be nine. If she failed to get someone else, and Miss Mapp couldn't squeeze it in, then there would be seven . . . Isabel wouldn't have a tranquil moment all day.

"Ah, do squeeze it in," she said in those horrid wheedling tones which for some reason Major Flint found so attractive. That was one of the weak points about him, and there were many, many others. But that was among those which Miss Mapp found it difficult to condone.

"If I possibly can," said Miss Mapp. "But at this late hour — Good-bye, dear, or only *au reservoir*, we hope."

She heard Isabel's polite laugh at this nearly new and delicious Malaprop before she rang off. Isabel collected malaprops and wrote them out in a note book. If you reversed the note-book and began at the other end, you would find the collection of Spoonerisms, which were very amusing, too.

Tea, followed by a bridge-party, was, in summer, the chief manifestation of the spirit of hospitality in Tilling. Mrs. Poppit, it is true, had attempted to do something in the way of dinner-parties, but though she was at liberty to give as many dinner-parties as she pleased, nobody else had followed her ostentatious example. Dinner-parties entailed a higher scale of living; Miss Mapp, for one, had accurately counted the cost of having three hungry people to dinner, and found that one such dinner-party was not nearly compensated for, in the way of expense, by being invited to three subsequent dinner-parties by your guests. Voluptuous teas were the rule, after which you really wanted no more than little bits of things, a cup of soup, a slice of cold tart, or a dished-up piece of fish and some toasted cheese. Then, after the excitement of bridge (and bridge was very exciting in Tilling), a jig-saw puzzle or Patience cooled your brain and composed your nerves. In winter, however, with its scarcity of daylight, Tilling commonly gave evening bridge-parties, and asked the requisite number of friends to drop in after dinner, though everybody knew that everybody else had only partaken of bits of things. Probably the ruinous price of coal had something to do with these evening bridge-parties, for the fire that warmed your room when you were alone would warm all your guests as well, and then, when your hospitality was returned, you could let your sitting-room fire go out. But though Miss Mapp was already planning something in connection with winter bridge, winter was a long way off yet . . .

Before Miss Mapp got back to her window in the garden-room

Mrs. Poppit's great offensive motor-car, which she always alluded to as "the Royce," had come round the corner and, stopping opposite Major Flint's house, was entirely extinguishing all survey of the street beyond. It was clear enough then that she had sent the Royce to take the two out to the golf-links, so that they should have time to play their round and catch the 2.20 back to Tilling again, so as to be in good time for the bridge-party. Even as she looked, Major Flint came out of his house on one side of the Royce and Captain Puffin on the other. The Royce obstructed their view of each other, and simultaneously each of them shouted across to the house of the other. Captain Puffin emitted a loud "Coo-ee, Major," (an Australian ejaculation, learned on his voyages), while Major Flint bellowed "Qui-hi, Captain," which, all the world knew, was of Oriental origin. The noise each of them made prevented him from hearing the other, and presently one in a fuming hurry to start ran round in front of the car at the precise moment that the other ran round behind it, and they both banged loudly on each other's knockers. These knocks were not so precisely simultaneous as the shouts had been, and this led to mutual discovery, hailed with peals of falsetto laughter on the part of Captain Puffin and the more manly guffaws of the Major . . . After that the Royce lumbered down the grass-grown cobbles of the street, and after a great deal of reversing managed to turn the corner.

Miss Mapp set off with her basket to do her shopping. She carried in it the weekly books, which she would leave, with payment but not without argument, at the tradesmen's shops. There was an item for suet which she intended to resist to the last breath in her body, though her butcher would probably surrender long before that. There was an item for eggs at the dairy which she might have to pay, though it was a monstrous overcharge. She had made up her mind about the laundry, she intended to pay that bill with an icy countenance and say "Good morning for ever," or words to that effect, unless the proprietor instantly produced the — the article of clothing which had been lost in the wash (like King John's treasures), or refunded an ample sum for the replacing of it. All these quarrelsome errands were meat and drink to Miss Mapp: Tuesday morning, the day on which she paid and disputed her weekly bills, was as enjoyable as Sunday mornings when, sitting close under the pulpit, she noted the glaring inconsistencies and grammatical errors in the discourse. After the bills were paid and business was done, there was pleasure to follow, for there was a fitting-on at the dress-maker's, the fitting-on of a tea-gown, to be worn at winter-evening bridge-parties, which, unless Miss Mapp was sadly mistaken, would astound and agonize by its magnificence all who set eyes on it. She had found the description of it, as worn by Mrs. Titus W. Trout, in an American fashion paper; it was of what was described as kingfisher blue, and had lumps and wedges of lace round the edge of the skirt, and orange chiffon round the neck. As she set off with her basket full of tradesmen's books, she pictured to herself with watering mouth the fury, the jealousy, the madness of envy which it would raise in all properly-constituted breasts.

In spite of her malignant curiosity and her cancerous suspicions about all her friends, in spite, too, of her restless activities, Miss Mapp was not, as might have been expected, a lady of lean and emaciated appearance. She was tall and portly, with plump hands, a broad, benignant face and dimpled, well-nourished cheeks. An acute observer might have detected a danger warning in the side-long glances of her rather bulgy eyes, and in a certain tightness at the corners of her expansive mouth, which boded ill for any who came within snapping distance, but to a more superficial view she was a rollicking, good-natured figure of a woman. Her mode of address, too, bore out this misleading impression: nothing, for instance, could have been more genial just now than her telephone voice to Isabel Poppit, or her smile to Withers, even while she so strongly suspected her of using the telephone for her own base purposes, and as she passed along the High Street, she showered little smiles and bows on acquaintances and friends. She markedly drew back her lips in speaking, being in no way ashamed of her long white teeth, and wore a practically perpetual smile when there was the least chance of being under observation. Though at sermon time on Sunday, as has been already remarked, she greedily noted the weaknesses and errors of which those twenty minutes was so rewardingly full, she sat all the time with down-dropped eyes and a pretty sacred smile on her lips, and now, when she spied on the other side of the street the figure of the vicar, she tripped slantingly across the road to him, as if by the move of a knight at chess, looking everywhere else, and only perceiving him with glad surprise at the very last moment. He was a great frequenter of tea parties and except in Lent an assiduous player of bridge, for a clergyman's duties, so he very properly held, were not confined to visiting the poor and exhorting the sinner. He should be a man of the world, and enter into the pleasures of his prosperous parishioners, as well as into the trials of the troubled. Being an accomplished card-player he entered not only into their pleasures but their pockets, and there was no lady of Tilling who was not pleased to have Mr. Bartlett for a partner. His winnings, so he said, he gave annually to charitable objects, though whether the charities he selected began at home was a point on which Miss Mapp had quite made up her mind. "Not a penny of that will the poor ever see," was the gist of her reflections when on disastrous days she paid him seven-and-ninepence. She always called him "Padre," and had never actually caught him looking over his adversaries' hands.

"Good morning, Padre," she said as soon as she perceived him. "What a lovely day! The white butterflies were enjoying themselves so in the sunshine in my garden. And the swallows!"

Miss Mapp, as every reader will have perceived, wanted to know whether he was playing bridge this afternoon at the Poppits. Major Flint and Captain Puffin certainly were, and it might be taken for granted that Godiva Plaistow was. With the Poppits and herself that made six . . .

Mr. Bartlett was humorously archaic in speech. He interlarded archaisms with Highland expressions, and his face was knobby, like a chest of drawers.

"Ha, good morrow, fair dame," he said. "And prithee, art not thou even as ye white butterflies?"

"Oh, Mr. Bartlett," said the fair dame with a provocative glance. "Naughty! Comparing me to a delicious butterfly!"

"Nay, prithee, why naughty?" said he. "Yea, indeed, it's a day to make ye little fowles rejoice! Ha! I perceive you are on the errands of the guid wife Martha." And he pointed to the basket.

"Yes; Tuesday morning," said Miss Mapp. "I pay all my household books on Tuesday. Poor but honest, dear Padre. What a rush life is to-day! I hardly know which way to turn. Little duties in all directions! And you; you're always busy! Such a busy bee!"

"Busy B? Busy Bartlett, quo' she! Yes, I'm a busy B to-day, Mistress Mapp. Sermon all morning: choir practice at three, a baptism at six. No time for a walk to-day, let alone a bit turn at the gowf."

Miss Mapp saw her opening, and made a busy bee line for it.

"Oh, but you should get regular exercise, Padre," said she. "You take no care of yourself. After the choir practice now, and before the baptism, you could have a brisk walk. To please me!"

"Yes. I had meant to get a breath of air then," said he. "But ye guid Dame Poppit has insisted that I take a wee hand at the cartes with them, the wifey and I. Prithee, shall we meet there?"

("That makes seven without me," thought Miss Mapp in parenthesis.) Aloud she said:

"If I can squeeze it in, Padre. I have promised dear Isabel to do my best."

"Well, and a lassie can do no mair," said he. "Au reservoir then."

Miss Mapp was partly pleased, partly annoyed by the agility with which the Padre brought out her own particular joke. It was she who had brought it down to Tilling, and she felt she had an option on it at the end of every interview, if she meant (as she had done on this occasion) to bring it out. On the other hand it was gratifying to see how popular it had become. She had heard it last month when on a visit to a friend at that sweet and refined village called Riseholme. It was rather looked down on there, as not being sufficiently intellectual. But within a week of Miss Mapp's return, Tilling rang with it, and she let it be understood that she was the original humorist.

Godiva Plaistow came whizzing along the pavement, a short, stout, breathless body who might, so thought Miss Mapp, have acted up to the full and fell associations of her Christian name without exciting the smallest curiosity on the part of the lewd. (Miss Mapp had much the same sort of figure, but her height, so she was perfectly satisfied to imagine, converted corpulence into majesty.) The swift alternation of those Dutch-looking feet gave the impression that Mrs. Plaistow was going at a prodigious speed, but they could stop revolving without any warning, and then she stood still. Just when a collision with Miss Mapp seemed imminent, she came to a dead halt.

It was as well to be quite certain that she was going to the Poppits, and Miss Mapp forgave and forgot about the worsted until she had found out. She could never quite manage the indelicacy of saying "Godiva," whatever Mrs. Plaistow's figure and age might happen to be, but always addressed her as "Diva," very affectionately, whenever they were on speaking terms.

"What a lovely morning, Diva darling," she said; and noticing that Mr. Bartlett was well out of earshot, "The white butterflies were enjoying themselves so in the sunshine in my garden. And the swallows."

Godiva was telegraphic in speech.

"Lucky birds," she said. "No teeth. Beaks."

Miss Mapp remembered her disappearance round the dentist's corner half an hour ago, and her own firm inference on the problem.

"Toothache, darling?" she said. "So sorry."

"Wisdom," said Godiva. "Out at one o'clock. Gas. Ready for bridge this afternoon. Playing? Poppits."

"If I can squeeze it in, dear," said Miss Mapp. "Such a hustle to-day."

Diva put her hand to her face as "wisdom" gave her an awful

twinge. Of course she did not believe in the "hustle," but her pangs prevented her from caring much.

"Meet you then," she said. "Shall be all comfortable then. Au —"

This was more than could be borne, and Miss Mapp hastily interrupted.

"Au reservoir, Diva dear," she said with extreme acerbity, and Diva's feet began swiftly revolving again.

The problem about the bridge-party thus seemed to be solved. The two Poppits, the two Bartletts, the Major and the Captain with Diva darling and herself made eight, and Miss Mapp with a sudden recrudescence of indignation against Isabel with regard to the red-currant fool and the belated invitation, made up her mind that she would not be able to squeeze it in, thus leaving the party one short. Even apart from the red-currant fool it served the Poppits right for not asking her originally, but only when, as seemed now perfectly clear, somebody else had disappointed them. But just as she emerged from the butcher's shop, having gained a complete victory in the matter of that suet, without expending the last breath in her body or anything like it, the whole of the seemingly solid structure came toppling to the ground. For on emerging, flushed with triumph, leaving the baffled butcher to try his tricks on somebody else if he chose but not on Miss Mapp, she ran straight into the Disgrace of Tilling and her sex, the suffragette, post-impressionist artist (who painted from the nude, both male and female), the socialist and the Germanophil, all incarnate in one frame. In spite of these execrable antecedents, it was quite in vain that Miss Mapp had tried to poison the collective mind of Tilling against this Creature. If she hated anybody, and she undoubtedly did, she hated Irene Coles. The bitterest part of it all was that if Miss Coles was amused at anybody, and she undoubtedly was, she was amused at Miss Mapp.

Miss Coles was strolling along in the attire to which Tilling generally had got accustomed, but Miss Mapp never. She had an old wide-awake hat jammed down on her head, a tall collar and stock, a large loose coat, knickerbockers and grey stockings. In her mouth was a cigarette, in her hand she swung the orthodox wicker-basket. She had certainly been to the other fishmonger's at the end of the High Street, for a lobster, revived perhaps after a sojourn on the ice, by this warm sun, which the butterflies and the swallows had been rejoicing in, was climbing with claws and waving legs over the edge of it.

Irene removed her cigarette from her mouth and did something in the gutter which is usually associated with the floor of third-class smoking carriages. Then her handsome, boyish face, more boyish because her hair was closely clipped, broke into a broad grin.

"Hullo, Mapp!" she said. "Been giving the tradesmen what for on Tuesday morning?"

Miss Mapp found it extremely difficult to bear this obviously insolent form of address without a spasm of rage. Irene called her Mapp because she chose to, and Mapp (more bitterness) felt it wiser not to provoke Coles. She had a dreadful, humorous tongue, an indecent disregard of public or private opinion, and her gift of mimicry was as appalling as her opinion about the Germans. Sometimes Miss Mapp alluded to her as "quaint Irene," but that was as far as she got in the way of reprisals.

"Oh, you sweet thing!" she said. "Treasure!"

Irene, in some ghastly way, seemed to take note of this. Why men like Captain Puffin and Major Flint found Irene "fetching" and "killing" was more than Miss Mapp could understand, or wanted to understand.

Quaint Irene looked down at her basket.

"Why, there's my lunch going over the top like those beastly British Tommies," she said, "Get back, love."

Miss Mapp could not quite determine whether "love" was a sarcastic echo of "Treasure." It seemed probable.

"Oh, what a dear little lobster," she said. "Look at his sweet claws."

"I shall do more than look at them soon," said Irene, poking it into her basket again. "Come and have tiffin, qui-hi, I've got to look after myself to-day."

"What has happened to your devoted Lucy?" asked Miss Mapp. Irene lived in a very queer way with one gigantic maid, who, but for her sex, might have been in the Guards.

"Ill. I suspect scarlet-fever," said Irene. "Very infectious, isn't it? I was up nursing her all last night."

Miss Mapp recoiled. She did not share Major Flint's robust views about microbes.

"But I hope, dear, you've thoroughly disinfected —"

"Oh, yes. Soap and water," said Irene. "By the way, are you Poppiting this afternoon?"

"If I can squeeze it in," said Miss Mapp.

"We'll meet again, then. Oh —"

"Au reservoir," said Miss Mapp instantly.

"No; not that silly old chestnut!" said Irene. "I wasn't going to say that. I was only going to say: 'Oh, do come to tiffin.' You and me and the lobster. Then you and me. But it's a bore about Lucy. I was painting her. Fine figure, gorgeous legs. You wouldn't like to sit for me till she's well again?"

Miss Mapp gave a little squeal and bolted into her dressmaker's. She always felt battered after a conversation with Irene, and needed kingfisher blue to restore her.

CHAPTER II

There is not in all England a town so blatantly picturesque as Tilling, nor one, for the lover of level marsh land, of tall reedy dykes, of enormous sunsets and rims of blue sea on the horizon, with so fortunate an environment. The hill on which it is built rises steeply from the level land, and, crowned by the great grave church so conveniently close to Miss Mapp's residence, positively consists of quaint corners, rough-cast and timber cottages, and mellow Georgian fronts. Corners and quaintnesses, gems, glimpses and bits are an obsession to the artist, and in consequence, during the summer months, not only did the majority of its inhabitants turn out into the cobbled ways with sketching-blocks, canvases and paintboxes, but every morning brought into the town charabancs from neighbouring places loaded with passengers, many of whom joined the artistic residents, and you would have thought (until an inspection of their productions convinced you of the contrary) that some tremendous outburst of Art was rivalling the Italian Renaissance. For those who were capable of tackling straight lines and the intricacies of perspective there were the steep cobbled streets of charming and irregular architecture, while for those who rightly felt themselves colourists rather than architectural draughtsmen, there was the view from the top of the hill over the marshes. There, but for one straight line to mark the horizon (and that could easily be misty) there were no petty conventionalities in the way of perspective, and the eager practitioner could almost instantly plunge into vivid greens and celestial blues, or, at sunset, into pinks and chromes and rose-madder.

Tourists who had no pictorial gifts would pick their way among the sketchers, and search the shops for cracked china and bits of brass. Few if any of them left without purchasing one of the famous Tilling money-boxes, made in the shape of a pottery pig, who bore on his back that remarkable legend of his authenticity which ran:

> "I won't be druv,
> Though I am willing.
> Good morning, my love,
> Said the Pig of Tilling."

Miss Mapp had a long shelf full of these in every colour to adorn her dining-room. The one which completed her collection, of a pleasant magenta colour, had only just been acquired. She called them "My sweet rainbow of piggies," and often when she came down to breakfast, especially if Withers was in the room, she said: "Good morning, quaint little piggies." When Withers had left the room she counted them.

The corner where the street took a turn towards the church, just below the window of her garden-room, was easily the most popular stance for sketchers. You were bewildered and bowled over by "bits." For the most accomplished of all there was that rarely attempted feat, the view of the steep downward street, which, in spite of all the efforts of the artist, insisted, in the sketch, on going up hill instead. Then, next in difficulty, was the street after it had turned, running by the gardener's cottage up to the churchyard and the church. This, in spite of its difficulty, was a very favourite subject, for it included, on the right of the street, just beyond Miss Mapp's garden wall, the famous crooked chimney, which was continually copied from every point of view. The expert artist would draw it rather more crooked than it really was, in order that there might be no question that he had not drawn it crooked by accident. This sketch was usually negotiated from the three steps in front of Miss Mapp's front door. Opposite the church-and-chimney-artists would sit others, drawing the front door itself (difficult), and moistening their pencils at their cherry lips, while a little further down the street was another battalion hard at work at the gabled front of the garden-room and its picturesque bow. It was a favourite occupation of Miss Mapp's, when there was a decent gathering of artists outside, to pull a table right into the window of the garden-room, in full view of them, and, quite unconscious of their presence, to arrange flowers there with a smiling and pensive countenance. She had other little playful public pastimes: she would get her kitten from the house, and induce it to sit on the table while she diverted it with the tassel of the blind, and she would kiss it on its sweet little sooty head, or she would write letters in the window, or play Patience there, and then suddenly become aware that there was no end of ladies and gentlemen looking at her. Sometimes she would come out of the house, if the steps were very full, with her own sketching paraphernalia in her hands and say, ever so coyly: "May I scriggle through?" or ask the squatters on her own steps if they could find a little corner for her. That was so interesting for them: they would remember afterwards that just while they were engaged on their sketches, the lady of that beautiful house at the corner, who had been playing with her kitten in the window, came out to sketch too. She addressed gracious and yet humble remarks to them: "I see you are painting my sweet little home. May I look? Oh, what a lovely little sketch!" Once, on a never-to-be-forgotten day, she observed one of them take a camera from his pocket and rapidly focus her as she stood on the top step. She turned full-faced and smiling to the camera just in time to catch the click of the shutter, but then it was too late to hide her face, and perhaps the picture might appear in the *Graphic* or the *Sketch*, or among the posturing nymphs of a neighbouring watering-place . . .

This afternoon she was content to "scriggle" through the sketchers, and humming a little tune, she passed up to the church-yard. ("Scriggle" was one of her own words, highly popular; it connoted squeezing and wriggling.) There she carefully concealed herself under the boughs of the weeping ash tree directly opposite the famous south porch of the church. She had already drawn in the lines of this south porch on her sketching-block, transferring them there by means of a tracing from a photograph, so that formed a very promising beginning to her sketch. But she was nicely placed not only with regard to her sketch, for, by peeping through the pretty foliage of the tree, she could command the front door of Mrs. Poppit's (M.B.E.) house.

Miss Mapp's plans for the bridge-party had, of course, been completely upset by the encounter with Irene in the High Street. Up till that moment she had imagined that, with the two ladies of the house and the Bartletts and the Major and the Captain and Godiva and herself, two complete tables of bridge would be formed, and she had, therefore, determined that she would not be able to squeeze the party into her numerous engagements, thereby spoiling the second table. But now everything was changed: there were eight without her, and unless, at a quarter to four, she saw reason to suppose, by noting the arrivals at the house, that three bridge tables were in contemplation, she had made up her mind to "squeeze it in," so that there would be nine gamblers, and Isabel or her mother, if they had any sense of hospitality to their guests, would be compelled to sit out for ever and ever. Miss Mapp had been urgently invited: sweet Isabel had made a great point of her squeezing it in, and if sweet Isabel, in order to be certain of a company of eight, had asked quaint Irene as well, it would serve her right. An additional reason, besides this piece of good-nature in managing to squeeze it in, for the sake of sweet Isabel, lay in the fact that she would be able to take some red-currant fool, and after one spoonful exclaim "Delicious," and leave the rest uneaten.

The white butterflies and the swallows were still enjoying themselves in the sunshine, and so, too, were the gnats, about whose pleasure, especially when they settled on her face, Miss Mapp did not care so much. But soon she quite ceased to regard them, for, before the quaint little gilded boys on each side of the clock above the north porch had hammered out the three-quarters after three on their bells, visitors began to arrive at the Poppits" door, and Miss Mapp was very active looking through the boughs of the weeping ash and sitting down again to smile and ponder over her sketch with her head a little on one side, if anybody approached. One by one the expected guests presented themselves and were admitted: Major Flint and Captain Puffin, the Padre and his wife, darling Diva with her head muffled in a "cloud," and finally Irene, still dressed as she had been in the morning, and probably reeking with scarlet-fever. With the two Poppits these made eight players, so as soon as Irene had gone in, Miss Mapp hastily put her sketching things away, and holding her admirably-accurate drawing with its wash of sky not quite dry, in her hand, hurried to the door, for it would never do to arrive after the two tables had started, since in that case it would be she who would have to sit out.

Boon opened the door to her three staccato little knocks, and sulkily consulted his list. She duly appeared on it and was admitted. Having banged the door behind her he crushed the list up in his hand and threw it into the fireplace: all those whose presence was desired had arrived, and Boon would turn his bovine eye on any subsequent caller, and say that his mistress was out.

"And may I put my sketching things down here, please, Boon," said Miss Mapp ingratiatingly. "And will no one touch my drawing? It's a little wet still. The church porch."

Boon made a grunting noise like the Tilling pig, and slouched away in front of her down the passage leading to the garden, sniffing. There they were, with the two bridge-tables set out in a shady corner of the lawn, and a buffet vulgarly heaped with all sorts of dainty confections which made Miss Mapp's mouth water, obliging her to swallow rapidly once or twice before she could manage a wide, dry smile: Isabel advanced.

"De-do, dear," said Miss Mapp. "Such a rush! But managed to squeeze it in, as you wouldn't let me off."

"Oh, that was nice of you, Miss Mapp," said Isabel.

A wild and awful surmise seized Miss Mapp.

"And your dear mother?" she said. "Where is Mrs. Poppit?"

"Mamma had to go to town this morning. She won't be back till close on dinner-time."

Miss Mapp's smile closed up like a furled umbrella. The trap had snapped behind her: it was impossible now to scriggle away. She had completed, instead of spoiling, the second table.

"So we're just eight," said Isabel, poking at her, so to speak, through the wires. "Shall we have a rubber first and then some tea? Or tea first. What says everybody?"

Restless and hungry murmurs, like those heard at the sea-lions' enclosure in the Zoological Gardens when feeding-time approaches, seemed to indicate tea first, and with gallant greetings from the Major, and archaistic welcomes from the Padre, Miss Mapp headed the general drifting movement towards the buffet. There may have been tea there, but there was certainly iced coffee and Lager beer and large jugs with dew on the outside and vegetables floating in a bubbling liquid in the inside, and it was all so vulgar and opulent that with one accord everyone set to work in earnest, in order that the garden should present a less gross and greedy appearance. But there was no sign at present of the red-currant fool, which was baffling . . .

"And have you had a good game of golf, Major?" asked Miss Mapp, making the best of these miserable circumstances. "Such a lovely day! The white butterflies were enjoying —"

She became aware that Diva and the Padre, who had already heard about the white butterflies, were in her immediate neighbourhood, and broke off.

"Which of you beat? Or should I say 'won!'" she asked.

Major Flint's long moustache was dripping with Lager beer, and he made a dexterous, sucking movement.

"Well, the Army and the Navy had it out," he said. "And if for once Britain's Navy was not invincible, eh, Puffin?"

Captain Puffin limped away pretending not to hear, and took his heaped plate and brimming glass in the direction of Irene.

"But I'm sure Captain Puffin played quite beautifully too," said Miss Mapp in the vain attempt to detain him. She liked to collect all the men round her, and then scold them for not talking to the other ladies.

"Well, a game's a game," said the Major. "It gets through the hours, Miss Mapp. Yes: we finished at the fourteenth hole, and hurried back to more congenial society. And what have you done to-day? Fairy-errands, I'll be bound. Titania! Ha!"

Suet errands and errands about a missing article of underclothing were really the most important things that Miss Mapp had done to-day, now that her bridge-party scheme had so miscarried, but naturally she would not allude to these.

"A little gardening," she said. "A little sketching. A little singing. Not time to change my frock and put on something less shabby. But I wouldn't have kept sweet Isabel's bridge-party waiting for anything, and so I came straight from my painting here. Padre, I've been trying to draw the lovely south porch. But so difficult! I shall give up trying to draw, and just enjoy myself with looking. And there's your dear Evie! How de do, Evie love?"

Godiva Plaistow had taken off her cloud for purposes of mastication, but wound it tightly round her head again as soon as she had eaten as much as she could manage. This had to be done on one side of her mouth, or with the front teeth in the nibbling manner of a rabbit. Everybody, of course, by now knew that she had had a wisdom tooth out at one p.m. with gas, and she could allude to it without explanation.

"Dreamed I was playing bridge," she said, "and had a hand of aces. As I played the first it went off in my hand. All over. Blood. Hope it'll come true. Bar the blood."

Miss Mapp found herself soon afterwards partnered with Major Flint and opposed by Irene and the Padre. They had hardly begun to consider their first hands when Boon staggered out into the garden under the weight of a large wooden bucket, packed with ice, that surrounded an interior cylinder.

"Red currant fool at last," thought Miss Mapp, adding aloud: "O poor little me, is it, to declare? Shall I say 'no trumps?'"

"Mustn't consult your partner, Mapp," said Irene, puffing the end of her cigarette out of its holder. Irene was painfully literal.

"I don't, darling," said Miss Mapp, beginning to fizz a little. "No trumps. Not a trump. Not any sort of trump. There! What are we playing for, by the way?"

"Bob a hundred," said the Padre, forgetting to be either Scotch or archaic.

"Oh, gambler! You want the poor-box to be the rich box, Padre," said Miss Mapp, surveying her magnificent hand with the greatest satisfaction. If it had not contained so many court-cards, she would have proposed playing for sixpence, not a shilling a hundred.

All semblance of manners was invariably thrown to the winds by the ladies of Tilling when once bridge began; primeval hatred took their place. The winners of any hand were exasperatingly condescending to the losers, and the losers correspondingly bitter and tremulous. Miss Mapp failed to get her contract, as her partner's contribution to success consisted of more twos and threes than were ever seen together before, and when quaint Irene at the end said, "Bad luck, Mapp," Miss Mapp's hands trembled so much with passion that she with difficulty marked the score. But she could command her voice sufficiently to say, "Lovely of you to be sympathetic, dear." Irene in answer gave a short, hoarse laugh and dealt.

By this time Boon had deposited at the left hand of each player a cup containing a red creamy fluid, on the surface of which bubbles intermittently appeared. Isabel, at this moment being dummy, had strolled across from the other table to see that everybody was comfortable and provided with sustenance in times of stress, and here was clearly the proper opportunity for Miss Mapp to take a spoonful of this attempt at red-currant fool, and with a wry face, hastily (but not too hastily) smothered in smiles, to push the revolting compound away from her. But the one spoonful that she took was so delicious and exhilarating, that she was positively unable to be good for Isabel. Instead, she drank her cup to the dregs in an absent manner, while considering how many trumps were out. The red-currant fool made a similarly agreeable impression on Major Flint.

"'Pon my word," he said. "That's amazingly good. Cooling on a hot day like this. Full of champagne."

Miss Mapp, seeing that it was so popular, had, of course, to claim it again as a family invention.

"No, dear Major," she said. "There's no champagne in it. It's my Grandmamma Mapp's famous red-currant fool, with little additions perhaps by me. No champagne: yolk of egg and a little cream. Dear Isabel has got it very nearly right."

The Padre had promised to take more tricks in diamonds than he had the slightest chance of doing. His mental worry communicated itself to his voice.

"And why should there be nary a wee drappie o' champagne in it?" he said, "though your Grandmamma Mapp did invent it. Weel, let's see your hand, partner. Eh, that's a sair sight."

"And there'll be a sair wee score agin us when ye're through with the playin' o' it," said Irene, in tones that could not be acquitted of a mocking intent. "Why the hell — hallelujah did you go on when I didn't support you?"

Even that one glass of red-currant fool, though there was no champagne in it, had produced, together with the certainty that her opponent had overbidden his hand, a pleasant exhilaration in Miss Mapp; but yolk of egg, as everybody knew, was a strong stimulant. Suddenly the name red-currant fool seemed very amusing to her.

"Red-currant fool!" she said. "What a quaint, old-fashioned name! I shall invent some others. I shall tell my cook to make some gooseberry-idiot, or strawberry-donkey . . . My play, I think. A ducky little ace of spades."

"Haw! haw! gooseberry idiot!" said her partner. "Capital! You won't beat that in a hurry! And a two of spades on the top of it."

"You wouldn't expect to find a two of spades at the bottom of it," said the Padre with singular acidity.

The Major was quick to resent this kind of comment from a man, cloth or no cloth.

"Well, by your leave, Bartlett, by your leave, I repeat," he said, "I shall expect to find twos of spades precisely where I please, and when I want your criticism —"

Miss Mapp hastily intervened.

"And after my wee ace, a little king-piece," she said. "And if my partner doesn't play the queen to it! Delicious! And I play just one more . . . Yes . . . lovely, partner puts wee trumpy on it! I'm not surprised; it takes more than that to surprise me; and then Padre's got another spade, I ken fine!"

"Hoots!" said the Padre with temperate disgust.

The hand proceeded for a round or two in silence, during which, by winks and gestures to Boon, the Major got hold of another cupful of red-currant fool. There was already a heavy penalty of tricks against Miss Mapp's opponents, and after a moment's refreshment, the Major led a club, of which, at this period, Miss Mapp seemed to have none. She felt happier than she had been ever since, trying to spoil Isabel's second table, she had only succeeded in completing it.

"Little trumpy again," she said, putting it on with the lightness of one of the white butterflies and turning the trick. "Useful little trumpy —"

She broke off suddenly from the chant of victory which ladies of Tilling were accustomed to indulge in during cross-roughs, for she discovered in her hand another more than useless little clubby . . . The silence that succeeded became tense in quality. Miss Mapp knew she had revoked and squeezed her brains to think how she could possibly dispose of the card, while there was a certain calmness about the Padre, which but too clearly indicated that he was quite content to wait for the inevitable disclosure. This came at the last trick, and though Miss Mapp made one forlorn attempt to thrust the horrible little clubby underneath the other cards and gather them up, the Padre pounced on it.

"What ho, fair lady!" he said, now completely restored. "Methinks thou art forsworn! Let me have a keek at the last trick but three! Verily I wis that thou didst trump ye club aforetime. I said so; there it is. Eh, that's bonny for us, partner!"

Miss Mapp, of course, denied it all, and a ruthless reconstruction of the tricks took place. The Major, still busy with red-currant fool, was the last to grasp the disaster, and then instantly deplored the unsportsmanlike greed of his adversaries.

"Well, I should have thought in a friendly game like this —" he said. "Of course, you're within your right, Bartlett: might is right, hey? but upon my word, a pound of flesh, you know . . . Can't think what made you do it, partner."

"You never asked me if I had any more clubs," said Miss Mapp shrilly, giving up for the moment the contention that she had not revoked. "I always ask if my partner has no more of a suit, and I always maintain that a revoke is more the partner's fault than the player's. Of course, if our adversaries claim it —"

"Naturally we do, Mapp," said Irene. "You were down on me sharp enough the other day."

Miss Mapp wrinkled her face up into the sweetest and extremest smile of which her mobile features were capable.

"Darling, you won't mind my telling you that just at this moment you are being dummy," she said, "and so you mustn't speak a single word. Otherwise there is no revoke, even if there was at all, which I consider far from proved yet."

There was no further proof possible beyond the clear and final evidence of the cards, and since everybody, including Miss Mapp herself, was perfectly well aware that she had revoked, their opponents merely marked up the penalty and the game proceeded. Miss Mapp, of course, following the rule of correct behaviour after revoking, stiffened into a state of offended dignity, and was extremely polite and distant with partner and adversaries alike. This demeanour became even more majestic when in the next hand the Major led out of turn. The moment he had done it, Miss Mapp hurriedly threw a random card out of her hand on to the table, in the hope that Irene, by some strange aberration, would think she had led first.

"Wait a second," said she. "I call a lead. Give me a trump, please."

Suddenly the awful expression as of some outraged empress faded from Miss Mapp's face, and she gave a little shriek of laughter which sounded like a squeaking slate pencil.

"Haven't got one, dear," she said. "Now may I have your permission to lead what I think best? Thank you."

There now existed between the four players that state of violent animosity which was the usual atmosphere towards the end of a rubber. But it would have been a capital mistake to suppose that they were not all enjoying themselves immensely. Emotion is the salt of life, and here was no end of salt. Everyone was overbidding his hand, and the penalty tricks were a glorious cause of vituperation, scarcely veiled, between the partners who had failed to make good, and caused epidemics of condescending sympathy from the adversaries which produced a passion in the losers far keener than their fury at having lost. What made the concluding stages of this contest the more exciting was that an evening breeze suddenly arising just as a deal was ended, made the cards rise in the air like a covey of partridges. They were recaptured, and all the hands were found to be complete with the exception of Miss Mapp's, which had a card missing. This, an ace of hearts, was discovered by the Padre, face upwards, in a bed of mignonette, and he was vehement in claiming a fresh deal, on the grounds that the card was exposed. Miss Mapp could not speak at all in answer to this preposterous claim: she could only smile at him, and proceed to declare trumps as if nothing had happened . . . The Major alone failed to come up to the full measure of these enjoyments, for though all the rest of them were as angry with him as they were with each other, he remained in a most indecorous state of good-humour, drinking thirstily of the red-currant fool, and when he was dummy, quite failing to mind whether Miss Mapp got her contract or not. Captain Puffin, at the other table, seemed to be behaving with the same impropriety, for the sound of his shrill, falsetto laugh was as regular as his visits to the bucket of red-currant fool. What if there was champagne in it after all, so Miss Mapp luridly conjectured! What if this unseemly good-humour was due to incipient intoxication? She took a little more of that delicious decoction herself.

It was unanimously determined, when the two rubbers came to an end almost simultaneously, that, as everything was so pleasant and agreeable, there should be no fresh sorting of the players. Besides, the second table was only playing stakes of sixpence a hundred, and it would be very awkward and unsettling that anyone should play these moderate points in one rubber and those high ones the next. But at this point Miss Mapp's table was obliged to endure a pause, for the Padre had to hurry away just before six to administer the rite of baptism in the church which was so conveniently close. The Major afforded a good deal of amusement, as soon as he was out of hearing, by hoping that he would not baptize the child the Knave of Hearts if it was a boy, or, if a girl, the Queen of Spades; but in order to spare the susceptibilities of Mrs. Bartlett, this admirable joke was not communicated to the next table, but enjoyed privately. The author of it, however, made a note in his mind to tell it to Captain Puffin, in the hopes that it would cause him to forget his ruinous half-crown defeat at golf this morning. Quite as agreeable was the arrival of a fresh supply of red-currant fool, and as this had been heralded a few minutes before by a loud pop from the butler's pantry, which looked on to the lawn, Miss Mapp began to waver in her belief that there was no champagne in it, particularly as it would not have suited the theory by which she accounted for the Major's unwonted good-humour, and her suggestion that the pop they had all heard so clearly was the opening of a bottle of stone ginger-beer was not delivered with conviction. To make sure, however, she took one more sip of the new supply, and, irradiated with smiles, made a great concession.

"I believe I was wrong," she said. "There is something in it beyond yolk of egg and cream. Oh, there's Boon; he will tell us."

She made a seductive face at Boon, and beckoned to him.

"Boon, will you think it very inquisitive of me," she asked archly, "if I ask you whether you have put a teeny drop of champagne into this delicious red-currant fool?"

"A bottle and a half, Miss," said Boon morosely, "and half a pint of old brandy. Will you have some more, Miss?"

Miss Mapp curbed her indignation at this vulgar squandering of precious liquids, so characteristic of Poppits. She gave a shrill little laugh.

"Oh, no, thank you, Boon!" she said. "I mustn't have any more. Delicious, though."

Major Flint let Boon fill up his cup while he was not looking.

"And we owe this to your grandmother, Miss Mapp?" he asked gallantly. "That's a second debt."

Miss Mapp acknowledged this polite subtlety with a reservation.

"But not the champagne in it, Major," she said. "Grandmamma Nap —"

The Major beat his thigh in ecstasy.

"Ha! That's a good Spoonerism for Miss Isabel's book," he said. "Miss Isabel, we've got a new —"

Miss Mapp was very much puzzled at this slight confusion in her speech, for her utterance was usually remarkably distinct. There might be some little joke made at her expense on the effect of Grandmamma Mapp's invention if this lovely Spoonerism was published. But if she who had only just tasted the red-currant fool tripped in her speech, how amply were Major Flint's good nature and Captain Puffin's incessant laugh accounted for. She herself felt very good-natured, too. How pleasant it all was!

"Oh, naughty!" she said to the Major. "Pray, hush! you're disturbing them at their rubber. And here's the Padre back again!"

The new rubber had only just begun (indeed, it was lucky that they cut their cards without any delay) when Mrs. Poppit appeared on her return from her expedition to London. Miss Mapp begged her to take her hand, and instantly began playing.

"It would really be a kindness to me, Mrs. Poppit," she said; "(No diamonds at all, partner?) but of course, if you won't — You've been missing such a lovely party. So much enjoyment!"

Suddenly she saw that Mrs. Poppit was wearing on her ample breast a small piece of riband with a little cross attached to it. Her entire stock of good-humour vanished, and she smiled her widest.

"We needn't ask what took you to London," she said. "Congratulations! How was the dear King?"

This rubber was soon over, and even as they were adding up the score, there arose a shrill outcry from the next table, where Mrs. Plaistow, as usual, had made the tale of her winnings sixpence in excess of what anybody else considered was due to her. The sound of that was so familiar that nobody looked up or asked what was going on.

"Darling Diva and her bawbees, Padre," said Miss Mapp in an aside. "So modest in her demands. Oh, she's stopped! Somebody has given her sixpence. Not another rubber? Well, perhaps it is rather late, and I must say good-night to my flowers before they close up for the night. All those shillings mine? Fancy!"

Miss Mapp was seething with excitement, curiosity and rage, as with Major Flint on one side of her and Captain Puffin on the other, she was escorted home. The excitement was due to her winnings, the rage to Mrs. Poppit's Order, the curiosity to the clue she believed she had found to those inexplicable lights that burned so late in the houses of her companions. Certainly it seemed that Major Flint was trying not to step on the joints of the paving-stones, and succeeding very imperfectly, while Captain Puffin, on her left, was walking very unevenly on the cobbles. Even making due allowance for the difficulty of walking evenly there at any time, Miss Mapp could not help thinking that a teetotaller would have made a better job of it than that. Both gentlemen talked at once, very agreeably but rather carefully, Major Flint promising himself a studious evening over some very interesting entries in his Indian Diary, while Captain Puffin anticipated the speedy solution of that problem about the Roman road which had puzzled him so long. As they said their "Au reservoirs" to her on her doorstep, they took off their hats more often than politeness really demanded.

Once in her house Miss Mapp postponed her good-nights to her sweet flowers, and hurried with the utmost speed of which she was capable to her garden-room, in order to see what her companions were doing. They were standing in the middle of the street, and Major Flint, with gesticulating forefinger, was being very impressive over something . . .

*****

Interesting as was Miss Mapp's walk home, and painful as was the light which it had conceivably thrown on the problem that had baffled her for so long, she might have been even more acutely disgusted had she lingered on with the rest of the bridge-party in Mrs. Poppit's garden, so revolting was the sycophantic loyalty of the newly-decorated Member of the British Empire . . . She described minutely her arrival at the Palace, her momentary nervousness as she entered the Throne-room, the instantaneousness with which that all vanished when she came face to face with her Sovereign.

"I assure you, he gave the most gracious smile," she said, "just as if we had known each other all our lives, and I felt at home at once. And he said a few words to me — such a beautiful voice he has. Dear Isabel, I wish you had been there to hear it, and then —"

"Oh, Mamma, what did he say?" asked Isabel, to the great relief of Mrs. Plaistow and the Bartletts, for while they were bursting with eagerness to know with the utmost detail all that had taken place, the correct attitude in Tilling was profound indifference to anybody of whatever degree who did not live at Tilling, and to anything that did not happen there. In particular, any manifestation of interest in kings or other distinguished people was held to be a very miserable failing . . . So they all pretended to look about them, and take no notice of what Mrs. Poppit was saying, and you might have heard a pin drop. Diva silently and hastily unwound her cloud from over her ears, risking catching cold in the hole where her tooth had been, so terrified was she of missing a single syllable.

"Well, it was very gratifying," said Mrs. Poppit; "he whispered to some gentleman standing near him, who I think was the Lord Chamberlain, and then told me how interested he had been in the good work of the Tilling hospital, and how especially glad he was to be able — and just then he began to pin my Order on — to be able to recognize it. Now I call that wonderful to know all about the Tilling hospital! And such neat, quick fingers he has: I am sure it would take me double the time to make a safety-pin hold, and then he gave me another smile, and passed me on, so to speak, to the Queen, who stood next him, and who had been listening to all he had said."

"And did she speak to you too?" asked Diva, quite unable to maintain the right indifference.

"Indeed she did: she said, 'So pleased,' and what she put into those two words I'm sure I can never convey to you. I could hear how sincere they were: it was no set form of words, as if she meant nothing by it. She *was* pleased: she was just as interested in what I had done for the Tilling hospital as the King was. And the crowds outside: they lined the Mall for at least fifty yards. I was bowing and smiling on this side and that till I felt quite dizzy."

"And was the Prince of Wales there?" asked Diva, beginning to wind her head up again. She did not care about the crowds.

"No, he wasn't there," said Mrs. Poppit, determined to have no embroidery in her story, however much other people, especially Miss Mapp, decorated remarkable incidents till you hardly recognized them. "He wasn't there. I daresay something had unexpectedly detained him, though I shouldn't wonder if before long we all saw him. For I noticed in the evening paper which I was reading on the way down here, after I had seen the King, that he was going to stay with Lord Ardingly for this very next week-end. And what's the station for Ardingly Park if it isn't Tilling? Though it's quite a private visit, I feel convinced that the right and proper thing for me to do is to be at the station, or, at any rate, just outside, with my Order on. I shall not claim acquaintance with him, or anything of that kind," said Mrs. Poppit, fingering her Order; "but after my reception to-day at the Palace, nothing can be more likely than that His Majesty might mention — quite casually, of course — to the Prince that he had just given a decoration to Mrs. Poppit of Tilling. And it would make me feel very awkward to think that that had happened, and I was not somewhere about to make my curtsy."

"Oh, Mamma, may I stand by you, or behind you?" asked Isabel, completely dazzled by the splendour of this prospect and prancing about the lawn . . .

This was quite awful: it was as bad as, if not worse than, the historically disastrous remark about super-tax, and a general rigidity, as of some partial cataleptic seizure, froze Mrs. Poppit's guests, rendering them, like incomplete Marconi installations, capable of receiving, but not of transmitting. They received these impressions, they also continued (mechanically) to receive more chocolates and sandwiches, and such refreshments as remained on the buffet; but no one could intervene and stop Mrs. Poppit from exposing herself further. One reason for this, of course, as already indicated, was that they all longed for her to expose herself as much as she possibly could, for if there was a quality — and, indeed, there were many — on which Tilling prided itself, it was on its immunity from snobbishness: there were, no doubt, in the great world with which Tilling concerned itself so little kings and queens and dukes and Members of the Order of the British Empire; but every Tillingite knew that he or she (particularly she) was just as good as any of them, and indeed better, being more fortunate than they in living in Tilling . . . And if there was a process in the world which Tilling detested, it was being patronized, and there was this woman telling them all what she felt it right and proper for her, as Mrs. Poppit of Tilling (M.B.E.), to do, when the Heir Apparent should pass through the town on Saturday. The rest of them, Mrs. Poppit implied, might do what they liked, for they did not matter; but she — she must put on her Order and make her curtsy. And Isabel, by her expressed desire to stand beside, or even behind, her mother for this degrading moment had showed of what stock she came.

Mrs. Poppit had nothing more to say on this subject; indeed, as Diva reflected, there was really nothing more that could be said, unless she suggested that they should all bow and curtsy to her for the future, and their hostess proceeded, as they all took their leave, to hope that they had enjoyed the bridge-party which she had been unavoidably prevented from attending.

"But my absence made it possible to include Miss Mapp," she said. "I should not have liked poor Miss Mapp to feel left out; I am always glad to give Miss Mapp pleasure. I hope she won her rubber; she does not like losing. Will no one have a little more red-currant fool? Boon has made it very tolerably to-day. A Scotch recipe of my great-grandmother's."

Diva gave a little cackle of laughter as she enfolded herself in her cloud again. She had heard Miss Mapp's ironical inquiry as to how the dear King was, and had thought at the time that it was probably a pity that Miss Mapp had said that.

*****

Though abhorrence of snobbery and immunity from any taint of it was so fine a characteristic of public social life at Tilling, the expected passage of this distinguished visitor through the town on Saturday next became very speedily known, and before the wicker-baskets of the ladies in their morning marketings next day were half full, there was no quarter which the news had failed to reach. Major Flint had it from Mrs. Plaistow, as he went down to the eleven-twenty tram out to the golf-links, and though he had not much time to spare (for his work last night on his old diaries had caused him to breakfast unusually late that morning to the accompaniment of a dismal headache from over-application), he had stopped to converse with Miss Mapp immediately afterwards, with one eye on the time, for naturally he could not fire off that sort of news point-blank at her, as if it was a matter of any interest or importance.

"Good morning, dear lady," he said. "By Jove! what a picture of health and freshness you are!"

Miss Mapp cast one glance at her basket to see that the paper quite concealed that article of clothing which the perfidious laundry had found. (Probably the laundry knew where it was all the time, and — in a figurative sense, of course — was "trying it on.")

"Early to bed and early to rise, Major," she said. "I saw my sweet flowers open their eyes this morning! Such a beautiful dew!"

"Well, my diaries kept me up late last night," he said. "When all you fascinating ladies have withdrawn is the only time at which I can bring myself to sit down to them."

"Let me recommend six to eight in the morning, Major," said Miss Mapp earnestly. "Such a freshness of brain then."

That seemed to be a cul-de-sac in the way of leading up to the important subject, and the Major tried another turning.

"Good, well-fought game of bridge we had yesterday," he said. "Just met Mrs. Plaistow; she stopped on for a chat after we had gone."

"Dear Diva; she loves a good gossip," said Miss Mapp effusively. "Such an interest she has in other people's affairs. So human and sympathetic. I'm sure our dear hostess told her all about her adventures at the Palace."

There was only seven minutes left before the tram started, and though this was not a perfect opening, it would have to do. Besides, the Major saw Mrs. Plaistow coming energetically along the High Street with whirling feet.

"Yes, and we haven't finished with — ha — royalty yet, "he said, getting the odious word out with difficulty. "The Prince of Wales will be passing through the town on Saturday, on his way to Ardingly Park, where he is spending the Sunday."

Miss Mapp was not betrayed into the smallest expression of interest.

"That will be nice for him," she said. "He will catch a glimpse of our beautiful Tilling."

"So he will! Well, I'm off for my game of golf. Perhaps the Navy will be a bit more efficient to-day."

"I'm sure you will both play perfectly!" said Miss Mapp.

Diva had "popped" into the grocer's. She always popped everywhere just now; she popped across to see a friend, and she popped home again; she popped into church on Sunday, and occasionally popped up to town, and Miss Mapp was beginning to feel that somebody ought to let her know, directly or by insinuation, that she popped too much. So, thinking that an opportunity might present itself now, Miss Mapp read the news-board outside the stationer's till Diva popped out of the grocer's again. The headlines of news, even the largest of them, hardly reached her brain, because it entirely absorbed in another subject. Of course, the first thing was to find out by what train . . .

Diva trundled swiftly across the street.

"Good morning, Elizabeth," she said. "You left the party too early yesterday. Missed a lot. How the King smiled! How the Queen said 'So pleased.'"

"Our dear hostess would like that," said Miss Mapp pensively. "She would be so pleased, too. She and the Queen would both be pleased. Quite a pair of them."

"By the way, on Saturday next —" began Diva.

"I know, dear," said Miss Mapp. "Major Flint told me. It seemed quite to interest him. Now I must pop into the stationer's —"

Diva was really very obtuse.

"I'm popping in there, too," she said. "Want a time-table of the trains."

Wild horses would not have dragged from Miss Mapp that this was precisely what she wanted.

"I only wanted a little ruled paper," she said. "Why, here's dear Evie popping out just as we pop in! Good morning, sweet Evie. Lovely day again."

Mrs. Bartlett thrust something into her basket which very much resembled a railway time-table. She spoke in a low, quick voice, as if afraid of being overheard, and was otherwise rather like a mouse. When she was excited she squeaked.

"So good for the harvest," she said. "Such an important thing to have a good harvest. I hope next Saturday will be fine; it would be a pity if he had a wet day. We were wondering, Kenneth and I, what would be the proper thing to do, if he came over for service — oh, here is Kenneth!"

She stopped abruptly, as if afraid that she had betrayed too much interest in next Saturday and Sunday. Kenneth would manage it much better.

"Ha! lady fair," he exclaimed. "Having a bit crack with wee wifey? Any news this bright morning?"

"No, dear Padre," said Miss Mapp, showing her gums. "At least, I've heard nothing of any interest. I can only give you the news of my garden. Such lovely new roses in bloom to-day, bless them!"

Mrs. Plaistow had popped into the stationer's, so this perjury was undetected.

The Padre was noted for his diplomacy. Just now he wanted to convey the impression that nothing which could happen next Saturday or Sunday could be of the smallest interest to him; whereas he had spent an almost sleepless night in wondering whether it would, in certain circumstances, be proper to make a bow at the beginning of his sermon and another at the end; whether he ought to meet the visitor at the west door; whether the mayor ought to be told, and whether there ought to be special psalms . . .

"Well, lady fair," he said. "Gossip will have it that ye Prince of Wales is staying at Ardingly for the Sunday; indeed, he will, I suppose, pass through Tilling on Saturday afternoon —"

Miss Mapp put her forefinger to her forehead, as if trying to recollect something.

"Yes, now somebody did tell me that," she said. "Major Flint, I believe. But when you asked for news I thought you meant something that really interested me. Yes, Padre?"

"Aweel, if he comes to service on Sunday — ?"

"Dear Padre, I'm sure he'll hear a very good sermon. Oh, I see what you mean! Whether you ought to have any special hymn? Don't ask poor little me! Mrs. Poppit, I'm sure, would tell you. She knows all about courts and etiquette."

Diva popped out of the stationer's at this moment.

"Sold out," she announced. "Everybody wanted time-tables this morning. Evie got the last. Have to go to the station."

"I'll walk with you, Diva, dear," said Miss Mapp. "There's a parcel that — Good-bye, dear Evie, au reservoir."

She kissed her hand to Mrs. Bartlett, leaving a smile behind it, as it fluttered away from her face, for the Padre.

Miss Mapp was so impenetrably wrapped in thought as she worked among her sweet flowers that afternoon, that she merely stared at a "love-in-a-mist," which she had absently rooted up instead of a piece of groundsel, without any bleeding of the heart for one of her sweet flowers. There were two trains by which He might arrive — one at 4.15, which would get him to Ardingly for tea, the other at 6.45. She was quite determined to see him, but more inflexible than that resolve was the Euclidean postulate that no one in Tilling should think that she had taken any deliberate step to do so. For the present she had disarmed suspicion by the blankness of her indifference as to what might happen on Saturday or Sunday; but she herself strongly suspected that everybody else, in spite of the public attitude of Tilling to such subjects, was determined to see him too. How to see and not be seen was the question which engrossed her, and though she might possibly happen to be at that sharp corner outside the station where every motor had to go slow, on the arrival of the 4.15, it would never do to risk being seen there again precisely at 6.45. Mrs. Poppit, shameless in her snobbery, would no doubt be at the station with her Order on at both these hours, if the arrival did not take place by the first train, and Isabel would be prancing by or behind her, and, in fact, dreadful though it was to contemplate, all Tilling, she reluctantly believed, would be hanging about . . . Then an idea struck her, so glorious, that she put the uprooted love-in-a-mist in the weed-basket, instead of planting it again, and went quickly indoors, up to the attics, and from there popped — really popped, so tight was the fit — through a trap-door on to the roof. Yes: the station was plainly visible, and if the 4.15 was the favoured train, there would certainly be a motor from Ardingly Park waiting there in good time for its arrival. From the house-roof she could ascertain that, and she would then have time to trip down the hill and get to her coal merchant's at that sharp corner outside the station, and ask, rather peremptorily, when the coke for her central heating might be expected. It was due now, and though it would be unfortunate if it arrived before Saturday, it was quite easy to smile away her peremptory manner, and say that Withers had not told her. Miss Mapp hated prevarication, but a major force sometimes came along . . . But if no motors from Ardingly Park were in waiting for the 4.15 (as spied from her house-roof), she need not risk being seen in the neighbourhood of the station, but would again make observations some few minutes before the 6.45 was due. There was positively no other train by which He could come . . .

The next day or two saw no traceable developments in the situation, but Miss Mapp's trained sense told her that there was underground work of some kind going on: she seemed to hear faint hollow taps and muffled knockings, and, so to speak, the silence of some unusual pregnancy. Up and down the High Street she observed short whispered conversations going on between her friends, which broke off on her approach. This only confirmed her view that these secret colloquies were connected with Saturday afternoon, for it was not to be expected that, after her freezing reception of the news, any projected snobbishness should be confided to her, and though she would have liked to know what Diva and Irene and darling Evie were meaning to do, the fact that they none of them told her, showed that they were aware that she, at any rate, was utterly indifferent to and above that sort of thing. She suspected, too, that Major Flint had fallen victim to this unTilling-like mania, for on Friday afternoon, when passing his door, which happened to be standing open, she quite distinctly saw him in front of his glass in the hall (standing on the head of one of the tigers to secure a better view of himself), trying on a silk top-hat. Her own errand at this moment was to the draper's, where she bought a quantity of pretty pale blue braid, for a little domestic dress-making which was in arrears, and some riband of the same tint. At this clever and unusual hour for shopping, the High Street was naturally empty, and after a little hesitation and many anxious glances to right and left, she plunged into the toy-shop and bought a pleasant little Union Jack with a short stick attached to it. She told Mr. Dabnet very distinctly that it was a present for her nephew, and concealed it inside her parasol, where it lay quite flat and made no perceptible bulge . . .

At four o'clock on Saturday afternoon, she remembered that the damp had come in through her bedroom ceiling in a storm last winter, and told Withers she was going to have a look to see if any tiles were loose. In order to ascertain this for certain, she took up through the trap door a pair of binocular glasses, through which it was also easy to identify anybody who might be in the open yard outside the station. Even as she looked, Mrs. Poppit and Isabel crossed the yard into the waiting-room and ticket-office. It was a little surprising that there were not more friends in the station-yard, but at the moment she heard a loud Qui-hi in the street below, and cautiously peering over the parapet, she got an admirable view of the Major in a frock-coat and tall hat. A "Coo-ee" answered him, and Captain Puffin, in a new suit (Miss Mapp was certain of it) and a Panama hat, joined him. They went down the street and turned the corner . . . Across the opening to the High Street there shot the figure of darling Diva.

While waiting for them to appear again in the station-yard, Miss Mapp looked to see what vehicles were standing there. It was already ten minutes past four, and the Ardingly motors must have been there by this time, if there was anything "doing" by the 4.15. But positively the only vehicle there was an open trolly laden with a piano in a sack. Apart from knowing all about that piano, for Mrs. Poppit had talked about little else than her new upright Bluthner before her visit to Buckingham Palace, a moment's reflection convinced Miss Mapp that this was a very unlikely mode of conveyance for any guest . . . She watched for a few moments more, but as no other friends appeared in the station-yard, she concluded that they were hanging about the street somewhere, poor things, and decided not to make inquiries about her coke just yet.

She had tea while she arranged flowers, in the very front of the window in her garden-room, and presently had the satisfaction of seeing many of the baffled loyalists trudging home. There was no need to do more than smile and tap the window and kiss her hand: they all knew that she had been busy with her flowers, and that she knew what they had been busy about . . . Out again they all came towards half-past six, and when she had watched the last of them down the hill, she hurried back to the roof again, to make a final inspection of the loose tiles through her binoculars. Brief but exciting was that inspection, for opposite the entrance to the station was drawn up a motor. So clear was the air and so serviceable her binoculars that she could distinguish the vulgar coronet on the panels, and as she looked Mrs. Poppit and Isabel hurried across the station-yard. It was then but the work of a moment to slip on the dust-cloak trimmed with blue braid, adjust the hat with the blue riband, and take up the parasol with its furled Union Jack inside it. The stick of the flag was uppermost; she could whip it out in a moment.

*****

Miss Mapp had calculated her appearance to a nicety. Just as she got to the sharp corner opposite the station, where all cars slowed down and her coal-merchant's office was situated, the train drew up. By the gates into the yard were standing the Major in his top-hat, the Captain in his Panama, Irene in a civilized skirt; Diva in a brand-new walking dress, and the Padre and wee wifey. They were all looking in the direction of the station, and Miss Mapp stepped into the coal-merchant's unobserved. Oddly enough the coke had been sent three days before, and there was no need for peremptoriness.

"So good of you, Mr. Wootten!" she said; "and why is everyone standing about this afternoon?"

Mr. Wootten explained the reason of this, and Miss Mapp, grasping her parasol, went out again as the car left the station. There were too many dear friends about, she decided, to use the Union Jack, and having seen what she wanted to she determined to slip quietly away again. Already the Major's hat was in his hand, and he was bowing low, so too were Captain Puffin and the Padre, while Irene, Diva and Evie were making little ducking movements . . . Miss Mapp was determined, when it came to her turn, to show them, as she happened to be on the spot, what a proper curtsy was.

The car came opposite her, and she curtsied so low that recovery was impossible, and she sat down in the road. Her parasol flew out of her hand and out of her parasol flew the Union Jack. She saw a young man looking out of the window, dressed in khaki, grinning broadly, but not, so she thought, graciously, and it suddenly struck her that there was something, beside her own part in the affair, which was not as it should be. As he put his head in again there was loud laughter from the inside of the car.

Mr. Wootten helped her up and the entire assembly of her friends crowded round her, hoping she was not hurt.

"No, dear Major, dear Padre, not at all, thanks," she said. "So stupid: my ancle turned. Oh, yes, the Union Jack I bought for my nephew, it's his birthday to-morrow. Thank you. I just came to see about my coke: of course I thought the Prince had arrived when you all went down to meet the 4.15. Fancy my running straight into it all! How well he looked."

This was all rather lame, and Miss Mapp hailed Mrs. Poppit's appearance from the station as a welcome diversion . . . Mrs. Poppit was looking vexed.

"I hope you saw him well, Mrs. Poppit," said Miss Mapp, "after meeting two trains, and taking all that trouble."

"Saw who?" said Mrs. Poppit with a deplorable lack both of manner and grammar. "Why" — light seemed to break on her odious countenance. "Why, you don't think that was the Prince, do you, Miss Mapp? He arrived here at one, so the station-master has just told me, and has been playing golf all afternoon."

The Major looked at the Captain, and the Captain at the Major. It was months and months since they had missed their Saturday afternoon's golf.

"It was the Prince of Wales who looked out of that car-window," said Miss Mapp firmly. "Such a pleasant smile. I should know it anywhere."

"The young man who got into the car at the station was no more the Prince of Wales than you are," said Mrs. Poppit shrilly. "I was close to him as he came out: I curtsied to him before I saw."

Miss Mapp instantly changed her attack: she could hardly hold her smile on to her face for rage.

"How very awkward for you," she said. "What a laugh they will all have over it this evening! Delicious!"

Mrs. Poppit's face suddenly took on an expression of the tenderest solicitude.

"I hope, Miss Mapp, you didn't jar yourself when you sat down in the road just now," she said.

"Not at all, thank you so much," said Miss Mapp, hearing her heart beat in her throat . . . If she had had a naval fifteen-inch gun handy, and had known how to fire it, she would, with a sense of duty accomplished, have discharged it point-blank at the Order of the Member of the British Empire, and at anybody else who might be within range . . .

*****

Sunday, of course, with all the opportunities of that day, still remained, and the seats of the auxiliary choir, which were advantageously situated, had never been so full, but as it was all no use, the Major and Captain Puffin left during the sermon to catch the 12.20 tram out to the links. On this delightful day it was but natural that the pleasant walk there across the marsh was very popular, and golfers that afternoon had a very trying and nervous time, for the ladies of Tilling kept bobbing up from behind sand-dunes and bunkers, as, regardless of the players, they executed swift flank marches in all directions. Miss Mapp returned exhausted about tea-time to hear from Withers that the Prince had spent an hour or more rambling about the town, and had stopped quite five minutes at the corner by the garden-room. He had actually sat down on Miss Mapp's steps and smoked a cigarette. She wondered if the end of the cigarette was there still: it was hateful to have cigarette-ends defiling the steps to her front-door, and often before now, when sketchers were numerous, she had sent her housemaid out to remove these untidy relics. She searched for it, but was obliged to come to the reluctant conclusion that there was nothing to remove . . .

CHAPTER III

Diva was sitting at the open drawing-room window of her house in the High Street, cutting with a pair of sharp nail scissors into the old chintz curtains which her maid had told her no longer "paid for the mending." So, since they refused to pay for their mending any more, she was preparing to make them pay, pretty smartly too, in other ways. The pattern was of little bunches of pink roses peeping out through trellis work, and it was these which she had just begun to cut out. Though Tilling was noted for the ingenuity with which its more fashionable ladies devised novel and quaint effects in their dress in an economical manner, Diva felt sure, ransack her memory though she might, that nobody had thought of *this* before.

The hot weather had continued late into September and showed no signs of breaking yet, and it would be agreeable to her and acutely painful to others that just at the end of the summer she should appear in a perfectly new costume, before the days of jumpers and heavy skirts and large woollen scarves came in. She was preparing, therefore, to take the light white jacket which she wore over her blouse, and cover the broad collar and cuffs of it with these pretty roses. The belt of the skirt would be similarly decorated, and so would the edge of it, if there were enough clean ones. The jacket and skirt had already gone to the dyer's, and would be back in a day or two, white no longer, but of a rich purple hue, and by that time she would have hundreds of these little pink roses ready to be tacked on. Perhaps a piece of the chintz, trellis and all, could be sewn over the belt, but she was determined to have single little bunches of roses peppered all over the collar and cuffs of the jacket and, if possible, round the edge of the skirt. She had already tried the effect, and was of the opinion that nobody could possibly guess what the origin of these roses was. When carefully sewn on they looked as if they were a design in the stuff.

She let the circumcised roses fall on to the window-seat, and from time to time, when they grew numerous, swept them into a cardboard box. Though she worked with zealous diligence, she had an eye to the movements in the street outside, for it was shopping-hour, and there were many observations to be made. She had not anything like Miss Mapp's genius for conjecture, but her memory was appallingly good, and this was the third morning running on which Elizabeth had gone into the grocer's. It was odd to go to your grocer's every day like that; groceries twice a week was sufficient for most people. From here on the floor above the street she could easily look into Elizabeth's basket, and she certainly was carrying nothing away with her from the grocer's, for the only thing there was a small bottle done up in white paper with sealing wax, which, Diva had no need to be told, certainly came from the chemist's, and was no doubt connected with too many plums.

Miss Mapp crossed the street to the pavement below Diva's house, and precisely as she reached it, Diva's maid opened the door into the drawing-room, bringing in the second post, or rather not bringing in the second post, but the announcement that there wasn't any second post. This opening of the door caused a draught, and the bunches of roses which littered the window-seat rose brightly in the air. Diva managed to beat most of them down again, but two fluttered out of the window. Precisely then, and at no other time, Miss Mapp looked up, and one settled on her face, the other fell into her basket. Her trained faculties were all on the alert, and she thrust them both inside her glove for future consideration, without stopping to examine them just then. She only knew that they were little pink roses, and that they had fluttered out of Diva's window . . .

She paused on the pavement, and remembered that Diva had not yet expressed regret about the worsted, and that she still "popped" as much as ever. Thus Diva deserved a punishment of some sort, and happily, at that very moment she thought of a subject on which she might be able to make her uncomfortable. The street was full, and it would be pretty to call up to her, instead of ringing her bell, in order to save trouble to poor overworked Janet. (Diva only kept two servants, though of course poverty was no crime.)

"Diva darling!" she cooed.

Diva's head looked out like a cuckoo in a clock preparing to chime the hour.

"Hullo!" she said. "Want me?"

"May I pop up for a moment, dear?" said Miss Mapp. "That's to say if you're not very busy."

"Pop away," said Diva. She was quite aware that Miss Mapp said "pop" in crude inverted commas, so to speak, for purposes of mockery, and so she said it herself more than ever. "I'll tell my maid to pop down and open the door."

While this was being done, Diva bundled her chintz curtains together and stored them and the roses she had cut out into her work-cupboard, for secrecy was an essential to the construction of these decorations. But in order to appear naturally employed, she pulled out the woollen scarf she was knitting for the autumn and winter, forgetting for the moment that the rose-madder stripe at the end on which she was now engaged was made of that fatal worsted which Miss Mapp considered to have been feloniously appropriated. That was the sort of thing Miss Mapp never forgot. Even among her sweet flowers. Her eye fell on it the moment she entered the room, and she tucked the two chintz roses more securely into her glove.

"I thought I would just pop across from the grocer's," she said. "What a pretty scarf, dear! That's a lovely shade of rose-madder. Where can I have seen something like it before?"

This was clearly ironical, and had best be answered by irony. Diva was no coward.

"Couldn't say, I'm sure," she said.

Miss Mapp appeared to recollect, and smiled as far back as her wisdom-teeth. (Diva couldn't do that.)

"I have it," she said. "It was the wool I ordered at Heynes's, and then he sold it you, and I couldn't get any more."

"So it was," said Diva. "Upset you a bit. There was the wool in the shop. I bought it."

"Yes, dear; I see you did. But that wasn't what I popped in about. This coal-strike, you know."

"Got a cellar full," said Diva.

"Diva, you've not been hoarding, have you?" asked Miss Mapp with great anxiety. "They can take away every atom of coal you've got, if so, and fine you I don't know what for every hundredweight of it."

"Pooh!" said Diva, rather forcing the indifference of this rude interjection.

"Yes, love, pooh by all means, if you like poohing!" said Miss Mapp. "But I should have felt very unfriendly if one morning I found you were fined — found you were fined — quite a play upon words — and I hadn't warned you."

Diva felt a little less poohish.

"But how much do they allow you to have?" she asked.

"Oh, quite a little: enough to go on with. But I daresay they won't discover you. I just took the trouble to come and warn you."

Diva did remember something about hoarding; there had surely been dreadful exposures of prudent housekeepers in the papers which were very uncomfortable reading.

"But all these orders were only for the period of the war," she said.

"No doubt you're right, dear," said Miss Mapp brightly. "I'm sure I hope you are. Only if the coal strike comes on, I think you'll find that the regulations against hoarding are quite as severe as they ever were. Food hoarding, too. Twemlow — such a civil man — tells me that he thinks we shall have plenty of food, or anyhow sufficient for everybody for quite a long time, provided that there's no hoarding. Not been hoarding food, too, dear Diva? You naughty thing: I believe that great cupboard is full of sardines and biscuits and bovril."

"Nothing of the kind," said Diva indignantly. "You shall see for yourself" — and then she suddenly remembered that the cupboard was full of chintz curtains and little bunches of pink roses, neatly cut out of them, and a pair of nail scissors.

There was a perfectly perceptible pause, during which Miss Mapp noticed that there were no curtains over the window. There certainly used to be, and they matched with the chintz cover of the window seat, which was decorated with little bunches of pink roses peeping through trellis. This was in the nature of a bonus: she had not up till then connected the chintz curtains with the little things that had fluttered down upon her and were now safe in her glove; her only real object in this call had been to instil a general uneasiness into Diva's mind about the coal strike and the danger of being well provided with fuel. That she humbly hoped that she had accomplished. She got up.

"Must be going," she said. "Such a lovely little chat! But what has happened to your pretty curtains?"

"Gone to the wash," said Diva firmly.

"Liar," thought Miss Mapp, as she tripped downstairs. "Diva would have sent the cover of the window-seat too, if that was the case. Liar," she thought again as she kissed her hand to Diva, who was looking gloomily out of the window.

*****

As soon as Miss Mapp had gained her garden-room, she examined the mysterious treasures in her left-hand glove. Without the smallest doubt Diva had taken down her curtains (and high time too, for they were sadly shabby), and was cutting the roses out of them. But what on earth was she doing that for? For what garish purpose could she want to use bunches of roses cut out of chintz curtains?

Miss Mapp had put the two specimens of which she had providentially become possessed in her lap, and they looked very pretty against the navy-blue of her skirt. Diva was very ingenious: she used up all sorts of odds and ends in a way that did credit to her undoubtedly parsimonious qualities. She could trim a hat with a toothbrush and a banana in such a way that it looked quite Parisian till you firmly analysed its component parts, and most of her ingenuity was devoted to dress: the more was the pity that she had such a roundabout figure that her waistband always reminded you of the equator . . .

"Eureka!" said Miss Mapp aloud, and, though the telephone bell was ringing, and the postulant might be one of the servants' friends ringing them up at an hour when their mistress was usually in the High Street, she glided swiftly to the large cupboard underneath the stairs which was full of the things which no right-minded person could bear to throw away: broken basket-chairs, pieces of brown paper, cardboard boxes without lids, and cardboard lids without boxes, old bags with holes in them, keys without locks and locks without keys and worn chintz covers. There was one — it had once adorned the sofa in the garden-room — covered with red poppies (very easy to cut out), and Miss Mapp dragged it dustily from its corner, setting in motion a perfect cascade of cardboard lids and some door-handles.

Withers had answered the telephone, and came to announce that Twemlow the grocer regretted he had only two large tins of corned beef, but —

"Then say I will have the tongue as well, Withers," said Miss Mapp. "Just a tongue — and then I shall want you and Mary to do some cutting out for me."

The three went to work with feverish energy, for Diva had got a start, and by four o'clock that afternoon there were enough poppies cut out to furnish, when in seed, a whole street of opium dens. The dress selected for decoration was, apart from a few mildew-spots, the colour of ripe corn, which was superbly appropriate for September. "Poppies in the corn," said Miss Mapp over and over to herself, remembering some sweet verses she had once read by Bernard Shaw or Clement Shorter or somebody like that about a garden of sleep somewhere in Norfolk . . .

"No one can work as neatly as you, Withers," she said gaily, "and I shall ask you to do the most difficult part. I want you to sew my lovely poppies over the collar and facings of the jacket, just spacing them a little and making a dainty irregularity. And then Mary — won't you, Mary? — will do the same with the waistband while I put a border of them round the skirt, and my dear old dress will look quite new and lovely. I shall be at home to nobody, Withers, this afternoon, even if the Prince of Wales came and sat on my doorstep again. We'll all work together in the garden, shall we, and you and Mary must scold me if you think I'm not working hard enough. It will be delicious in the garden."

Thanks to this pleasant plan, there was not much opportunity for Withers and Mary to be idle . . .

*****

Just about the time that this harmonious party began their work, a far from harmonious couple were being just as industrious in the grand spacious bunker in front of the tee to the last hole on the golf links. It was a beautiful bunker, consisting of a great slope of loose, steep sand against the face of the hill, and solidly shored up with timber. The Navy had been in better form to-day, and after a decisive victory over the Army in the morning and an indemnity of half-a-crown, its match in the afternoon, with just the last hole to play, was all square. So Captain Puffin, having the honour, hit a low, nervous drive that tapped loudly at the timbered wall of the bunker, and cuddled down below it, well protected from any future assault.

"Phew! That about settles it," said Major Flint boisterously. "Bad place to top a ball! Give me the hole?"

This insolent question needed no answer, and Major Flint drove, skying the ball to a prodigious height. But it had to come to earth sometime, and it fell like Lucifer, son of the morning, in the middle of the same bunker . . . So the Army played three more, and, sweating profusely, got out. Then it was the Navy's turn, and the Navy had to lie on its keel above the boards of the bunker, in order to reach its ball at all, and missed it twice.

"Better give it up, old chap," said Major Flint. "Unplayable."

"Then see me play it," said Captain Puffin, with a chewing motion of his jaws.

"We shall miss the tram," said the Major, and, with the intention of giving annoyance, he sat down in the bunker with his back to Captain Puffin, and lit a cigarette. At his third attempt nothing happened; at the fourth the ball flew against the boards, rebounded briskly again into the bunker, trickled down the steep, sandy slope and hit the Major's boot.

"Hit you, I think," said Captain Puffin. "Ha! So it's my hole, Major!"

Major Flint had a short fit of aphasia. He opened and shut his mouth and foamed. Then he took a half-crown from his pocket.

"Give that to the Captain," he said to his caddie, and without looking round, walked away in the direction of the tram. He had not gone a hundred yards when the whistle sounded, and it puffed away homewards with ever-increasing velocity.

*****

Weak and trembling from passion, Major Flint found that after a few tottering steps in the direction of Tilling he would be totally unable to get there unless fortified by some strong stimulant, and turned back to the Club-house to obtain it. He always went dead-lame when beaten at golf, while Captain Puffin was lame in any circumstances, and the two, no longer on speaking terms, hobbled into the Club-house, one after the other, each unconscious of the other's presence. Summoning his last remaining strength Major Flint roared for whisky, and was told that, according to regulation, he could not be served until six. There was lemonade and stone ginger-beer . . . You might as well have offered a man-eating tiger bread and milk. Even the threat that he would instantly resign his membership unless provided with drink produced no effect on a polite steward, and he sat down to recover as best he might with an old volume of *Punch*. This seemed to do him little good. His forced abstemiousness was rendered the more intolerable by the fact that Captain Puffin, hobbling in immediately afterwards, fetched from his locker a large flask full of the required elixir, and proceeded to mix himself a long, strong tumblerful. After the Major's rudeness in the matter of the half-crown, it was impossible for any sailor of spirit to take the first step towards reconciliation.

Thirst is a great leveller. By the time the refreshed Puffin had penetrated half-way down his glass, the Major found it impossible to be proud and proper any longer. He hated saying he was sorry (no man more) and wouldn't have been sorry if he had been able to get a drink. He twirled his moustache a great many times and cleared his throat — it wanted more than that to clear it — and capitulated.

"Upon my word, Puffin, I'm ashamed of myself for — ha! — for not taking my defeat better," he said. "A man's no business to let a game ruffle him."

Puffin gave his alto cackling laugh.

"Oh, that's all right, Major," he said. "I know it's awfully hard to lose like a gentleman."

He let this sink in, then added:

"Have a drink, old chap?"

Major Flint flew to his feet.

"Well, thank ye, thank ye," he said. "Now where's that soda water you offered me just now?" he shouted to the steward.

The speed and completeness of the reconciliation was in no way remarkable, for when two men quarrel whenever they meet, it follows that they make it up again with corresponding frequency, else there could be no fresh quarrels at all. This one had been a shade more acute than most, and the drop into amity again was a shade more precipitous.

Major Flint in his eagerness had put most of his moustache into the life-giving tumbler, and dried it on his handkerchief.

"After all, it was a most amusing incident," he said. "There was I with my back turned, waiting for you to give it up, when your bl — wretched little ball hit my foot. I must remember that. I'll serve you with the same spoon some day, at least I would if I thought it sportsmanlike. Well, well, enough said. Astonishing good whisky, that of yours."

Captain Puffin helped himself to rather more than half of what now remained in the flask.

"Help yourself, Major," he said.

"Well, thank ye, I don't mind if I do," he said, reversing the flask over the tumbler. "There's a good tramp in front of us now that the last tram has gone. Tram and tramp! Upon my word, I've half a mind to telephone for a taxi."

This, of course, was a direct hint. Puffin ought clearly to pay for a taxi, having won two half-crowns to-day. This casual drink did not constitute the usual drink stood by the winner, and paid for with cash over the counter. A drink (or two) from a flask was not the same thing . . . Puffin naturally saw it in another light. He had paid for the whisky which Major Flint had drunk (or owed for it) in his wine-merchant's bill. That was money just as much as a florin pushed across the counter. But he was so excessively pleased with himself over the adroitness with which he had claimed the last hole, that he quite overstepped the bounds of his habitual parsimony.

"Well, you trot along to the telephone and order a taxi," he said, "and I'll pay for it."

"Done with you," said the other.

Their comradeship was now on its most felicitous level again, and they sat on the bench outside the club-house till the arrival of their unusual conveyance.

"Lunching at the Poppits' to-morrow?" asked Major Flint.

"Yes. Meet you there? Good. Bridge afterwards, suppose."

"Sure to be. Wish there was a chance of more red-currant fool. That was a decent tipple, all but the red-currants. If I had had all the old brandy that was served for my ration in one glass, and all the champagne in another, I should have been better content."

Captain Puffin was a great cynic in his own misogynistic way.

"Camouflage for the fair sex," he said. "A woman will lick up half a bottle of brandy if it's called plum-pudding, and ask for more, whereas if you offered her a small brandy and soda, she would think you were insulting her."

"Bless them, the funny little fairies," said the Major.

"Well, what I tell you is true, Major," said Puffin. "There's old Mapp. Teetotaller she calls herself, but she played a bo'sun's part in that red-currant fool. Bit rosy, I thought her, as we escorted her home."

"So she was," said the Major. "So she was. Said good-bye to us on her doorstep as if she thought she was a perfect Venus Ana — Ana something."

"Anno Domini," giggled Puffin.

"Well, well, we all get long in the tooth in time," said Major Flint charitably. "Fine figure of a woman, though."

"Eh?" said Puffin archly.

"Now none of your sailor-talk ashore, Captain," said the Major, in high good humour. "I'm not a marrying man any more than you are. Better if I had been perhaps, more years ago than I care to think about. Dear me, my wound's going to trouble me to-night."

"What do you do for it, Major?" asked Puffin.

"Do for it? Think of old times a bit over my diaries."

"Going to let the world have a look at them some day?" asked Puffin.

"No, sir, I am not," said Major Flint. "Perhaps a hundred years hence — the date I have named in my will for their publication — someone may think them not so uninteresting. But all this toasting and buttering and grilling and frying your friends, and serving them up hot for all the old cats at a tea-table to mew over — Pah!"

Puffin was silent a moment in appreciation of these noble sentiments.

"But you put in a lot of work over them," he said at length. "Often when I'm going up to bed, I see the light still burning in your sitting-room window."

"And if it comes to that," rejoined the Major, "I'm sure I've often dozed off when I'm in bed and woken again, and pulled up my blind, and what not, and there's your light still burning. Powerful long roads those old Romans must have made, Captain."

The ice was not broken, but it was cracking in all directions under this unexampled thaw. The two had clearly indicated a mutual suspicion of each other's industrious habits after dinner . . . They had never got quite so far as this before: some quarrel had congealed the surface again. But now, with a desperate disagreement just behind them, and the unusual luxury of a taxi just in front, the vernal airs continued blowing in the most springlike manner.

"Yes, that's true enough," said Puffin. "Long roads they were, and dry roads at that, and if I stuck to them from after my supper every evening till midnight or more, should be smothered in dust."

"Unless you washed the dust down just once in a while," said Major Flint.

"Just so. Brain-work's an exhausting process; requires a little stimulant now and again," said Puffin. "I sit in my chair, you understand, and perhaps doze for a bit after my supper, and then I'll get my maps out, and have them handy beside me. And then, if there's something interesting the evening paper, perhaps I'll have a look at it, and bless me, if by that time it isn't already half-past ten or eleven, and it seems useless to tackle archæology then. And I just — just while away the time till I'm sleepy. But there seems to be a sort of legend among the ladies here, that I'm a great student of local topography and Roman roads, and all sorts of truck, and I find it better to leave it at that. Tiresome to go into long explanations. In fact," added Puffin in a burst of confidence, "the study I've done on Roman roads these last six months wouldn't cover a threepenny piece."

Major Flint gave a loud, choking guffaw and beat his fat leg.

"Well, if that's not the best joke I've heard for many a long day," he said. "There I've been in the house opposite you these last two years, seeing your light burning late night after night, and thinking to myself, 'There's my friend Puffin still at it! Fine thing to be an enthusiastic archæologist like that. That makes short work of a lonely evening for him if he's so buried in his books or his maps — Mapps, ha! ha! — that he doesn't seem to notice whether it's twelve o'clock or one or two, maybe!' And all the time you've been sitting snoozing and boozing in your chair, with your glass handy to wash the dust down."

Puffin added his falsetto cackle to this merriment.

"And, often I've thought to myself," he said, "'There's my friend the Major in his study opposite, with all his diaries round him, making a note here, and copying an extract there, and conferring with the Viceroy one day, and reprimanding the Maharajah of Bom-be-boo another. He's spending the evening on India's coral strand, he is, having tiffin and shooting tigers and Gawd knows what — '"

The Major's laughter boomed out again.

"And I never kept a diary in my life!" he cried. "Why there's enough cream in this situation to make a dishful of meringues. You and I, you know, the students of Tilling! The serious-minded students who do a hard day's work when all the pretty ladies have gone to bed. Often and often has old — I mean has that fine woman, Miss Mapp, told me that I work too hard at night! Recommended me to get earlier to bed, and do my work between six and eight in the morning! Six and eight in the morning! That's a queer time of day to recommend an old campaigner to be awake at! Often she's talked to you, too, I bet my hat, about sitting up late and exhausting the nervous faculties."

Major Flint choked and laughed and inhaled tobacco smoke till he got purple in the face.

"And you sitting up one side of the street," he gasped, "pretending to be interested in Roman roads, and me on the other pulling a long face over my diaries, and neither of us with a Roman road or a diary to our names. Let's have an end to such unsociable arrangements, old friend; you bring your Roman roads and the bottle to lay the dust over to me one night, and I'll bring my diaries and my peg over to you the next. Never drink alone — one of my maxims in life — if you can find someone to drink with you. And there were you within a few yards of me all the time sitting by your old solitary self, and there was I sitting by my old solitary self, and we each thought the other a serious-minded old buffer, busy on his life-work. I'm blessed if I heard of two such pompous old frauds as you and I, Captain! What a sight of hypocrisy there is in the world, to be sure! No offence — mind: I'm as bad as you, and you're as bad as me, and we're both as bad as each other. But no more solitary confinement of an evening for Benjamin Flint, as long as you're agreeable."

The advent of the taxi was announced, and arm in arm they limped down the steep path together to the road. A little way off to the left was the great bunker which, primarily, was the cause of their present amity. As they drove by it, the Major waggled his red hand at it.

"Au reservoir," he said. "Back again soon!"

*****

It was late that night when Miss Mapp felt that she was physically incapable of tacking on a single poppy more to the edge of her skirt, and went to the window of the garden-room where she had been working, to close it. She glanced up at the top story of her own house, and saw that the lights in the servants' rooms were out: she glanced to the right and concluded that her gardener had gone to bed: finally, she glanced down the street and saw with a pang of pleasure that the windows of the Major's house showed no sign of midnight labour. This was intensely gratifying: it indicated that her influence was at work in him, for in response to her wish, so often and so tactfully urged on him, that he would go to bed earlier and not work so hard at night, here was the darkened window, and she dismissed as unworthy the suspicion which had been aroused by the red-currant fool. The window of his bedroom was dark too: he must have already put out his light, and Miss Mapp made haste over her little tidyings so that she might not be found a transgressor to her own precepts. But there was a light in Captain Puffin's house: he had a less impressionable nature than the Major and was in so many ways far inferior. And did he really find Roman roads so wonderfully exhilarating? Miss Mapp sincerely hoped that he did, and that it was nothing else of less pure and innocent allurement that kept him up . . . As she closed the window very gently, it did just seem to her that there had been something equally baffling in Major Flint's egoistical vigils over his diaries; that she had wondered whether there was not something else (she had hardly formulated what) which kept his lights burning so late. But she would now cross him — dear man — and his late habits, out of the list of riddles about Tilling which awaited solution. Whatever it had been (diaries or what not) that used to keep him up, he had broken the habit now, whereas Captain Puffin had not. She took her poppy-bordered skirt over her arm, and smiled her thankful way to bed. She could allow herself to wonder with a little more definiteness, now that the Major's lights were out and he was abed, what it could be which rendered Captain Puffin so oblivious to the passage of time, when he was investigating Roman roads. How glad she was that the Major was not with him . . . "Benjamin Flint!" she said to herself as, having put her window open, she trod softly (so as not to disturb the slumberer next door) across her room on her fat white feet to her big white bed. "Good-night, Major Benjy," she whispered, as she put her light out.

*****

It was not to be supposed that Diva would act on Miss Mapp's alarming hints that morning as to the fate of coal-hoarders, and give, say, a ton of fuel to the hospital at once, in lieu of her usual smaller Christmas contribution, without making further inquiries in the proper quarters as to the legal liabilities of having, so she ascertained, three tons in her cellar, and as soon as her visitor had left her this morning, she popped out to see Mr. Wootten, her coal-merchant. She returned in a state of fury, for there were no regulations whatever in existence with regard to the amount of coal that any householder might choose to amass, and Mr. Wootten complimented her on her prudence in having got in a reasonable supply, for he thought it quite probable that, if the coal strike took place, there would be some difficulty in month's time from now in replenishing cellars. "But we've had a good supply all the summer," added agreeable Mr. Wootten, "and all my customers have got their cellars well stocked."

Diva rapidly recollected that the perfidious Elizabeth was among them.

"O but, Mr. Wootten," she said, "Miss Mapp popped — dropped in to see me just now. Told me she had hardly got any."

Mr. Wootten turned up his ledger. It was not etiquette to disclose the affairs of one client to another, but if there was a cantankerous customer, one who was never satisfied with prices and quality, that client was Miss Mapp . . . He allowed a broad grin to overspread his agreeable face.

"Well, ma'am, if in a month's time I'm short of coal, there are friends of yours in Tilling who can let you have plenty," he permitted himself to say . . .

It was idle to attempt to cut out bunches of roses while her hand was so feverish, and she trundled up and down the High Street to cool off. Had she not been so prudent as to make inquiries, as likely as not she would have sent a ton of coal that very day to the hospital, so strongly had Elizabeth's perfidious warning inflamed her imagination as to the fate of hoarders, and all the time Elizabeth's own cellars were glutted, though she had asserted that she was almost fuelless. Why, she must have in her possession more coal than Diva herself, since Mr. Wootten had clearly implied that it was Elizabeth who could be borrowed from! And all because of a wretched piece of rose-madder worsted . . .

By degrees she calmed down, for it was no use attempting to plan revenge with a brain at fever-heat. She must be calm and icily ingenious. As the cooling-process went on she began to wonder whether it was worsted alone that had prompted her friend's diabolical suggestion. It seemed more likely that another motive (one strangely Elizabethan) was the cause of it. Elizabeth might be taken for certain as being a coal-hoarder herself, and it was ever so like her to divert suspicion by pretending her cellar was next to empty. She had been equally severe on any who might happen to be hoarding food, in case transport was disarranged and supplies fell short, and with a sudden flare of authentic intuition, Diva's mind blazed with the conjecture that Elizabeth was hoarding food as well.

Luck ever attends the bold and constructive thinker: the apple, for instance, fell from the tree precisely when Newton's mind was groping after the law of gravity, and as Diva stepped into her grocer's to begin her morning's shopping (for she had been occupied with roses ever since breakfast) the attendant was at the telephone at the back of the shop. He spoke in a lucid telephone-voice.

"We've only two of the big tins of corned beef," he said; and there was a pause, during which, to a psychic, Diva's ears might have seemed to grow as pointed with attention as a satyr's. But she could only hear little hollow quacks from the other end.

"Tongue as well. Very good. I'll send them up at once," he added, and came forward into the shop.

"Good morning," said Diva. Her voice was tremulous with anxiety and investigation. "Got any big tins of corned beef? The ones that contain six pounds."

"Very sorry, ma'am. We've only got two, and they've just been ordered."

"A small pot of ginger then, please," said Diva recklessly. "Will you send it round immediately?"

"Yes, ma'am. The boy's just going out."

That was luck. Diva hurried into the street, and was absorbed by the headlines of the news outside the stationer's. This was a favourite place for observation, for you appeared to be quite taken up by the topics of the day, and kept an oblique eye on the true object of your scrutiny . . . She had not got to wait long, for almost immediately the grocer's boy came out of the shop with a heavy basket on his arm, delivered the small pot of ginger at her own door, and proceeded along the street. He was, unfortunately, a popular and a conversational youth, who had a great deal to say to his friends, and the period of waiting to see if he would turn up the steep street that led to Miss Mapp's house was very protracted. At the corner he deliberately put down the basket altogether and lit a cigarette, and never had Diva so acutely deplored the spread of the tobacco-habit among the juvenile population.

Having refreshed himself he turned up the steep street.

He passed the fishmonger's and the fruiterer's; he did not take the turn down to the dentist's and Mr. Wyse's. He had no errand to the Major's house or to the Captain's. Then, oh then, he rang the bell at Miss Mapp's back door. All the time Diva had been following him, keeping her head well down so as to avert the possibility of observation from the window of the garden-room, and walking so slowly that the motion of her feet seemed not circular at all . . . Then the bell was answered, and he delivered into Withers' hands one, two tins of corned beef and a round ox-tongue. He put the basket on his head and came down the street again, shrilly whistling. If Diva had had any reasonably small change in her pocket, she would assuredly have given him some small share in it. Lacking this, she trundled home with all speed, and began cutting out roses with swift and certain strokes of the nail-scissors.

Now she had already noticed that Elizabeth had paid visits to the grocer's on three consecutive days (three consecutive days: think of it!), and given that her purchases on other occasions had been on the same substantial scale as to-day, it became a matter of thrilling interest as to where she kept these stores. She could not keep them in the coal cellar, for that was already bursting with coal, and Diva, who had assisted her (the base one) in making a prodigious quantity of jam that year from her well-stocked garden, was aware that the kitchen cupboards were like to be as replete as the coal-cellar, before those hoardings of dead oxen began. Then there was the big cupboard under the stairs, but that could scarcely be the site of this prodigious cache, for it was full of cardboard and curtains and carpets and all the rubbishy accumulations which Elizabeth could not bear to part with. Then she had large cupboards in her bedroom and spare rooms full to overflowing of mouldy clothes, but there was positively not another cupboard in the house that Diva knew of, and she crushed her temples in her hands in the attempt to locate the hiding-place of the hoard.

Diva suddenly jumped up with a happy squeal of discovery, and in her excitement snapped her scissors with so random a stroke that she completely cut in half the bunch of roses that she was engaged on. There was another cupboard, the best and biggest of all and the most secret and the most discreet. It lay embedded in the wall of the garden-room, cloaked and concealed behind the shelves a false bookcase, which contained no more than the simulacra of books, just books with titles that had never yet appeared on any honest book. There were twelve volumes of "The Beauties of Nature," a shelf full of "Elegant Extracts," there were volumes simply called "Poems," there were "Commentaries," there were "Travels" and "Astronomy" and the lowest and tallest shelf was full of "Music." A card-table habitually stood in front of this false repository learning, and it was only last week that Diva, prying casually round the room while Elizabeth had gone to take off her gardening-gloves, had noticed a modest catch let into the wood-work. Without doubt, then, the bookcase was the door of the cupboard, and with a stroke of intuition, too sure to be called a guess, Diva was aware that she had correctly inferred the storage of this nefarious hoard. It only remained to verify her conclusion, and, if possible, expose it with every circumstance of public ignominy. She was in no hurry: she could bide her time, aware that, in all probability, every day that passed would see an addition to its damning contents. Some day, when she was playing bridge and the card-table had been moved out, in some rubber when she herself was dummy and Elizabeth greedily playing the hand, she would secretly and accidentally press the catch which her acute vision had so providentially revealed to her . . .

She attacked her chintz curtains again with her appetite for the pink roses agreeably whetted. Another hour's work would give her sufficient bunches for her purpose, and unless the dyer was as perfidious as Elizabeth, her now purple jacket and skirt would arrive that afternoon. Two days' hard work would be sufficient for so accomplished a needlewoman as herself to make these original decorations.

In the meantime, for Diva was never idle, and was chiefly occupied with dress, she got out a certain American fashion paper. There was in it the description of a tea-gown worn by Mrs. Titus W. Trout which she believed was within her dressmaking capacity. She would attempt it, anyhow, and if it proved to be beyond her, she could entrust the more difficult parts to that little dressmaker whom Elizabeth employed, and who was certainly very capable. But the costume was of so daring and splendid a nature that she feared to take anyone into her confidence about it, lest some hint or gossip — for Tilling was a gossipy place — might leak out. Kingfisher blue! It made her mouth water to dwell on the sumptuous syllables!

*****

Miss Mapp was so feverishly occupied all next morning with the application of poppies to the corn-coloured skirt that she paid very little attention to the opening gambits of the day, either as regards the world in general, or, more particularly, Major Benjy. After his early retirement last night he was probably up with the lark this morning, and when between half-past ten and eleven his sonorous "Qui-hi!" sounded through her open window, the shock she experienced interrupted for a moment her floral industry. It was certainly very odd that, having gone to bed at so respectable an hour last night, he should be calling for his porridge only now, but with an impulse of unusual optimism, she figured him as having been at work on his diaries before breakfast, and in that absorbing occupation having forgotten how late it was growing. That, no doubt, was the explanation, though it would be nice to know for certain, if the information positively forced itself on her notice . . . As she worked, (framing her lips with elaborate motions to the syllables) she dumbly practised the phrase "Major Benjy." Sometimes in moments of gallantry he called her "Miss Elizabeth," and she meant, when she had got accustomed to it by practice, to say "Major

Benjy" to him by accident, and he would, no doubt, beg her to make a habit of that friendly slip of the tongue . . . "Tongue" led to a new train of thought, and presently she paused in her work, and pulling the card-table away from the deceptive bookcase, she pressed the concealed catch of the door, and peeped in.

There was still room for further small precautions against starvation owing to the impending coal-strike, and she took stock of her provisions. Even if the strike lasted quite a long time, there would now be no immediate lack of the necessaries of life, for the cupboard glistened with tinned meats, and the flour-merchant had sent a very sensible sack. This with considerable exertion she transferred to a high shelf in the cupboard, instead of allowing it to remain standing on the floor, for Withers had informed her of an unpleasant rumour about a mouse, which Mary had observed, lost in thought in front of the cupboard. "So mousie shall only find tins on the floor now," thought Miss Mapp. "Mousie shall try his teeth on tins." . . . There was tea and coffee in abundance, jars of jam filled the kitchen shelves, and if this morning she laid in a moderate supply of dried fruits, there was no reason to face the future with anything but fortitude. She would see about that now, for, busy though she was, she could not miss the shopping-parade. Would Diva, she wondered, be at her window, snipping roses out of chintz curtains? The careful, thrifty soul. Perhaps this time to-morrow, Diva, looking out of her window, would see that somebody else had been quicker about being thrifty than she. That would be fun!

The Major's dining-room window was open, and as Miss Mapp passed it, she could not help hearing loud, angry remarks about eggs coming from inside. That made it clear that he was still at breakfast, and that if he had been working at his diaries in the fresh morning hours and forgetting the time, early rising, in spite of his early retirement last night, could not be supposed to suit his Oriental temper. But a change of habits was invariably known to be upsetting, and Miss Mapp was hopeful that in a day or two he would feel quite a different man. Further down the street was quaint Irene lounging at the door of her new studio (a converted coach-house), smoking a cigarette and dressed like a jockey.

"Hullo, Mapp," she said. "Come and have a look round my new studio. You haven't seen it yet. I shall give a house-warming next week. Bridge-party!"

Miss Mapp tried to steel herself for the hundredth time to appear quite unconscious that she was being addressed when Irene said "Mapp" in that odious manner. But she never could summon up sufficient nerve to be rude to so awful a mimic . . .

"Good morning, dear one," she said sycophantically. "Shall I peep in for a moment?"

The decoration of the studio was even more appalling than might have been expected. There was a German stove in the corner made of pink porcelain, the rafters and roof were painted scarlet, the walls were of magenta distemper and the floor was blue. In the corner was a very large orange-coloured screen. The walls were hung with specimens of Irene's art, there was a stout female with no clothes on at all, whom it was impossible not to recognize as being Lucy; there were studies of fat legs and ample bosoms, and on the easel was a picture, evidently in process of completion, which represented a man. From this Miss Mapp instantly averted her eyes.

"Eve," said Irene, pointing to Lucy.

Miss Mapp naturally guessed that the gentleman who was almost in the same costume was Adam, and turned completely away from him.

"And what a lovely idea to have a blue floor, dear," she said. "How original you are. And that pretty scarlet ceiling. But don't you find when you're painting that all these bright colours disturb you?"

"Not a bit: they stimulate your sense of colour."

Miss Mapp moved towards the screen.

"What a delicious big screen," she said.

"Yes, but don't go behind it, Mapp," said Irene, "or you'll see my model undressing."

Miss Mapp retreated from it precipitately, as from a wasp's nest, and examined some of the studies on the wall, for it was more than probable from the unfinished picture on the easel that Adam lurked behind the delicious screen. Terrible though it all was, she was conscious of an unbridled curiosity to know who Adam was. It was dreadful to think that there could be any man in Tilling so depraved as to stand to be looked at with so little on . . .

Irene strolled round the walls with her.

"Studies of Lucy," she said.

"I see, dear," said Miss Mapp. "How clever! Legs and things! But when you have your bridge-party, won't you perhaps cover some of them up, or turn them to the wall? We should all be looking at your pictures instead of attending to our cards. And if you were thinking of asking the Padre, you know . . ."

They were approaching the corner of the room where the screen stood, when a movement there as if Adam had hit it with his elbow made Miss Mapp turn round. The screen fell flat on the ground and within a yard of her stood Mr. Hopkins, the proprietor of the fish-shop just up the street. Often and often had Miss Mapp had pleasant little conversations with him, with a view to bringing down the price of flounders. He had little bathing-drawers on . . .

"Hullo, Hopkins, are you ready?" said Irene. "You know Miss Mapp, don't you?"

Miss Mapp had not imagined that Time and Eternity combined could hold so embarrassing a moment. She did not know where to look, but wherever she looked, it should not be at Hopkins. But (wherever she looked) she could not be unaware that Hopkins raised his large bare arm and touched the place where his cap would have been, if he had had one.

"Good-morning, Hopkins," she said. "Well, Irene darling, I must be trotting, and leave you to your —" she hardly knew what to call it — "to your work."

She tripped from the room, which seemed to be entirely full of unclothed limbs, and redder than one of Mr. Hopkins's boiled lobsters hurried down the street. She felt that she could never face him again, but would be obliged to go to the establishment in the High Street where Irene dealt, when it was fish she wanted from a fish-shop . . . Her head was in a whirl at the brazenness of mankind, especially womankind. How had Irene started the overtures that led to this? Had she just said to Hopkins one morning: "Will you come to my studio and take off all your clothes?" If Irene had not been such a wonderful mimic, she would certainly have felt it her duty to go straight to the Padre, and, pulling down her veil, confide to him the whole sad story. But as that was out of the question, she went into Twenlow's and ordered four pounds of dried apricots.

CHAPTER IV

The dyer, as Diva had feared, proved perfidious, and it was not till the next morning that her maid brought her the parcel containing the coat and skirt of the projected costume. Diva had already done her marketing, so that she might have no other calls on her time to interfere with the tacking on of the bunches of pink roses, and she hoped to have the dress finished in time for Elizabeth's afternoon bridge-party next day, an invitation to which had just reached her. She had also settled to have a cold lunch to-day, so that her cook as well as her parlour-maid could devote themselves to the job.

She herself had taken the jacket for decoration, and was just tacking the first rose on to the collar, when she looked out of the window, and what she saw caused her needle to fall from her nerveless hand. Tripping along the opposite pavement was Elizabeth. She had on a dress, the material of which, after a moment's gaze, Diva identified: it was that corn-coloured coat and skirt which she had worn so much last spring. But the collar, the cuffs, the waistband and the hem of the skirt were covered with staring red poppies. Next moment, she called to remembrance the chintz that had once covered Elizabeth's sofa in the garden-room.

Diva wasted no time, but rang the bell. She had to make certain.

"Janet," she said, "go straight out into the High Street, and walk close behind Miss Mapp. Look very carefully at her dress; see if the poppies on it are of chintz."

Janet's face fell.

"Why, ma'am, she's never gone and —" she began.

"Quick!" said Diva in a strangled voice.

Diva watched from her window. Janet went out, looked this way and that, spied the quarry, and skimmed up the High Street on feet that twinkled as fast as her mistress's. She came back much out of breath with speed and indignation.

"Yes, ma'am," she said. "They're chintz sure enough. Tacked on, too, just as you were meaning to do. Oh, ma'am —"

Janet quite appreciated the magnitude of the calamity and her voice failed.

"What are we to do, ma'am?" she added.

Diva did not reply for a moment, but sat with eyes closed in profound and concentrated thought. It required no reflection to decide how impossible it was to appear herself to-morrow in a dress which seemed to ape the costume which all Tilling had seen Elizabeth wearing to-day, and at first it looked as if there was nothing to be done with all those laboriously acquired bunches of rosebuds; for it was clearly out of the question to use them as the decoration for any costume, and idle to think of sewing them back into the snipped and gashed curtains. She looked at the purple skirt and coat that hungered for their flowers, and then she looked at Janet. Janet was a short, roundabout person; it was ill-naturedly supposed that she had much the same figure as her mistress . . .

Then the light broke, dazzling and diabolical, and Diva bounced to her feet, blinded by its splendour.

"My coat and skirt are yours, Janet," she said. "Get with the work both of you. Bustle. Cover it with roses. Have it finished to-night. Wear it to-morrow. Wear it always."

She gave a loud cackle of laughter and threaded her needle.

"Lor, ma'am!" said Janet, admiringly. "That's a teaser! And thank you, ma'am!"

"It was roses, roses all the way." Diva had quite miscalculated the number required, and there were sufficient not only to cover collar, cuffs and border of the skirt with them but to make another line of them six inches above the hem. Original and gorgeous as the dress would be, it was yet a sort of parody of Elizabeth's costume which was attracting so much interest and attention as she popped in and out of shops to-day. To-morrow that would be worn by Janet, and Janet (or Diva was much mistaken) should encourage her friends to get permission to use up old bits of chintz. Very likely chintz decoration would become quite a vogue among the servant maids of Tilling . . . How Elizabeth had got hold of the idea mattered nothing, but anyhow she would be surfeited with the idea before Diva had finished with her. It was possible, of course (anything was possible), that it had occurred to her independently, but Diva was loath to give so innocent an ancestry to her adoption of it. It was far more sensible to take for granted that she had got wind of Diva's invention by some odious, underhand piece of spying. What that might be must be investigated (and probably determined) later, but at present the business of Janet's roses eclipsed every other interest.

Miss Mapp's shopping that morning was unusually prolonged, for it was important that every woman in Tilling should see the poppies on the corn-coloured ground, and know that she had worn that dress before Diva appeared in some mean adaptation of it. Though the total cost of her entire purchases hardly amounted to a shilling, she went in and out of an amazing number of shops, and made a prodigious series of inquiries into the price of commodities that ranged from motor-cars to sealing-wax, and often entered a shop twice because (wreathed in smiling apologies for her stupidity) she had forgotten what she was told the first time. By twelve o'clock she was satisfied that practically everybody, with one exception, had seen her, and that her costume had aroused a deep sense of jealousy and angry admiration. So cunning was the handiwork of herself, Withers and Mary that she felt fairly sure that no one had the slightest notion of how this decoration of poppies was accomplished, for Evie had run round her in small mouse-like circles, murmuring to herself: "Very effective idea; is it woven into the cloth, Elizabeth? Dear me, I wonder where I could get some like it," and Mrs. Poppit had followed her all up the street, with eyes glued to the hem of her skirt, and a completely puzzled face: "but then," so thought Elizabeth sweetly "even members of the Order of the British Empire can't have everything their own way." As for the Major, he had simply come to a dead stop when he bounced out of his house as she passed, and said something very gallant and appropriate. Even the absence of that one inhabitant of Tilling, dear Diva, did not strike a jarring note in this pæan of triumph, for Miss Mapp was quite satisfied that Diva was busy indoors, working her fingers to the bone over the application of bunches of roses, and, as usual, she was perfectly correct in her conjecture. But dear Diva would have to see the new frock to-morrow afternoon, at the latest, when she came to the bridge-party. Perhaps she would then, for the first time, be wearing the roses herself, and everybody would very pleasantly pity her. This was so rapturous a thought, that when Miss Mapp, after her prolonged shopping and with her almost empty basket, passed Mr. Hopkins standing outside his shop on her return home again, she gave him her usual smile, though without meeting his eye, and tried to forget how much of him she had seen yesterday. Perhaps she might speak to him to-morrow and gradually resume ordinary relations, for the prices at the other fish shop were as high as the quality of the fish was low . . . She told herself that there was nothing actually immoral in the human skin, however embarrassing it was.

*****

Miss Mapp had experienced a cruel disappointment last night, though the triumph of this morning had done something to soothe it, for Major Benjy's window had certainly been lit up to a very late hour, and so it was clear that he had not been able, twice in succession, to tear himself away from his diaries, or whatever else detained him, and go to bed at a proper time. Captain Puffin, however, had not sat up late; indeed he must have gone to bed quite unusually early, for his window was dark by half-past nine. To-night, again the position was reversed, and it seemed that Major Benjy was "good" and Captain Puffin was "bad." On the whole, then, there was cause for thankfulness, and as she added a tin of biscuits and two jars of bovril to her prudent stores, she found herself a conscious sceptic about those Roman roads. Diaries (perhaps) were a little different, for egoism was a more potent force than archæology, and for her part she now definitely believed that Roman roads spelt some form of drink. She was sorry to believe it, but it was her duty to believe something of the kind, and she really did not know what else to believe. She did not go so far as mentally to accuse him of drunkenness, but considering the way he absorbed red-currant fool, it was clear that he was no foe to alcohol and probably watered the Roman roads with it. With her vivid imagination she pictured him —

Miss Mapp recalled herself from this melancholy reflection and put up her hand just in time to save a bottle of bovril which she had put on the top shelf in front of the sack of flour from tumbling to the ground. With the latest additions she had made to her larder, it required considerable ingenuity to fit all the tins and packages in, and for a while she diverted her mind from Captain Puffin's drinking to her own eating. But by careful packing and balancing she managed to stow everything away with sufficient economy of space to allow her to shut the door, and then put the card-table in place again. It was then late, and with a fond look at her sweet flowers sleeping in the moonlight, she went to bed. Captain Puffin's sitting-room was still alight, and even as she deplored this, his shadow in profile crossed the blind. Shadows were queer things — she could make a beautiful shadow-rabbit on the wall by a dexterous interlacement of fingers and thumbs — and certainly this shadow, in the momentary glance she had of it, appeared to have a large moustache. She could make nothing whatever out of that, except to suppose that just as fingers and thumbs became a rabbit, so his nose became a moustache, for he could not have grown one since he came back from golf . . .

*****

She was out early for her shopping next morning, for there were some delicacies to be purchased for her bridge-party, more particularly some little chocolate cakes she had lately discovered which looked very small and innocent, were in reality of so cloying and substantial a nature, that the partaker thereof would probably not feel capable of making any serious inroads into other provisions. Naturally she was much on the alert to-day, for it was more than possible that Diva's dress was finished and in evidence. What colour it would be she did not know, but a large quantity of rosebuds would, even at a distance, make identification easy. Diva was certainly not at her window this morning, so it seemed more than probable that they would soon meet.

Far away, just crossing the High Street at the further end, she caught sight of a bright patch of purple, very much of the required shape. There was surely a pink border round the skirt and a pink panel on the collar, and just as surely Mrs. Bartlett, recognizable for her gliding mouse-like walk, was moving in its fascinating wake. Then the purple patch vanished into a shop, and Miss Mapp, all smiles and poppies, went with her basket up the street. Presently she encountered Evie, who, also all smiles, seemed to have some communication to make, but only got as far as "Have you seen" — when she gave a little squeal of laughter, quite inexplicable, and glided into some dark entry. A minute afterwards, the purple patch suddenly appeared from a shop and almost collided with her. It was not Diva at all, but Diva's Janet.

The shock was so indescribably severe that Miss Mapp's smile was frozen, so to speak, as by some sudden congealment on to her face, and did not thaw off it till she had reached the sharp turn at the end of the street, where she leaned heavily on the railing and breathed through her nose. A light autumnal mist overlay the miles of marsh, but the sun was already drinking it up, promising the Tillingites another golden day. The tidal river was at the flood, and the bright water lapped the bases of the turf-covered banks that kept it within its course. Beyond that was the tram-station towards which presently Major Benjy and Captain Puffin would be hurrying to catch the tram that would take them out to the golf links. The straight road across the marsh was visible, and the railway bridge. All these things were pitilessly unchanged, and Miss Mapp noted them blankly, until rage began to restore the numbed current of her mental processes.

*****

If the records of history contained any similar instance of such treachery and low cunning as was involved in this plot of Diva's to dress Janet in the rosebud chintz, Miss Mapp would have liked to be told clearly and distinctly what it was. She could trace the workings of Diva's base mind with absolute accuracy, and if all the archangels in the hierarchy of heaven had assured her that Diva had originally intended the rosebuds for Janet, she would have scorned them for their clumsy perjury. Diva had designed and executed that dress for herself, and just because Miss Mapp's ingenuity (inspired by the two rosebuds that had fluttered out of the window) had forestalled her, she had taken this fiendish revenge. It was impossible to pervade the High Street covered with chintz poppies when a parlour-maid was being equally pervasive in chintz rosebuds, and what was to be done with this frock executed with such mirth and malice by Withers, Mary and herself she had no idea. She might just as well give it Withers, for she could no longer wear it herself, or tear the poppies from the hem and bestrew the High Street with them . . . Miss Mapp's face froze into immobility again, for here, trundling swiftly towards her, was Diva herself.

Diva appeared not to see her till she got quite close.

"Morning, Elizabeth," she said. "Seen my Janet anywhere?"

"No," said Miss Mapp.

Janet (no doubt according to instructions received) popped out of a shop, and came towards her mistress.

"Here she is," said Diva. "All right, Janet. You go home. I'll see to the other things."

"It's a lovely day," said Miss Mapp, beginning to lash her tail. "So bright."

"Yes. Pretty trimming of poppies," said Diva. "Janet's got rose-buds."

This was too much.

"Diva, I didn't think it of you," said Miss Mapp in a shaking voice. "You saw my new frock yesterday, and you were filled with malice and envy, Diva, just because I had thought of using flowers off an old chintz as well as you, and came out first with it. You had meant to wear that purple frock yourself — though I must say it fits Janet perfectly — and just because I was first in the field you did this. You gave Janet that frock, so that I should be dressed in the same style as your parlour-maid, and you've got a black heart, Diva!"

"That's nonsense," said Diva firmly. "Heart's as red as any-body's, and talking of black hearts doesn't become *you*, Elizabeth. You knew I was cutting out roses from my curtains —"

Miss Mapp laughed shrilly.

"Well, if I happen to notice that you've taken your chintz cur-tains down," she said with an awful distinctness that showed the wisdom-teeth of which Diva had got three at the most, "and pink bunches of roses come flying out of your window into the High Street, even my poor wits, small as they are, are equal to drawing the conclusion that you are cutting roses out of curtains. Your well-known fondness for dress did the rest. With your permission, Diva, I intend to draw exactly what conclusions I please on every occa-sion, including this one."

"Ho! That's how you got the idea then," said Diva. "I knew you had cribbed it from me."

"Cribbed?" asked Miss Mapp, in ironical ignorance of what so vulgar and slangy an expression meant.

"Cribbed means taking what isn't yours," said Diva. "Even then, if you had only acted in a straightforward manner —"

Miss Mapp, shaken as with palsy, regretted that she had let slip, out of pure childlike joy, in irony, the manner in which she had obtained the poppy-notion, but in a quarrel regrets are useless, and she went on again.

"And would you very kindly explain how or when I have acted in a manner that was not straightforward," she asked with laborious politeness. "Or do I understand that a monopoly of cutting up chintz curtains for personal adornment has been bestowed on you by Act of Parliament?"

"You knew I was meaning to make a frock with chintz roses on it," said Diva. "You stole my idea. Worked night and day to be first. Just like you. Mean behaviour."

"It was meaner to give that frock to Janet," said Miss Mapp.

"You can give yours to Withers," snapped Diva.

"Much obliged, Mrs. Plaistow," said Miss Mapp.

*****

Diva had been watching Janet's retreating figure, and feeling that though revenge was sweet, revenge was also strangely expensive, for she had sacrificed one of the most strikingly successful frocks she had ever made on that smoking altar. Now her revenge was gratified, and deeply she regretted the frock. Miss Mapp's heart was similarly wrung by torture: revenge too had been hers (general revenge on Diva for existing), but this dreadful counter-stroke had made it quite impossible for her to enjoy the use of this frock any more, for she could not habit herself like a housemaid. Each, in fact, had, as matters at present stood, completely wrecked the other, like two express trains meeting in top-speed collision, and, since the quarrel had clearly risen to its utmost height, there was no farther joy of battle to be anticipated, but only the melancholy task of counting the corpses. So they paused, breathing very quickly and trembling, while both sought for some way out. Besides Miss Mapp had a bridge-party this afternoon, and if they parted now in this extreme state of tension, Diva might conceivably not come, thereby robbing herself of her bridge and spoiling her hostess's table. Naturally any permanent quarrel was not contemplated by either of them, for if quarrels were permanent in Tilling, nobody would be on speaking terms any more with anyone else in a day or two, and (hardly less disastrous) there could be no fresh quarrels with anybody, since you could not quarrel without words. There might be songs without words, as Mendelssohn had proved, but not rows without words. By what formula could this deadly antagonism be bridged without delay?

Diva gazed out over the marsh. She wanted desperately to regain her rosebud-frock, and she knew that Elizabeth was starving for further wearing of her poppies. Perhaps the wide, serene plain below inspired her with a hatred of littleness. There would be no loss of dignity in making a proposal that her enemy, she felt sure, would accept: it merely showed a Christian spirit, and set an example to Elizabeth, to make the first move. Janet she did not consider.

"If you are in a fit state to listen to reason, Elizabeth," she began.

Miss Mapp heaved a sigh of relief. Diva had thought of something. She swallowed the insult at a gulp.

"Yes, dear," she said.

"Got an idea. Take away Janet's frock, and wear it myself. Then you can wear yours. Too pretty for parlour-maids. Eh?"

A heavenly brightness spread over Miss Mapp's face.

"Oh, how wonderful of you to have thought of that, Diva," she said. "But how shall we explain it all to everybody?"

Diva clung to her rights. Though clearly Christian, she was human.

"Say I thought of tacking chintz on and told you," she said.

"Yes, darling," said Elizabeth. "That's beautiful, I agree. But poor Janet!"

"I'll give her some other old thing," said Diva. "Good sort, Janet. Wants me to win."

"And about her having been seen wearing it?"

"Say she hasn't ever worn it. Say they're mad," said Diva.

Miss Mapp felt it better to tear herself away before she began distilling all sorts of acidities that welled up in her fruitful mind. She could, for instance, easily have agreed that nothing was more probable than that Janet had been mistaken for her mistress . . .

"Au reservoir then, dear," she said tenderly. "See you at about four? And will you wear your pretty rosebud frock?"

This was agreed to, and Diva went home to take it away from Janet.

*****

The reconciliation of course was strictly confined to matters relating to chintz and did not include such extraneous subjects as coal-strike or food-hoarding, and even in the first glowing moments of restored friendliness, Diva began wondering whether she would have the opportunity that afternoon of testing the truth of her conjecture about the cupboard in the garden-room. Cudgel her brains as she might she could think of no other *cache* that could contain the immense amount of provisions that Elizabeth had probably accumulated, and she was all on fire to get to practical grips with the problem. As far as tins of corned beef and tongues went, Elizabeth might possibly have buried them in her garden in the manner of a dog, but it was not likely that a hoarder would limit herself to things in tins. No: there was a cupboard somewhere ready to burst with strong supporting foods . . .

Diva intentionally arrived a full quarter of an hour on the hither side of punctuality, and was taken by Withers out into the garden-room, where tea was laid, and two card-tables were in readiness. She was, of course, the first of the guests, and the moment Withers withdrew to tell her mistress that she had come, Diva stealthily glided to the cupboard, from in front of which the bridge-table had been removed, feeling the shrill joy of some romantic treasure hunter. She found the catch, she pressed it, she pulled open the door and the whole of the damning profusion of provisions burst upon her delighted eyes. Shelf after shelf was crowded with eatables; there were tins of corned beef and tongues (that she knew already), there was a sack of flour, there were tubes of Bath Oliver biscuits, bottles of bovril, the yield of a thousand condensed Swiss cows, jars of prunes . . . All these were in the front row, flush with the door, and who knew to what depth the cupboard extended? Even as she feasted her eyes on this incredible store, some package on the top shelf wavered and toppled, and she had only just time to shut the door again, in order to prevent it falling out on to the floor. But this displacement prevented the door from wholly closing, and push and shove as Diva might, she could not get the catch to click home, and the only result of her energy and efforts was to give rise to a muffled explosion from within, just precisely as if something made of cardboard had burst. That mental image was so vivid that to her fevered imagination it seemed to be real. This was followed by certain faint taps from within against "Elegant Extracts" and "Astronomy."

Diva grew very red in the face, and said "Drat it" under her breath. She did not dare open the door again in order to push things back, for fear of an uncontrollable stream of "things" pouring out. Some nicely balanced equilibrium had clearly been upset in those capacious shelves, and it was impossible to tell, without looking, how deep and how extensive the disturbance was. And in order to look, she had to open the bookcase again . . . Luckily the pressure against the door was not sufficiently heavy to cause it to swing wide, so the best she could do was to leave it just ajar with temporary quiescence inside. Simultaneously she heard Miss Mapp's step, and had no more than time to trundle at the utmost speed of her whirling feet across to the window, where she stood looking out, and appeared quite unconscious of her hostess's entry.

"Diva darling, how sweet of you to come so early!" she said. "A little cosy chat before the others arrive."

Diva turned round, much startled.

"Hullo!" she said. "Didn't hear you. Got Janet's frock you see."

("What makes Diva's face so red?" thought Miss Mapp.)

"So I see, darling," she said. "Lovely rose-garden. How well it suits you, dear! Did Janet mind?"

"No. Promised her a new frock at Christmas."

"That will be nice for Janet," said Elizabeth enthusiastically. "Shall we pop into the garden, dear, till my guests come?"

Diva was glad to pop into the garden and get away from the immediate vicinity of the cupboard, for though she had planned and looked forward to the exposure of Elizabeth's hoarding, she had not meant it to come, as it now probably would, in crashes of tins and bursting of bovril bottles. Again she had intended to have opened that door quite casually and innocently while she was being dummy, so that everyone could see how accidental the exposure was, and to have gone poking about the cupboard in Elizabeth's absence was a shade too professional, so to speak, for the usual detective work of Tilling. But the fuse was set now. Sooner or later the explosion must come. She wondered as they went out to commune with Elizabeth's sweet flowers till the other guests arrived how great a torrent would be let loose. She did not repent her exploration — far from it — but her pleasurable anticipations were strongly diluted with suspense.

Miss Mapp had found such difficulty in getting eight players together to-day, that she had transgressed her principles and asked Mrs. Poppit as well as Isabel, and they, with Diva, the two Bartletts, and the Major and the Captain, formed the party. The moment Mrs. Poppit appeared, Elizabeth hated her more than ever, for she put up her glasses, and began to give her patronizing advice about her garden, which she had not been allowed to see before.

"You have quite a pretty little piece of garden, Miss Mapp," she said, "though, to be sure, I fancied from what you said that it was more extensive. Dear me, your roses do not seem to be doing very well. Probably they are old plants and want renewing. You must send your gardener round — you keep a gardener? — and I will let you have a dozen vigorous young bushes."

Miss Mapp licked her dry lips. She kept a kind of gardener: two days a week.

"Too good of you," she said, "but that rose-bed is quite sacred, dear Mrs. Poppit. Not all the vigorous young bushes in the world would tempt me. It's my 'Friendship's Border:' some dear friend gave me each of my rose-trees."

Mrs. Poppit transferred her gaze to the wistaria that grew over the steps up to the garden-room. Some of the dear friends she thought must be centenarians.

"Your wistaria wants pruning sadly," she said. "Your gardener does not understand wistarias. That corner there was made, I may say, for fuchsias. You should get a dozen choice fuchsias."

Miss Mapp laughed.

"Oh, you must excuse me," she said with a glance at Mrs. Poppit's brocaded silk. "I can't bear fuchsias. They always remind me of over-dressed women. Ah, there's Mr. Bartlett. How de do, Padre. And dear Evie!"

Dear Evie appeared fascinated by Diva's dress.

"Such beautiful rosebuds," she murmured, "and what lovely shade of purple. And Elizabeth's poppies too, quite a pair of you. But surely this morning, Diva, didn't I see your good Janet in just such another dress, and I thought at the time how odd it was that —"

"If you saw Janet this morning," said Diva quite firmly, "you saw her in her print dress."

"And here's Major Benjy," said Miss Mapp, who had made her slip about his Christian name yesterday, and had been duly entreated to continue slipping. "And Captain Puffin. Well, that is nice! Shall we go into my little garden shed, dear Mrs. Poppit, and have our tea?"

Major Flint was still a little lame, for his golf to-day had been of the nature of gardening, and he hobbled up the steps behind the ladies, with that little cock-sparrow sailor following him and telling the Padre how badly and yet how successfully he himself had played.

"Pleasantest room in Tilling, I always say, Miss Elizabeth," said he, diverting his mind from a mere game to the fairies.

"My dear little room," said Miss Mapp, knowing that it was much larger than anything in Mrs. Poppit's house. "So tiny!"

"Oh, not a bad-sized little room," said Mrs. Poppit encouragingly. "Much the same proportions, on a very small scale, as the throne-room at Buckingham Palace."

"That beautiful throne-room!" exclaimed Miss Mapp. "A cup

of tea, dear Mrs. Poppit? None of that naughty red-currant fool, I am afraid. And a little chocolate-cake?"

These substantial chocolate cakes soon did their fell work of producing the sense of surfeit, and presently Elizabeth's guests dropped off gorged from the tea-table. Diva fortunately remembered their consistency in time, and nearly cleared a plate of jumbles instead, which the hostess had hoped would form a pleasant accompaniment to her dessert at her supper this evening, and was still crashingly engaged on them when the general drifting movement towards the two bridge-tables set in. Mrs. Poppit, with her glasses up, followed by Isabel, was employed in making a tour of the room, in case, as Miss Mapp had already determined, she never saw it again, examining the quality of the carpet, the curtains, the chair-backs with the air of a doubtful purchaser.

"And quite a quantity of books, I see," she announced as she came opposite the fatal cupboard. "Look, Isabel, what a quantity of books. There is something strange about them, though; I do not believe they are real."

She put out her hand and pulled at the back of one of the volumes of "Elegant Extracts." The door swung open, and from behind it came a noise of rattling, bumping and clattering. Something soft and heavy thumped on to the floor, and a cloud of floury dust arose. A bottle of bovril embedded itself quietly there without damage, and a tin of Bath Oliver biscuits beat a fierce tattoo on one of corned beef. Innumerable dried apricots from the burst package flew about like shrapnel, and tapped at the tins. A jar of prunes, breaking its fall on the flour, rolled merrily out into the middle of the floor.

The din was succeeded by complete silence. The Padre had said "What ho, i' fegs?" during the tumult, but his voice had been drowned by the rattling of the dried apricots. The Member of the Order of the British Empire stepped free of the provisions that bumped round her, and examined them through her glasses. Diva crammed the last jumble into her mouth and disposed of it with the utmost rapidity. The birthday of her life had come, as Miss Rossetti said.

"Dear Elizabeth!" she exclaimed. "What a disaster! All your little stores in case of the coal strike. Let me help to pick them up. I do not think anything is broken. Isn't that lucky?"

Evie hurried to the spot.

"Such a quantity of good things," she said rapidly under her breath. "Tinned meats and bovril and prunes, and ever so many apricots. Let me pick them all up, and with a little dusting . . . Why, what a big cupboard, and such a quantity of good things."

Miss Mapp had certainly struck a streak of embarrassments. What with naked Mr. Hopkins, and Janet's frock and this unveiling of her hoard, life seemed at the moment really to consist of nothing else than beastly situations. How on earth that catch of the door had come undone, she had no idea, but much as she would have liked to suspect foul play from somebody, she was bound to conclude that Mrs. Poppit with her prying hands had accidentally pressed it. It was like Diva, of course, to break the silence with odious allusions to hoarding, and bitterly she wished that she had not started the topic the other day, but had been content to lay in her stores without so pointedly affirming that she was doing nothing of the kind. But this was no time for vain laments, and restraining a natural impulse to scratch and beat Mrs. Poppit, she exhibited an admirable inventiveness and composure. Though she knew it would deceive nobody, everybody had to pretend he was deceived.

"Oh, my poor little Christmas presents for your needy parishioners, Padre," she said. "You've seen them before you were meant to, and you must forget all about them. And so little harm done, just an apricot or two. Withers will pick them all up, so let us get to our bridge."

Withers entered the room at this moment to clear away tea, and Miss Mapp explained it all over again.

"All our little Christmas presents have come tumbling out, Withers," she said. "Will you put as many as you can back in the cupboard and take the rest indoors? Don't tread on the apricots."

It was difficult to avoid doing this, as the apricots were everywhere, and their colour on the brown carpet was wonderfully protective. Miss Mapp herself had already stepped on two, and their adhesive stickiness was hard to get rid of. In fact, for the next few minutes the coal-shovel was in strong request for their removal from the soles of shoes, and the fender was littered with their squashed remains . . . The party generally was distinctly thoughtful as it sorted itself out into two tables, for every single member of it was trying to assimilate the amazing proposition that Miss Mapp had, half-way through September, loaded her cupboard with Christmas presents on a scale that staggered belief. The feat required thought: it required a faith so childlike as to verge on the imbecile. Conversation during deals had an awkward tendency towards discussion of the coal strike. As often as it drifted there the subject was changed very abruptly, just as if there was some occult reason for not speaking of so natural a topic. It concerned everybody, but it was rightly felt to concern Miss Mapp the most . . .

CHAPTER V

It was the Major's turn to entertain his friend, and by half-past nine, on a certain squally October evening, he and Puffin were seated by the fire in the diary-room, while the rain volleyed at the windows and occasional puffs of stinging smoke were driven down the chimney by the gale that squealed and buffeted round the house. Puffin, by way of keeping up the comedy of Roman roads, had brought a map of the district across from his house, but the more essential part of his equipment for this studious evening was a bottle of whisky. Originally the host had provided whisky for himself and his guest at these pleasant chats, but there were undeniable objections to this plan, because the guest always proved unusually thirsty, which tempted his host to keep pace with him, while if they both drank at their own expense, the causes of economy and abstemiousness had a better chance. Also, while the Major took his drinks short and strong in a small tumbler, Puffin enriched his with lemons and sugar in a large one, so that nobody could really tell if equality as well as fraternity was realized. But if each brought his own bottle . . .

It had been a trying day, and the Major was very lame. A drenching storm had come up during their golf, while they were far from the club-house, and Puffin, being three up, had very naturally refused to accede to his opponent's suggestion to call the match off. He was perfectly willing to be paid his half-crown and go home, but Major Flint, remembering that Puffin's game usually went to pieces if it rained, had rejected this proposal with the scorn that it deserved. There had been other disagreeable incidents as well. His driver, slippery from rain, had flown out of the Major's hands on the twelfth tee, and had "shot like a streamer of the northern morn," and landed in a pool of brackish water left by an unusually high tide. The ball had gone into another pool nearer the tee. The ground was greasy with moisture, and three holes further on Puffin had fallen flat on his face instead of lashing his fifth shot home on to the green, as he had intended. They had given each other stimies, and each had holed his opponent's ball by mistake; they had wrangled over the correct procedure if you lay in a rabbit-scrape or on the tram lines; the Major had lost a new ball; there was a mushroom on one of the greens between Puffin's ball and the hole . . . All these untoward incidents had come crowding in together, and from the Major's point of view, the worst of them all had been the collective incident that Puffin, so far from being put off by the rain, had, in spite of mushroom and falling down, played with a steadiness of which he was usually quite incapable. Consequently Major Flint was lame and his wound troubled him, while Puffin, in spite of his obvious reasons for complacency, was growing irritated with his companion's ill-temper, and was half blinded by wood-smoke.

He wiped his streaming eyes.

"You should get your chimney swept," he observed.

Major Flint had put his handkerchief over his face to keep the wood-smoke out of his eyes. He blew it off with a loud, indignant puff.

"Oh! Ah! Indeed!" he said.

Puffin was rather taken aback by the violence of these interjections; they dripped with angry sarcasm.

"Oh, well! No offence," he said.

"A man," said the Major impersonally, "makes an offensive remark, and says 'No offence.' If your own fireside suits you better than mine, Captain Puffin, all I can say is that you're at liberty to enjoy it!"

This was all rather irregular: they had indulged in a good stiff breeze this afternoon, and it was too early to ruffle the calm again. Puffin plucked and proffered an olive-branch.

"There's your handkerchief," he said, picking it up. "Now let's have one of our comfortable talks. Hot glass of grog and a chat over the fire: that's the best thing after such a wetting as we got this afternoon. I'll take a slice of lemon, if you'll be so good as to give it me, and a lump of sugar."

The Major got up and limped to his cupboard. It struck him precisely at that moment that Puffin scored considerably over lemons and sugar, because he was supplied with them gratis every other night; whereas he himself, when Puffin's guest, took nothing off his host but hot water. He determined to ask for some biscuits, anyhow, to-morrow . . .

"I hardly know whether there's a lemon left," he grumbled. "I must lay in a store of lemons. As for sugar —"

Puffin chose to disregard this suggestion.

"Amusing incident the other day," he said brightly, "when Miss Mapp's cupboard door flew open. The old lady didn't like it. Don't suppose the poor of the parish will see much of that corned beef."

The Major became dignified.

"Pardon me," he said. "When an esteemed friend like Miss Elizabeth tells me that certain provisions are destined for the poor of the parish, I take it that her statement is correct. I expect others of my friends, while they are in my presence, to do the same. I have the honour to give you a lemon, Captain Puffin, and a slice of sugar. I should say a lump of sugar. Pray make yourself comfortable."

This dignified and lofty mood was often one of the after-effects of an unsuccessful game of golf. It generally yielded quite quickly to a little stimulant. Puffin filled his glass from the bottle and the kettle, while his friend put his handkerchief again over his face.

"Well, I shall just have my grog before I turn in," he observed, according to custom. "Aren't you going to join me, Major?"

"Presently, sir," said the Major.

Puffin knocked out the consumed cinders in his pipe against the edge of the fender. Major Flint apparently was waiting for this, for he withdrew his handkerchief and closely watched the process. A minute piece of ash fell from Puffin's pipe on to the hearthrug, and he jumped to his feet and removed it very carefully with the shovel.

"I have your permission, I hope?" he said witheringly.

"Certainly, certainly," said Puffin. "Now get your glass, Major. You'll feel better in a minute or two."

Major Flint would have liked to have kept up this magnificent attitude, but the smell of Puffin's steaming glass beat dignity down, and after glaring at him, he limped back to the cupboard for his whisky bottle. He gave a lamentable cry when he beheld it.

"But I got that bottle in only the day before yesterday," he shouted, "and there's hardly a drink left in it."

"Well, you did yourself pretty well last night," said Puffin. "Those small glasses of yours, if frequently filled up, empty a bottle quicker than you seem to realize."

Motives of policy prevented the Major from receiving this with the resentment that was proper to it, and his face cleared. He would get quits over these incessant lemons and lumps of sugar.

"Well, you'll have to let me borrow from you to-night," he said genially, as he poured the rest of the contents of his bottle into the glass. "Ah, that's more the ticket! A glass of whisky a day keeps the doctor away."

The prospect of sponging on Puffin was most exhilarating, and he put his large slippered feet on to the fender.

"Yes, indeed, that was a highly amusing incident about Miss Mapp's cupboard," he said. "And wasn't Mrs. Plaistow down on her like a knife about it? Our fair friends, you know, have a pretty sharp eye for each other's little failings. They've no sooner finished one squabble than they begin another, the pert little fairies. They can't sit and enjoy themselves like two old cronies I could tell you of, and feel at peace with all the world."

He finished his glass at a gulp, and seemed much surprised to find it empty.

"I'll be borrowing a drop from you, old friend," he said.

"Help yourself, Major," said Puffin, with a keen eye as to how much he took.

"Very obliging of you. I feel as if I caught a bit of a chill this afternoon. My wound."

"Be careful not to inflame it," said Puffin.

"Thank ye for the warning. It's this beastly climate that touches it up. A winter in England adds years on to a man's life unless he takes care of himself. Take care of yourself, old boy. Have some more sugar."

Before long the Major's hand was moving slowly and instinctively towards Puffin's whisky bottle again.

"I reckon that big glass of yours, Puffin," he said, "holds between three and a half times to four times what my little tumbler holds. Between three and a half and four I should reckon. I may be wrong."

"Reckoning the water in, I daresay you're not far out, Major," said he. "And according to my estimate you mix your drink somewhere about three and a half times to four stronger than I mix mine."

"Oh, come, come!" said the Major.

"Three and a half to four times, *I* should say," repeated Puffin. "You won't find I'm far out."

He replenished his big tumbler, and instead of putting the bottle back on the table, absently deposited it on the floor on the far side of his chair. This second tumbler usually marked the most convivial period of the evening, for the first would have healed whatever unhappy discords had marred the harmony of the day, and, those being disposed of, they very contentedly talked through their hats about past prowesses, and took a rosy view of the youth and energy which still beat in their vigorous pulses. They would begin, perhaps, by extolling each other: Puffin, when informed that his friend would be fifty-four next birthday, flatly refused (without offence) to believe it, and, indeed, he was quite right in so doing, because the Major was in reality fifty-six. In turn, Major Flint would say that his friend had the figure of a boy of twenty, which caused Puffin presently to feel a little cramped and to wander negligently in front of the big looking-glass between the windows, and find this compliment much easier to swallow than the Major's age. For the next half-hour they would chiefly talk about themselves in a pleasant glow of self-satisfaction. Major Flint, looking at the various implements and trophies that adorned the room, would suggest putting a sporting challenge in the *Times*.

"'Pon my word, Puffin," he would say, "I've half a mind to do it. Retired Major of His Majesty's Forces — the King, God bless him!" (and he took a substantial sip); "'Retired Major, aged fifty-four, challenges any gentleman of fifty years or over.'"

"Forty," said Puffin sycophantically, as he thought over what he would say about himself when the old man had finished.

"Well, we'll halve it, we'll say forty-five, to please you, Puffin — let's see, where had I got to? — 'Retired Major challenges any gentleman of forty-five years or over to — to a shooting match in the morning, followed by half a dozen rounds with four-ounce gloves, a game of golf, eighteen holes, in the afternoon, and a billiard match of two hundred up after tea.' Ha! ha! I shouldn't feel much anxiety as to the result."

"My confounded leg!" said Puffin. "But I know a retired captain from His Majesty's merchant service — the King, God bless him! — aged fifty —"

"Ho! ho! Fifty, indeed!" said the Major, thinking to himself that a dried-up little man like Puffin might be as old as an Egyptian mummy. Who can tell the age of a kipper? . . .

"Not a day less, Major. 'Retired Captain, aged fifty, who'll take on all comers of forty-two and over, at a steeplechase, round of golf, billiard match, hopping match, gymnastic competition, swinging Indian clubs — ' No objection, gentlemen? Then carried *nem. con.*"

This gaseous mood, athletic, amatory or otherwise (the amatory ones were the worst), usually faded slowly, like the light from the setting sun or an exhausted coal in the grate, about the end of Puffin's second tumbler, and the gentlemen after that were usually somnolent, but occasionally laid the foundation for some disagreement next day, which they were too sleepy to go into now. Major Flint by this time would have had some five small glasses of whisky (equivalent, as he bitterly observed, to one in pre-war days), and as he measured his next with extreme care and a slightly jerky movement, would announce it as being his night-cap, though you would have thought he had plenty of night-caps on already. Puffin correspondingly took a thimbleful more (the thimble apparently belonging to some housewife of Anak), and after another half-hour of sudden single snores and startings awake again, of pipes frequently lit and immediately going out, the guest, still perfectly capable of coherent speech and voluntary motion in the required direction, would stumble across the dark cobbles to his house, and doors would be very carefully closed for fear of attracting the attention of the lady who at this period of the evening was usually known as "Old Mappy." The two were perfectly well aware of the sympathetic interest that Old Mappy took in all that concerned them, and that she had an eye on their evening séances was evidenced by the frequency with which the corner of her blind in the window of the garden-room was raised between, say, half-past nine and eleven at night. They had often watched with giggles the pencil of light that escaped, obscured at the lower end by the outline of Old Mappy's head, and occasionally drank to the "Guardian Angel." Guardian Angel, in answer to direct inquiries, had been told by Major Benjy during the last month that he worked at his diaries on three nights in the week and went to bed early on the others, to the vast improvement of his mental grasp.

"And on Sunday night, dear Major Benjy?" asked Old Mappy in the character of Guardian Angel.

"I don't think you knew my beloved, my revered mother, Miss Elizabeth," said Major Benjy. "I spend Sunday evening as — Well, well."

The very next Sunday evening Guardian Angel had heard the sound of singing. She could not catch the words, and only fragments of the tune, which reminded her of "The roseate morn hath passed away." Brimming with emotion, she sang it softly to herself as she undressed, and blamed herself very much for ever having thought that dear Major Benjy — She peeped out of her window when she had extinguished her light, but fortunately the singing had ceased.

*****

To-night, however, the epoch of Puffin's second big tumbler was not accompanied by harmonious developments. Major Benjy was determined to make the most of this unique opportunity of drinking his friend's whisky, and whether Puffin put the bottle on the further side of him, or under his chair, or under the table, he came padding round in his slippers and standing near the ambush while he tried to interest his friend in tales of love or tiger-shooting so as to distract his attention. When he mistakenly thought he had done so, he hastily refilled his glass, taking unusually stiff doses for fear of not getting another opportunity, and altogether omitting to ask Puffin's leave for these maraudings. When this had happened four or five times, Puffin, acting on the instinct of the polar bear who eats her babies for fear that anybody else should get them, surreptitiously poured the rest of his bottle into his glass, and filled it up to the top with hot water, making a mixture of extraordinary power.

Soon after this Major Flint came rambling round the table again. He was not sure whether Puffin had put the bottle by his chair or behind the coal-scuttle, and was quite ignorant of the fact that wherever it was, it was empty. Amorous reminiscences to-night had been the accompaniment to Puffin's second tumbler.

"Devilish fine woman she was," he said, "and that was the last that Benjamin Flint ever saw of her. She went up to the hills next morning —"

"But the last you saw of her just now was on the deck of the P. and O. at Bombay," objected Puffin. "Or did she go up to the hills on the deck of the P. and O.? Wonderful line!"

"No, sir," said Benjamin Flint, "that was Helen, *la belle Hélène*. It was *la belle Hélène* whom I saw off at the Apollo Bunder. I don't know if I told you — By Gad, I've kicked the bottle over. No idea you'd put it there. Hope the cork's in."

"No harm if it isn't," said Puffin, beginning on his third most fiery glass. The strength of it rather astonished him.

"You don't mean to say it's empty?" asked Major Flint. "Why just now there was close on a quarter of a bottle left."

"As much as that?" asked Puffin. "Glad to hear it."

"Not a drop less. You don't mean to say — Well, if you can drink that and can say hippopotamus afterwards, I should put that among your challenges, to men of four hundred and two: I should say forty-two. It's a fine thing to have a strong head, though if I drank what you've got in your glass, I should be tipsy, sir."

Puffin laughed in his irritating falsetto manner.

"Good thing that it's in my glass then, and not your glass," he said. "And lemme tell you, Major, in case you don't know it, that when I've drunk every drop of this and sucked the lemon, you'll have had far more out of my bottle this evening than I have. My usual twice and — and my usual night-cap, as you say, is what's my ration, and I've had no more than my ration. Eight Bells."

"And a pretty good ration you've got there," said the baffled Major. "Without your usual twice."

Puffin was beginning to be aware of that as he swallowed the fiery mixture, but nothing in the world would now have prevented his drinking every single drop of it. It was clear to him, among so much that was dim owing to the wood-smoke, that the Major would miss a good many drives to-morrow morning.

"And whose whisky is it?" he said, gulping down the fiery stuff.

"I know whose it's going to be," said the other.

"And I know whose it is now," retorted Puffin, "and I know whose whisky it is that's filled you up ti' as a drum. Tight as a drum," he repeated very carefully.

Major Flint was conscious of an unusual activity of brain, and, when he spoke, of a sort of congestion and entanglement of words. It pleased him to think that he had drunk so much of somebody's else whisky, but he felt that he ought to be angry.

"That's a very unmentionable sor' of thing to say," he remarked. "An' if it wasn't for the sacred claims of hospitality, I'd make you explain just what you mean by that, and make you eat your words. Pologize, in fact."

Puffin finished his glass at a gulp, and rose to his feet.

"Pologies be blowed," he said. "Hittopopamus!"

"And were you addressing that to me?" asked Major Flint with deadly calm.

"Of course, I was. Hippot — same animal as before. Pleasant old boy. And as for the lemon you lent me, well, I don't want it any more. Have a suck at it, ole fellow! I don't want it any more."

The Major turned purple in the face, made a course for the door like a knight's move at chess (a long step in one direction and a short one at right angles to the first) and opened it. The door thus served as an aperture from the room and a support to himself. He spoke no word of any sort or kind: his silence spoke for him in a far more dignified manner than he could have managed for himself.

Captain Puffin stood for a moment wreathed in smiles, and fingering the slice of lemon, which he had meant playfully to throw at his friend. But his smile faded, and by some sort of telepathic perception he realized how much more decorous it was to say (or, better, to indicate) good-night in a dignified manner than to throw lemons about. He walked in dots and dashes like a Morse code out of the room, bestowing a naval salute on the Major as he passed. The latter returned it with a military salute and a suppressed hiccup. Not a word passed.

Then Captain Puffin found his hat and coat without much difficulty, and marched out of the house, slamming the door behind him with a bang that echoed down the street and made Miss Mapp dream about a thunderstorm. He let himself into his own house, and bent down before his expired fire, which he tried to blow into life again. This was unsuccessful, and he breathed in a quantity of wood-ash.

He sat down by his table and began to think things out. He told himself that he was not drunk at all, but that he had taken an unusual quantity of whisky, which seemed to produce much the same effect as intoxication. Allowing for that, he was conscious that he was extremely angry about something, and had a firm idea that the Major was very angry too.

"But woz'it all been about?" he vainly asked himself. "Woz'it all been about?"

He was roused from his puzzling over this unanswerable conundrum by the clink of the flap in his letter-box. Either this was the first post in the morning, in which case it was much later than he thought, and wonderfully dark still, or it was the last post at night, in which case it was much earlier than he thought. But, whichever it was, a letter had been slipped into his box, and he brought it in. The gum on the envelope was still wet, which saved trouble in opening it. Inside was a half sheet containing but a few words. This curt epistle ran as follows:

"Sir,

"My seconds will wait on you in the course of to-morrow morning.

"Your faithful obedient servant,

"Benjamin Flint.

Captain Puffin."

Puffin felt as calm as a tropic night, and as courageous as a captain. Somewhere below his courage and his calm was an appalling sense of misgiving. That he successfully stifled.

"Very proper," he said aloud. "Qui' proper. Insults. Blood. Seconds won't have to wait a second. Better get a good sleep."

He went up to his room, fell on to his bed and instantly began to snore.

*****

It was still dark when he awoke, but the square of his window was visible against the blackness, and he concluded that though it was not morning yet, it was getting on for morning, which seemed a pity. As he turned over on to his side his hand came in contact with his coat, instead of a sheet, and he became aware that he had all his clothes on. Then, as with a crash of cymbals and the beating of a drum in his brain, the events of the evening before leaped into reality and significance. In a few hours now arrangements would have been made for a deadly encounter. His anger was gone, his whisky was gone, and in particular his courage was gone. He expressed all this compendiously by moaning "Oh, God!"

He struggled to a sitting position, and lit a match at which he kindled his candle. He looked for his watch beside it, but it was not there. What could have happened — then he remembered that it was in its accustomed place in his waistcoat pocket. A consultation of it followed by holding it to his ear only revealed the fact that it had stopped at half-past five. With the lucidity that was growing brighter in his brain, he concluded that this stoppage was due to the fact that he had not wound it up . . . It was after half-past five then, but how much later only the Lords of Time knew — Time which bordered so closely on Eternity.

He felt that he had no use whatever for Eternity but that he must not waste Time. Just now, that was far more precious.

*****

From somewhere in the Cosmic Consciousness there came to him a thought, namely, that the first train to London started at half-past six in the morning. It was a slow train, but it got there, and in any case it went away from Tilling. He did not trouble to consider how that thought came to him: the important point was that it had come. Coupled with that was the knowledge that it was now an undiscoverable number of minutes after half-past five.

There was a Gladstone bag under his bed. He had brought it back from the Club-house only yesterday, after that game of golf which had been so full of disturbances and wet stockings, but which now wore the shimmering security of peaceful, tranquil days long past. How little, so he thought to himself, as he began swiftly storing shirts, ties, collars and other useful things into his bag, had he appreciated the sweet amenities of life, its pleasant conversations and companionships, its topped drives, and mushrooms and incalculable incidents. Now they wore a glamour and a preciousness that was bound up with life itself. He starved for more of them, not knowing while they were his how sweet they were.

The house was not yet astir, when ten minutes later he came downstairs with his bag. He left on his sitting-room table, where it would catch the eye of his housemaid, a sheet of paper on which he wrote "Called away" (he shuddered as he traced the words). "Forward no letters. Will communicate . . ." (Somehow the telegraphic form seemed best to suit the urgency of the situation.) Then very quietly he let himself out of his house.

He could not help casting an apprehensive glance at the windows of his quondam friend and prospective murderer. To his horror he observed that there was a light behind the blind of the Major's bedroom, and pictured him writing to his seconds — he wondered who the "seconds" were going to be — or polishing up his pistols. All the rumours and hints of the Major's duels and affairs of honour, which he had rather scorned before, not wholly believing them, poured like a red torrent into his mind, and he found that now he believed them with a passionate sincerity. Why had he ever attempted (and with such small success) to call this fire-eater a hippopotamus?

The gale of the night before had abated, and thick chilly rain was falling from a sullen sky as he tiptoed down the hill. Once round the corner and out of sight of the duellist's house, he broke into a limping run, which was accelerated by the sound of an engine-whistle from the station. It was mental suspense of the most agonizing kind not to know how long it was after his watch had stopped that he had awoke, and the sound of that whistle, followed by several short puffs of steam, might prove to be the six-thirty bearing away to London, on business or pleasure, its secure and careless pilgrims. Splashing through puddles, lopsidedly weighted by his bag, with his mackintosh flapping against his legs, he gained the sanctuary of the waiting-room and booking-office, which was lighted by a dim expiring lamp, and scrutinized the face of the murky clock . . .

With a sob of relief he saw that he was in time. He was, indeed, in exceptionally good time, for he had a quarter of an hour to wait. An anxious internal debate followed as to whether or not he should take a return ticket. Optimism, that is to say, the hope that he would return to Tilling in peace and safety before the six months for which the ticket was available inclined him to the larger expense, but in these disquieting circumstances, it was difficult to be optimistic and he purchased a first-class single, for on such a morning, and on such a journey, he must get what comfort he could from looking-glasses, padded seats and coloured photographs of places of interest on the line. He formed no vision at all of the future: that was a dark well into which it was dangerous to peer. There was no bright speck in its unplumbable depths: unless Major Flint died suddenly without revealing the challenge he had sent last night, and the promptitude with which its recipient had disappeared rather than face his pistol, he could not frame any grouping of events which would make it possible for him to come back to Tilling again, for he would either have to fight (and this he was quite determined not to do) or be pointed at by the finger of scorn as the man who had refused to do so, and this was nearly as unthinkable as the other. Bitterly he blamed himself for having made a friend (and worse than that, an enemy) of one so obsolete and old-fashioned as to bring duelling into modern life . . . As far as he could be glad of anything he was glad that he had taken a single, not a return ticket.

He turned his eyes away from the blackness of the future and let his mind dwell on the hardly less murky past. Then, throwing up his hands, he buried his face in them with a hollow groan. By some miserable forgetfulness he had left the challenge on his chimney-piece, where his housemaid would undoubtedly find and read it. That would explain his absence far better than the telegraphic instructions he had left on his table. There was no time to go back for it now, even if he could have faced the risk of being seen by the Major, and in an hour or two the whole story, via Withers, Janet, etc., would be all over Tilling.

It was no use then thinking of the future nor of the past, and in order to anchor himself to the world at all and preserve his sanity he had to confine himself to the present. The minutes, long though each tarried, were slipping away and provided his train was punctual, the passage of five more of these laggards would see him safe. The news-boy took down the shutters of his stall, a porter quenched the expiring lamp, and Puffin began to listen for the rumble of the approaching train. It stayed three minutes here: if up to time it would be in before a couple more minutes had passed.

There came from the station-yard outside the sound of heavy footsteps running. Some early traveller like himself was afraid of missing the train. The door burst open, and, streaming with rain and panting for breath, Major Flint stood at the entry. Puffin looked wildly round to see whether he could escape, still perhaps unobserved, on to the platform, but it was too late, for their eyes met.

In that instant of abject terror, two things struck Puffin. One was that the Major looked at the open door behind him as if meditating retreat, the second that he carried a Gladstone bag. Simultaneously Major Flint spoke, if indeed that reverberating thunder of scornful indignation can be called speech.

"Ha! I guessed right then," he roared. "I guessed, sir, that you might be meditating flight, and I — in fact, I came down to see whether you were running away. I was right. You are a coward, Captain Puffin! But relieve your mind, sir. Major Flint will not demean himself to fight with a coward."

Puffin gave one long sigh of relief, and then, standing in front of his own Gladstone bag, in order to conceal it, burst into a cackling laugh.

"Indeed!" he said. "And why, Major, was it necessary for you to pack a Gladstone bag in order to stop me from running away? I'll tell you what has happened. You were running away, and you know it. I guessed you would. I came to stop you, you, you quaking runaway. Your wound troubled you, hey? Didn't want another, hey?"

There was an awful pause, broken by the entry from behind the Major of the outside porter, panting under the weight of a large portmanteau.

"You had to take your portmanteau, too," observed Puffin witheringly, "in order to stop me. That's a curious way of stopping me. You're a coward, sir! But go home. You're safe enough. This will be a fine story for tea-parties."

Puffin turned from him in scorn, still concealing his own bag. Unfortunately the flap of his coat caught it, precariously perched on the bench, and it bumped to the ground.

"What's that?" said Major Flint.

They stared at each other for a moment and then simultaneously burst into peals of laughter. The train rumbled slowly into the station, but neither took the least notice of it, and only shook their heads and broke out again when the station-master urged them to take their seats. The only thing that had power to restore Captain Puffin to gravity was the difficulty of getting the money for his ticket refunded, while the departure of the train with his portmanteau in it did the same for the Major.

*****

The events of that night and morning, as may easily be imagined, soon supplied Tilling with one of the most remarkable conundrums that had ever been forced upon its notice. Puffin's housemaid, during his absence at the station, found and read not only the notice intended for her eyes, but the challenge which he had left on the chimney-piece. She conceived it to be her duty to take it down to Mrs. Gashly, his cook, and while they were putting the bloodiest construction on these inscriptions, their conference was interrupted by the return of Captain Puffin in the highest spirits, who, after a vain search for the challenge, was quite content, as its purport was no longer fraught with danger and death, to suppose that he had torn it up. Mrs. Gashly, therefore, after preparing breakfast at this unusually early hour, went across to the back door of the Major's house, with the challenge in her hand, to borrow a nutmeg grater, and gleaned the information that Mrs. Dominic's employer (for master he could not be called) had gone off in a great hurry to the station early that morning with a Gladstone bag and a portmanteau, the latter of which had been seen no more, though the Major had returned. So Mrs. Gashly produced the challenge, and having watched Miss Mapp off to the High Street at half-past ten, Dominic and Gashly went together to her house, to see if Withers could supply anything of importance, or, if not, a nutmeg grater. They were forced to be content with the grater, but pored over the challenge with Withers, and she having an errand to Diva's house, told Janet, who without further ceremony bounded upstairs to tell her mistress. Hardly had Diva heard, than she plunged into the High Street, and, with suitable additions, told Miss Mapp, Evie, Irene and the Padre under promise in each case, of the strictest secrecy. Ten minutes later Irene had asked the defenceless Mr.

Hopkins, who was being Adam again, what he knew about it, and Evie, with her mouse-like gait that looked so rapid and was so deliberate, had the mortification of seeing Miss Mapp outdistance her and be admitted into the Poppits' house, just as she came in view of the front-door. She rightly conjectured that, after the affair of the store-cupboard in the garden-room, there could be nothing of lesser importance than "the duel" which could take that lady through those abhorred portals. Finally, at ten minutes past eleven, Major Flint and Captain Puffin were seen by one or two fortunate people (the morning having cleared up) walking together to the tram, and, without exception, everybody knew that they were on their way to fight their duel in some remote hollow of the sand-dunes.

Miss Mapp had gone straight home from her visit to the Poppits just about eleven, and stationed herself in the window where she could keep an eye on the houses of the duellists. In her anxiety to outstrip Evie and be the first to tell the Poppits, she had not waited to hear that they had both come back and knew only of the challenge and that they had gone to the station. She had already formed a glorious idea of her own as to what the history of the duel (past or future) was, and intoxicated with emotion had retired from the wordy fray to think about it, and, as already mentioned, to keep an eye on the two houses just below. Then there appeared in sight the Padre, walking swiftly up the hill, and she had barely time under cover of the curtain to regain the table where her sweet chrysanthemums were pining for water when Withers announced him. He wore a furrowed brow and quite forgot to speak either Scotch or Elizabethan English. A few rapid words made it clear that they both had heard the main outlines.

"A terrible situation," said the Padre. "Duelling is direct contravention of all Christian principles, and, I believe, of the civil law. The discharge of a pistol, in unskilful hands, may lead to deplorable results. And Major Flint, so one has heard, is an experienced duellist . . . That, of course, makes it even more dangerous."

It was at this identical moment that Major Flint came out of his house and qui-hied cheerily to Puffin. Miss Mapp and the Padre, deep in these bloody possibilities, neither saw nor heard them. They passed together down the road and into the High Street, unconscious that their very look and action was being more commented on than the Epistle to the Hebrews. Inside the garden-room Miss Mapp sighed, and bent her eyes on her chrysanthemums.

"Quite terrible!" she said. "And in our peaceful, tranquil Tilling!"

"Perhaps the duel has already taken place, and — and they've missed," said the Padre. "They were both seen to return to their houses early this morning."

"By whom?" asked Miss Mapp jealously. She had not heard that.

"By Hopkins," said he. "Hopkins saw them both return."

"I shouldn't trust that man too much," said Miss Mapp. "Hopkins may not be telling the truth. I have no great opinion of his moral standard."

"Why is that?"

This was no time to discuss the nudity of Hopkins and Miss Mapp put the question aside.

"That does not matter now, dear Padre," she said. "I only wish I thought the duel had taken place without accident. But Major Benjy's — I mean Major Flint's — portmanteau has not come back to his house. Of that I'm sure. What if they have sent it away to some place where they are unknown, full of pistols and things?"

"Possible — terribly possible," said the Padre. "I wish I could see my duty clear. I should not hesitate to — well, to do the best I could to induce them to abandon this murderous project. And what do you imagine was the root of the quarrel?"

"I couldn't say, I'm sure," said Miss Mapp. She bent her head over the chrysanthemums.

"Your distracting sex," said he with a moment's gallantry, "is usually the cause of quarrel. I've noticed that they both seemed to admire Miss Irene very much."

Miss Mapp raised her head and spoke with great animation.

"Dear, quaint Irene, I'm sure, has nothing whatever to do with it," she said with perfect truth. "Nothing whatever!"

There was no mistaking the sincerity of this, and the Padre, Tillingite to the marrow, instantly concluded that Miss Mapp knew what (or who) was the cause of all this unique disturbance. And as she bent her head again over the chrysanthemums, and quite distinctly grew brick-red in the face, he felt that delicacy prevented his inquiring any further.

"What are you going to do, dear Padre?" she asked in a low voice, choking with emotion. "Whatever you decide will be wise and Christian. Oh, these violent men! Such babies, too!"

The Padre was bursting with curiosity, but since his delicacy forbade him to ask any of the questions which effervesced like sherbet round his tongue, he propounded another plan.

"I think my duty is to go straight to the Major," he said, "who seems to be the principal in the affair, and tell him that I know all —

and guess the rest," he added.

"Nothing that I have said," declared Miss Mapp in great confusion, "must have anything to do with your guesses. Promise me that, Padre."

This intimate and fruitful conversation was interrupted by the sound of two pairs of steps just outside, and before Withers had had time to say "Mrs. Plaistow," Diva burst in.

"They have both taken the 11.20 tram," she said, and sank into the nearest chair.

"Together?" asked Miss Mapp, feeling a sudden chill of disappointment at the thought of a duel with pistols trailing off into one with golf clubs.

"Yes, but that's a blind," panted Diva. "They were talking and laughing together. Sheer blind! Duel among the sand-dunes!"

"Padre, it is your duty to stop it," said Miss Mapp faintly.

"But if the pistols are in a portmanteau —" he began.

"What portmanteau?" screamed Diva, who hadn't heard about that.

"Darling, I'll tell you presently," said Miss Mapp. "That was only a guess of mine, Padre. But there's no time to lose."

"But there's no tram to catch," said the Padre. "It has gone by this time."

"A taxi then, Padre! Oh, lose no time!"

"Are you coming with me?" he said in a low voice. "Your presence —"

"Better not," she said. "It might — Better not," she repeated.

He skipped down the steps and was observed running down the street.

"What about the portmanteau?" asked the greedy Diva.

*****

It was with strong misgivings that the Padre started on his Christian errand, and had not the sense of adventure spiced it, he would probably have returned to his sermon instead, which was Christian, too. To begin with, there was the ruinous expense of taking a taxi out to the golf-links, but by no other means could he hope to arrive in time to avert an encounter that might be fatal. It must be said to his credit that, though this was an errand distinctly due to his position as the spiritual head of Tilling, he rejected, as soon as it occurred to him, the idea of charging the hire of the taxi to Church Expenses, and as he whirled along the flat road across the marsh, the thing that chiefly buoyed up his drooping spirits and annealed his courage was the romantic nature of his mission. He no longer, thanks to what Miss Mapp had so clearly refrained from saying, had the slightest doubt that she, in some manner that scarcely needed conjecture, was the cause of the duel he was attempting to avert. For years it had been a matter of unwearied and confidential discussion as to whether and when she would marry either Major Flint or Captain Puffin, and it was superfluous to look for any other explanation. It was true that she, in popular parlance, was "getting on," but so, too, and at exactly the same rate, were the representatives of the United Services, and the sooner that two out of the three of them "got on" permanently, the better. No doubt some crisis had arisen, and inflamed with love . . . He intended to confide all this to his wife on his return.

On his return! The unspoken words made his heart sink. What if he never did return? For he was about to place himself in a position of no common danger. His plan was to drive past the club-house, and then on foot, after discharging the taxi, to strike directly into the line of tumbled sand-dunes which, remote and undisturbed and full of large convenient hollows, stretched along the coast above the flat beach. Any of those hollows, he knew, might prove to contain the duellists in the very act of firing, and over the rim of each he had to pop his unprotected head. He (if in time) would have to separate the combatants, and who knew whether, in their very natural chagrin at being interrupted, they might not turn their combined pistols on him first, and settle with each other afterwards? One murder the more made little difference to desperate men. Other shocks, less deadly but extremely unnerving, might await him. He might be too late, and pop his head over the edge of one of these craters, only to discover it full of bleeding if not mangled bodies. Or there might be only one mangled body, and the other, unmangled, would pursue him through the sand-dunes and offer him life at the price of silence. That, he painfully reflected, would be a very difficult decision to make. Luckily, Captain Puffin (if he proved to be the survivor) was lame . . .

With drawn face and agonized prayers on his lips, he began a systematic search of the sand-dunes. Often his nerve nearly failed him, and he would sink panting among the prickly bents before he dared to peer into the hollow up the sides of which he had climbed. His ears shuddered at the anticipation of hearing from near at hand the report of pistols, and once a back-fire from a motor passing along the road caused him to leap high in the air. The sides of these dunes were steep, and his shoes got so full of sand, that from time to time, in spite of the urgency of his errand, he was forced to pause in order to empty them out. He stumbled in rabbit holes, he caught his foot and once his trousers in strands of barbed wire, the remnant of coast defences in the Great War, he crashed among potsherds and abandoned kettles; but with a thoroughness that did equal credit to his wind and his Christian spirit, he searched a mile of perilous dunes from end to end, and peered into every important hollow. Two hours later, jaded and torn and streaming with perspiration, he came, in the vicinity of the club-house, to the end of his fruitless search.

He staggered round the corner of it and came in view of the eighteenth green. Two figures were occupying it, and one of these was in the act of putting. He missed. Then he saw who the figures were: it was Captain Puffin who had just missed his putt, it was Major Flint who now expressed elated sympathy.

"Bad luck, old boy," he said. "Well, a jolly good match and we halve it. Why, there's the Padre. Been for a walk? Join us in a round this afternoon, Padre! Blow your sermon!"

CHAPTER VI

The same delightful prospect at the end of the High Street, over the marsh, which had witnessed not so long ago the final encounter in the Wars of the Roses and the subsequent armistice, was, of course, found to be peculiarly attractive that morning to those who knew (and who did not?) that the combatants had left by the 11.20 steam-tram to fight among the sand-dunes, and that the intrepid Padre had rushed after them in a taxi. The Padre's taxi had returned empty, and the driver seemed to know nothing whatever about anything, so the only thing for everybody to do was to put off lunch and wait for the arrival of the next tram, which occurred at 1.37. In consequence, all the doors in Tilling flew open like those of cuckoo clocks at ten minutes before that hour, and this pleasant promenade was full of those who so keenly admired autumn tints.

From here the progress of the tram across the plain was in full view; so, too, was the shed-like station across the river, which was the terminus of the line, and expectation, when the two-waggoned little train approached the end of its journey, was so tense that it was almost disagreeable. A couple of hours had elapsed since, like the fishers who sailed away into the West and were seen no more till the corpses lay out on the shining sand, the three had left for the sand-dunes, and a couple of hours, so reasoned the Cosmic Consciousness of Tilling, gave ample time for a duel to be fought, if the Padre was not in time to stop it, and for him to stop it if he was. No surgical assistance, as far as was known, had been summoned, but the reason for that might easily be that a surgeon's skill was no longer, alas! of any avail for one, if not both, of the combatants. But if such was the case, it was nice to hope that the Padre had been in time to supply spiritual aid to anyone whom first-aid and probes were powerless to succour.

The variety of *dénouements* which the approaching tram, that had now cut off steam, was capable of providing was positively bewildering. They whirled through Miss Mapp's head like the autumn leaves which she admired so much, and she tried in vain to catch them all, and, when caught, to tick them off on her fingers. Each, moreover, furnished diverse and legitimate conclusions. For instance (taking the thumb)

- I. If nobody of the slightest importance arrived by the tram, that might be because o (*a*) Nothing had happened, and they were all playing golf.

o (*b*) The worst had happened, and, as the Padre had feared, the duellists had first shot him and then each other.

o (*c*) The next worst had happened, and the Padre was arranging for the reverent removal of the corpse of
- (i) Major Benjy, or
- (ii) Captain Puffin, or those of
- (iii) Both.

Miss Mapp let go of her thumb and lightly touched her forefinger.

- II. The Padre might arrive alone.

In that case anything or nothing might have happened to either or both of the others, and the various contingencies hanging on this arrival were so numerous that there was not time to sort them out.

- III. The Padre might arrive with two limping figures whom he assisted.

Here it must not be forgotten that Captain Puffin always limped, and the Major occasionally. Miss Mapp did not forget it.

- IV. The Padre might arrive with a stretcher. Query — Whose?
- V. The Padre might arrive with two stretchers.
- VI. Three stretchers might arrive from the shining sands, at the town where the women were weeping and wringing their hands.

In that case Miss Mapp saw herself busily employed in strengthening poor Evie, who now was running about like a mouse from group to group picking up crumbs of Cosmic Consciousness.

Miss Mapp had got as far as sixthly, though she was aware she had not exhausted the possibilities, when the tram stopped. She furtively took out from her pocket (she had focussed them before she put them in) the opera-glasses through which she had watched the station-yard on a day which had been very much less exciting than this. After one glance she put them back again, feeling vexed and disappointed with herself, for the *dénouement* which they had so unerringly disclosed was one that had not entered her mind at all.

In that moment she had seen that out of the tram there stepped three figures and no stretcher. One figure, it is true, limped, but in a manner so natural, that she scorned to draw any deductions from that halting gait. They proceeded, side by side, across the bridge over the river towards the town.

It is no use denying that the Cosmic Consciousness of the ladies of Tilling was aware of a disagreeable anti-climax to so many hopes and fears. It had, of course, hoped for the best, but it had not expected that the best would be quite as bad as this. The best, to put it frankly, would have been a bandaged arm, or something of that kind. There was still room for the more hardened optimist to hope that something of some sort had occurred, or that something of some sort had been averted, and that the whole affair was not, in the delicious new slang phrase of the Padre's, which was spreading like wildfire through Tilling, a "wash-out." Pistols might have been innocuously discharged for all that was known to the contrary. But it looked bad.

Miss Mapp was the first to recover from the blow, and took Diva's podgy hand.

"Diva, darling," she said, "I feel so deeply thankful. What a wonderful and beautiful end to all our anxiety!"

There was a subconscious regret with regard to the anxiety. The anxiety was, so to speak, a dear and beloved departed . . . And Diva did not feel so sure that the end was so beautiful and wonderful. Her grandfather, Miss Mapp had reason to know, had been a butcher, and probably some inherited indifference to slaughter lurked in her tainted blood.

"There's the portmanteau still," she said hopefully. "Pistols in the portmanteau. Your idea, Elizabeth."

"Yes, dear," said Elizabeth; "but thank God I must have been very wrong about the portmanteau. The outside-porter told me that he brought it up from the station to Major Benjy's house half an hour ago. Fancy your not knowing that! I feel sure he is a truthful man, for he attends the Padre's confirmation class. If there had been pistols in it, Major Benjy and Captain Puffin would have gone away too. I am quite happy about that now. It went away and it has come back. That's all about the portmanteau."

She paused a moment.

"But what does it contain, then?" she said quickly, more as if she was thinking aloud than talking to Diva. "Why did Major Benjy pack it and send it to the station this morning? Where has it come back from? Why did it go there?"

She felt that she was saying too much, and pressed her hand to her head.

"Has all this happened this morning?" she said. "What a full morning, dear! Lovely autumn leaves! I shall go home and have my lunch and rest. Au reservoir, Diva."

Miss Mapp's eternal reservoirs had begun to get on Diva's nerves, and as she lingered here a moment more a great idea occurred to her, which temporarily banished the disappointment about the duellists. Elizabeth, as all the world knew, had accumulated a great reservoir of provisions in the false bookcase in her garden-room, and Diva determined that, if she could think of a neat phrase, the very next time Elizabeth said *au reservoir* to her, she would work in an allusion to Elizabeth's own reservoir of corned beef, tongue, flour, bovril, dried apricots and condensed milk. She would have to frame some stinging rejoinder which would "escape her" when next Elizabeth used that stale old phrase: it would have to be short, swift and spontaneous, and therefore required careful thought. It would be good to bring "pop" into it also. "Your reservoir in the garden-room hasn't gone 'pop' again, I hope, darling?" was the first draft that occurred to her, but that was not sufficiently condensed. "Pop goes the reservoir," on the analogy of the weasel, was better. And, better than either, was there not some sort of corn called pop-corn, which Americans ate? . . . "Have you any pop-corn in your reservoir?" That would be a nasty one . . .

But it all required thinking over, and the sight of the Padre and the duellists crossing the field below, as she still lingered on this escarpment of the hill, brought the duel back to her mind. It would have been considered inquisitive even at Tilling to put direct questions to the combatants, and (still hoping for the best) ask them point-blank "Who won?" or something of that sort; but until she arrived at some sort of information, the excruciating pangs of curiosity that must be endured could be likened only to some acute toothache of the mind with no dentist to stop or remove the source of the trouble. Elizabeth had already succumbed to these pangs of surmise and excitement, and had frankly gone home to rest, and her absence, the fact that for the next hour or two she could not, except by some extraordinary feat on the telephone, get hold of anything which would throw light on the whole prodigious situation, inflamed Diva's brain to the highest pitch of inventiveness. She knew that she was Elizabeth's inferior in point of reconstructive imagination, and the present moment, while the other was recuperating her energies for fresh assaults on the unknown, was Diva's opportunity. The one person who might be presumed to know more than anybody else was the Padre, but while he was with the duellists, it was as impossible to ask him what had happened as to ask the duellists who had won. She must, while Miss Mapp rested, get hold of the Padre without the duellists.

Even as Athene sprang full grown and panoplied from the brain of Zeus, so from Diva's brain there sprang her plan complete. She even resisted the temptation to go on admiring autumn tints, in order to see how the interesting trio "looked" when, as they must presently do, they passed close to where she stood, and hurried home, pausing only to purchase, pay for, and carry away with her from the provision shop a large and expensively-dressed crab, a dainty of which the Padre was inordinately fond. Ruinous as this was, there was a note of triumph in her voice when, on arrival, she called loudly for Janet, and told her to lay another place at the luncheon table. Then putting a strong constraint on herself, she waited three minutes by her watch, in order to give the Padre time to get home, and then rang him up and reminded him that he had promised to lunch with her that day. It was no use asking him to lunch in such a way that he might refuse: she employed without remorse this pitiless *force majeure*.

The engagement was short and brisk. He pleaded that not even now could he remember even having been asked (which was not surprising), and said that he and wee wifie had begun lunch. On which Diva unmasked her last gun, and told him that she had ordered a crab on purpose. That silenced further argument, and he said that he and wee wifie would be round in a jiffy, and rang off. She did not particularly want wee wifie, but there was enough crab.

Diva felt that she had never laid out four shillings to better purpose, when, a quarter of an hour later, the Padre gave her the full account of his fruitless search among the sand-dunes, so deeply impressive was his sense of being buoyed up to that incredibly fatiguing and perilous excursion by some Power outside himself. It never even occurred to her to think that it was an elaborate practical joke on the part of the Power outside himself, to spur him on to such immense exertions to no purpose at all. He had only got as far as this over his interrupted lunch with wee wifie, and though she, too, was in agonized suspense as to what happened next, she bore the repetition with great equanimity, only making small mouse-like noises of impatience which nobody heard. He was quite forgetting to speak either Scotch or Elizabethan English, so obvious was the absorption of his hearers, without these added aids to command attention.

"And then I came round the corner of the club-house," he said, "and there were Captain Puffin and the Major finishing their match on the eighteenth hole."

"Then there's been no duel at all," said Diva, scraping the shell of the crab.

"I feel sure of it. There wouldn't have been time for a duel and a round of golf, in addition to the impossibility of playing golf immediately after a duel. No nerves could stand it. Besides, I asked one of their caddies. They had come straight from the tram to the club-house, and from the club-house to the first tee. They had not been alone for a moment."

"Wash-out," said Diva, wondering whether this had been worth four shillings, so tame was the conclusion.

Mrs. Bartlett gave a little squeak which was her preliminary to speech.

"But I do not see why there may not be a duel yet, Kenneth," she said. "Because they did not fight this morning — excellent crab, dear Diva, so good of you to ask us — there's no reason why there shouldn't be a duel this afternoon. O dear me, and cold beef as well: I shall be quite stuffed. Depend upon it a man doesn't take the trouble to write a challenge and all that, unless he means business."

The Padre held up his hand. He felt that he was gradually growing to be the hero of the whole affair. He had certainly looked over the edge of numberless hollows in the sand-dunes with vivid anticipations of having a bullet whizz by him on each separate occasion. It behoved him to take a sublime line.

"My dear," he said, "business is hardly a word to apply to murder. That within the last twenty-four hours there was the intention of fighting a duel, I don't deny. But something has decidedly happened which has averted that deplorable calamity. Peace and reconciliation is the result of it, and I have never seen two men so unaffectedly friendly."

Diva got up and whirled round the table to get the port for the Padre, so pleased was she at a fresh idea coming to her while still dear Elizabeth was resting. She attributed it to the crab.

"We've all been on a false scent," she said. "Peace and reconciliation happened before they went out to the sand-dunes at all. It happened at the station. They met at the station, you know. It is proved that Major Flint went there. Major wouldn't send portmanteau off alone. And it's proved that Captain Puffin went there too, because the note which his housemaid found on the table before she saw the challenge from the Major, which was on the chimney-piece, said that he had been called away very suddenly. No: they both went to catch the early train in order to go away before they could be stopped, and kill each other. But why didn't they go? What happened? Don't suppose the outside porter showed them how wicked they were, confirmation-class or no confirmation-class. Stumps me. Almost wish Elizabeth was here. She's good at guessing."

The Padre's eye brightened. Reaction after the perils of the morning, crab and port combined to make a man of him.

"Eh, 'tis a bonny wee drappie of port whatever, Mistress Plaistow," he said. "And I dinna ken that ye're far wrang in jaloosing that Mistress Mapp might have a wee bitty word to say aboot it a', 'gin she had the mind."

"She was wrong about the portmanteau," said Diva. "Confessed she was wrong."

"Hoots! I'm not mindin' the bit pochmantie," said the Padre.

"What else does she know?" asked Diva feverishly.

There was no doubt that the Padre had the fullest attention of the two ladies again, and there was no need to talk Scotch any more.

"Begin at the beginning," he said. "What do we suppose was the cause of the quarrel?"

"Anything," said Diva. "Golf, tiger-skins, coal-strike, summer-time."

He shook his head.

"I grant you words may pass on such subjects," he said. "We feel keenly, I know, about summer-time in Tilling, though we shall all be reconciled over that next Sunday, when real time, God's time, as I am venturing to call it in my sermon, comes in again."

Diva had to bite her tongue to prevent herself bolting off on this new scent. After all, she had invested in crab to learn about duelling, not about summer-time.

"Well?" she said.

"We may have had words on that subject," said the Padre, booming as if he was in the pulpit already, "but we should, I hope, none of us go so far as to catch the earliest train with pistols, in defence of our conviction about summer-time. No, Mrs. Plaistow, if you are right, and there is something to be said for your view, in thinking that they both went to such lengths as to be in time for the early train, in order to fight a duel undisturbed, you must look for a more solid cause than that."

Diva vainly racked her brains to think of anything more worthy of the highest pitches of emotion than this. If it had been she and Miss Mapp who had been embroiled, hoarding and dress would have occurred to her. But as it was, no one in his senses could dream that the Captain and the Major were sartorial rivals, unless they had quarrelled over the question as to which of them wore the snuffiest old clothes.

"Give it up," she said. "What did they quarrel about?"

"Passion!" said the Padre, in those full, deep tones in which next Sunday he would allude to God's time. "I do not mean anger, but the flame that exalts man to heaven or — or does exactly the opposite!"

"But whomever for?" asked Diva, quite thrown off her bearings. Such a thing had never occurred to her, for, as far as she was aware, passion, except in the sense of temper, did not exist in Tilling. Tilling was far too respectable.

The Padre considered this a moment.

"I am betraying no confidence," he said, "because no one has confided in me. But there certainly is a lady in this town — I do not allude to Miss Irene — who has long enjoyed the Major's particular esteem. May not some deprecating remark —"

Wee wifie gave a much louder squeal than usual.

"He means poor Elizabeth," she said in a high, tremulous voice. "Fancy, Kenneth!"

Diva, a few seconds before, had seen no reason why the Padre should drink the rest of her port, and was now in the act of drinking some of that unusual beverage herself. She tried to swallow it, but it was too late, and next moment all the openings in her face were fountains of that delicious wine. She choked and she gurgled, until the last drop had left her windpipe — under the persuasion of pattings on the back from the others — and then she gave herself up to loud, hoarse laughter, through which there shrilled the staccato squeaks of wee wifie. Nothing, even if you are being laughed at yourself, is so infectious as prolonged laughter, and the Padre felt himself forced to join it. When one of them got a little better, a relapse ensued by reason of infection from the others, and it was not till exhaustion set in, that this triple volcano became quiescent again.

"Only fancy!" said Evie faintly. "How did such an idea get into your head, Kenneth?"

His voice shook as he answered.

"Well, we were all a little worked up this morning," he said. "The idea — really, I don't know what we have all been laughing at —"

"I do," said Diva. "Go on. About the idea —"

A feminine, a diabolical inspiration flared within wee wifie's mind.

"Elizabeth suggested it herself," she squealed.

Naturally Diva could not help remembering that she had found Miss Mapp and the Padre in earnest conversation together when she forced her way in that morning with the news that the duellists had left by the 11.20 tram. Nobody could be expected to have so short a memory as to have forgotten *that*. Just now she forgave Elizabeth for anything she had ever done. That might have to be reconsidered afterwards, but at present it was valid enough.

"Did she suggest it?" she asked.

The Padre behaved like a man, and lied like Ananias.

"Most emphatically she did not," he said.

The disappointment would have been severe, had the two ladies believed this confident assertion, and Diva pictured a delightful interview with Elizabeth, in which she would suddenly tell her the wild surmise the Padre had made with regard to the cause of the duel, and see how she looked then. Just see how she looked then: that was all — self-consciousness and guilt would fly their colours . . .

*****

Miss Mapp had been tempted when she went home that morning, after enjoying the autumn tints, to ask Diva to lunch with her, but remembered in time that she had told her cook to broach one of the tins of corned-beef which no human wizard could coax into the store-cupboard again, if he shut the door after it. Diva would have been sure to say something acid and allusive, to remark on its excellence being happily not wasted on the poor people in the hospital, or, if she had not said anything at all about it, her silence as she ate a great deal would have had a sharp flavour. But Miss Mapp would have liked, especially when she went to take her rest afterwards on the big sofa in the garden-room, to have had somebody to talk to, for her brain seethed with conjectures as to what had happened, was happening and would happen, and discussion was the best method of simplifying a problem, of narrowing it down to the limits of probability, whereas when she was alone now with her own imaginings, the most fantastic of them seemed plausible. She had, however, handed a glorious suggestion to the Padre, the one, that is, which concerned the cause of the duel, and it had been highly satisfactory to observe the sympathy and respect with which he had imbibed it. She had, too, been so discreet about it; she had not come within measurable distance of asserting that the challenge had been in any way connected with her. She had only been very emphatic on the point of its not being connected with poor dear Irene, and then occupied herself with her sweet flowers. That had been sufficient, and she felt in her bones and marrow that he inferred what she had meant him to infer . . .

The vulture of surmise ceased to peck at her for a few moments as she considered this, and followed up a thread of gold . . . Though the Padre would surely be discreet, she hoped that he would "let slip" to dear Evie in the course of the vivid conversation they would be sure to have over lunch, that he had a good guess as to the cause which had led to that savage challenge. Upon which dear Evie would be certain to ply him with direct squeaks and questions, and when she "got hot" (as in animal, vegetable and mineral) his reticence would lead her to make a good guess too. She might be incredulous, but there the idea would be in her mind, while if she felt that these stirring days were no time for scepticism, she could hardly fail to be interested and touched. Before long (how soon Miss Mapp was happily not aware) she would "pop in" to see Diva, or Diva would "pop in" to see her, and, Evie observing a discretion similar to that of the Padre and herself, would soon enable dear Diva to make a good guess too. After that, all would be well, for dear Diva ("such a gossiping darling") would undoubtedly tell everybody in Tilling, under vows of secrecy (so that she should have the pleasure of telling everybody herself) just what her good guess was. Thus, very presently, all Tilling would know exactly that which Miss Mapp had not said to the dear Padre, namely, that the duel which had been fought (or which hadn't been fought) was "all about" her. And the best of it was, that though everybody knew, it would still be a great and beautiful secret, reposing inviolably in every breast or chest, as the case might be. She had no anxiety about anybody asking direct questions of the duellists, for if duelling, for years past, had been a subject which no delicately-minded person alluded to purposely in Major Benjy's presence, how much more now after this critical morning would that subject be taboo? That certainly was a good thing, for the duellists if closely questioned might have a different explanation, and it would be highly inconvenient to have two contradictory stories going about. But, as it was, nothing could be nicer: the whole of the rest of Tilling, under promise of secrecy, would know, and even if under further promises of secrecy they communicated their secret to each other, there would be no harm done . . .

After this excursion into Elysian fields, poor Miss Mapp had to get back to her vulture again, and the hour's rest that she had felt was due to herself as the heroine of a duel became a period of extraordinary cerebral activity. Puzzle as she might, she could make nothing whatever of the portmanteau and the excursion to the early train, and she got up long before her hour was over, since she found that the more she thought, the more invincible were the objections to any conclusion that she drowningly grasped at. Whatever attack she made on this mystery, the garrison failed to march out and surrender but kept their flag flying, and her conjectures were woefully blasted by the forces of the most elementary reasons. But as the agony of suspense, if no fresh topic of interest intervened, would be frankly unendurable, she determined to concentrate no more on it, but rather to commit it to the ice-house or safe of her subconscious mind, from which at will, when she felt refreshed and reinvigorated, she could unlock it and examine it again. The whole problem was more superlatively baffling than any that she could remember having encountered in all these inquisitive years, just as the subject of it was more majestic than any, for it concerned not hoarding, nor visits of the Prince of Wales, nor poppy-trimmed gowns, but life and death and firing of deadly pistols. And should love be added to this august list? Certainly not by her, though Tilling might do what it liked. In fact Tilling always did.

She walked across to the bow-window from which she had conducted so many exciting and successful investigations. But to-day the view seemed as stale and unprofitable as the world appeared to Hamlet, even though Mrs. Poppit at that moment went waddling down the street and disappeared round the corner where the dentist and Mr. Wyse lived. With a sense of fatigue Miss Mapp recalled the fact that she had seen the housemaid cleaning Mr. Wyse's windows yesterday — ("Children dear, was it yesterday?") — and had noted her industry, and drawn from it the irresistible conclusion that Mr. Wyse was probably expected home. He usually came back about mid-October, and let slip allusions to his enjoyable visits in Scotland and his *villeggiatura* (so he was pleased to express it) with his sister the Contessa di Faraglione at Capri. That Contessa Faraglione was rather a mythical personage to Miss Mapp's mind: she was certainly not in a mediæval copy of "Who's Who?" which was the only accessible handbook in matters relating to noble and notable personages, and though Miss Mapp would not have taken an oath that she did not exist, she saw no strong reason for supposing that she did. Certainly she had never been to Tilling, which was strange as her brother lived there, and there was nothing but her brother's allusions to certify her. About Mrs. Poppit now: had she gone to see Mr. Wyse or had she gone to the dentist? One or other it must be, for apart from them that particular street contained nobody who counted, and at the bottom it simply conducted you out into the uneventful country. Mrs. Poppit was all dressed up, and she would never walk in the country in such a costume. It would do either for Mr. Wyse or the dentist, for she was the sort of woman who would like to appear grand in the dentist's chair, so that he might be shy of hurting such a fine lady. Then again, Mrs. Poppit had wonderful teeth, almost too good to be true, and before now she had asked who lived at that pretty little house just round the corner, as if to show that she didn't know where the dentist lived! Or had she found out by some underhand means that Mr. Wyse had come back, and had gone to call on him and give him the first news of the duel, and talk to him about Scotland? Very likely they had neither of them been to Scotland at all: they conspired to say that they had been to Scotland and stayed at shooting-lodges (keepers' lodges more likely) in order to impress Tilling with their magnificence . . .

Miss Mapp sat down on the central-heating pipes in her window, and fell into one of her reconstructive musings. Partly, if Mr. Wyse was back, it was well just to run over his record; partly she wanted to divert her mind from the two houses just below, that of Major Benjy on the one side and that of Captain Puffin on the other, which contained the key to the great, insoluble mystery, from conjecture as to which she wanted to obtain relief. Mr. Wyse, anyhow, would serve as a mild opiate, for she had never lost an angry interest in him. Though he was for eight months of the year, or thereabouts, in Tilling, he was never, for a single hour, *of* Tilling. He did not exactly invest himself with an air of condescension and superiority — Miss Mapp did him that justice — but he made other people invest him with it, so that it came to the same thing: he was invested. He did not drag the fact of his sister being the Contessa Faraglione into conversation, but if talk turned on sisters, and he was asked about his, he confessed to her nobility. The same phenomenon appeared when the innocent county of Hampshire was mentioned, for it turned out that he knew the county well, being one of the Wyses of Whitchurch. You couldn't say he talked about it, but he made other people talk about it . . . He was quite impervious to satire on such points, for when, goaded to madness, Miss Mapp had once said that she was one of the Mapps of Maidstone, he had merely bowed and said: "A very old family, I believe," and when the conversation branched off on to old families he had rather pointedly said "we" to Miss Mapp. So poor Miss Mapp was sorry she had been satirical . . . But for some reason, Tilling never ceased to play up to Mr. Wyse, and there was not a tea-party or a bridge-party given during the whole period of his residence there to which he was not invited. Hostesses always started with him, sending him round a note with "To await answer," written in the top left-hand corner, since he had clearly stated that he considered the telephone an undignified instrument only fit to be used for household purposes, and had installed his in the kitchen, in the manner of the Wyses of Whitchurch. That alone, apart from Mr. Wyse's old-fashioned notions on the subject, made telephoning impossible, for your summons was usually answered by his cook, who instantly began scolding the butcher irrespective and disrespectful of whom you were. When her mistake was made known to her, she never apologized, but grudgingly said she would call Mr. Figgis, who was Mr. Wyse's valet. Mr. Figgis always took a long time in coming, and when he came he sneezed or did something disagreeable and said: "Yes, yes; what is it?" in a very testy manner. After explanations he would consent to tell his master, which took another long time, and even then Mr. Wyse did not come himself, and usually refused the proffered invitation. Miss Mapp had tried the expedient of sending Withers to the telephone when she wanted to get at Mr. Wyse, but this had not succeeded, for Withers and Mr. Wyse's cook quarrelled so violently before they got to business that Mr. Figgis had to calm the cook and Withers to complain to Miss Mapp . . . This, in brief, was the general reason why Tilling sent notes to Mr. Wyse. As for chatting through the telephone, which was the main use of telephones, the thing was quite out of the question.

Miss Mapp revived a little as she made this piercing analysis of Mr. Wyse, and the warmth of the central heating pipes, on this baffling day of autumn tints, was comforting . . . No one could say that Mr. Wyse was not punctilious in matters of social etiquette, for though he refused three-quarters of the invitations which were showered on him, he invariably returned the compliment by an autograph note hoping that he might have the pleasure of entertaining you at lunch on Thursday next, for he always gave a small luncheon-party on Thursday. These invitations were couched in Chesterfield-terms: Mr. Wyse said that he had met a mutual friend just now who had informed him that you were in residence, and had encouraged him to hope that you might give him the pleasure of your company, etc. This was alluring diction: it presented the image of Mr. Wyse stepping briskly home again, quite heartened up by this chance encounter, and no longer the prey to melancholy at the thought that you might not give him the joy. He was encouraged to hope . . . These polite expressions were traced in a neat upright hand on paper which, when he had just come back from Italy, often bore a coronet on the top with "Villa Faraglione, Capri" printed on the right-hand top corner and "Amelia" (the name of his putative sister) in sprawling gilt on the left, the whole being lightly erased. Of course he was quite right to filch a few sheets, but it threw rather a lurid light on his character that they should be such grand ones.

Last year only, in a fit of passion at Mr. Wyse having refused six invitations running on the plea of other engagements, Miss Mapp had headed a movement, the object of which was that Tilling should not accept any of Mr. Wyse's invitations unless he accepted its. This had met with theoretical sympathy; the Bartletts, Diva, Irene, the Poppits had all agreed — rather absently — that it would be a very proper thing to do, but the very next Thursday they had all, including the originator, met on Mr. Wyse's doorstep for a luncheon-party, and the movement then and there collapsed. Though they all protested and rebelled against such a notion, the horrid fact remained that everybody basked in Mr. Wyse's effulgence whenever it was disposed to shed itself on them. Much as they distrusted the information they dragged out of him, they adored hearing about the Villa Faraglione, and dressed themselves in their very best clothes to do so. Then again there was the quality of the lunch itself: often there was caviare, and it was impossible (though the interrogator who asked whether it came from Twemlow's feared the worst) not to be mildly excited to know, when Mr. Wyse referred the question to Figgis, that the caviare had arrived from Odessa that morning. The haunch of roe-deer came from Perthshire; the wine, on the subject of which the Major could not be silent, and which often made him extremely talkative, was from "my brother-in-law's vineyard." And Mr. Wyse would taste it with the air of a connoisseur and say: "Not quite as good as last year: I must tell the Cont — I mean my sister."

Again when Mr. Wyse did condescend to honour a tea-party or a bridge-party, Tilling writhed under the consciousness that their general deportment was quite different from that which they ordinarily practised among themselves. There was never any squabbling at Mr. Wyse's table, and such squabbling as took place at the other tables was conducted in low hissings and whispers, so that Mr. Wyse should not hear. Diva never haggled over her gains or losses when he was there, the Padre never talked Scotch or Elizabethan English. Evie never squeaked like a mouse, no shrill recriminations or stately sarcasms took place between partners, and if there happened to be a little disagreement about the rules, Mr. Wyse's decision, though he was not a better player than any of them, was accepted without a murmur. At intervals for refreshment, in the same way, Diva no longer filled her mouth and both hands with nougat-chocolate; there was no scrambling or jostling, but the ladies were waited on by the gentlemen, who then refreshed themselves. And yet Mr. Wyse in no way asserted himself, or reduced them all to politeness by talking about the polished manners of Italians; it was Tilling itself which chose to behave in this unusual manner in his presence. Sometimes Diva might forget herself for a moment, and address something withering to her partner, but the partner never replied in suitable terms, and Diva became honey-mouthed again. It was, indeed, if Mr. Wyse had appeared at two or three parties, rather a relief not to find him at the next, and breathe freely in less rarefied air. But whether he came or not he always returned the invitation by one to a Thursday luncheon-party, and thus the high circles of Tilling met every week at his house.

Miss Mapp came to the end of this brief retrospect, and determined, when once it was proved that Mr. Wyse had arrived, to ask him to tea on Tuesday. That would mean lunch with him on Thursday, and it was unnecessary to ask anybody else unless Mr. Wyse accepted. If he refused, there would be no tea-party . . . But, after the events of the last twenty-four hours, there was no vividness in these plans and reminiscences, and her eye turned to the profile of the Colonel's house.

"The portmanteau," she said to herself . . . No: she must take her mind off that subject. She would go for a walk, not into the High Street, but into the quiet level country, away from the turmoil of passion (in the Padre's sense) and quarrels (in her own), where she could cool her curiosity and her soul with contemplation of the swallows and the white butterflies (if they had not all been killed by the touch of frost last night) and the autumn tints of which there were none whatever in the treeless marsh . . . Decidedly the shortest way out of the town was that which led past Mr. Wyse's house. But before leaving the garden-room she practised several faces at the looking-glass opposite the door, which should suitably express, if she met anybody to whom the cause of the challenge was likely to have spread, the bewildering emotion which the unwilling cause of it must feel. There must be a wistful wonder, there must be a certain pride, there must be the remains of romantic excitement, and there must be deep womanly anxiety. The carriage of the head "did" the pride, the wide-open eyes "did" the wistful wonder and the romance, the deep womanly anxiety lurked in the tremulous smile, and a violent rubbing of the cheeks produced the colour of excitement. In answer to any impertinent questions, if she encountered such, she meant to give an absent answer, as if she had not understood. Thus equipped she set forth.

It was rather disappointing to meet nobody, but as she passed Mr. Wyse's bow-window she adjusted the chrysanthemums she wore, and she had a good sight of his profile and the back of Mrs. Poppit's head. They appeared deep in conversation, and Miss

Mapp felt that the tiresome woman was probably giving him a very incomplete account of what had happened. She returned late for tea, and broke off her apologies to Withers for being such a trouble because she saw a note on the hall table. There was a coronet on the back of the envelope, and it was addressed in the neat, punctilious hand which so well expressed its writer. Villa Faraglione, Capri, a coronet and Amelia all lightly crossed out headed the page, and she read:

"Dear Miss Mapp,

"It is such a pleasure to find myself in our little Tilling again, and our mutual friend Mrs. Poppit, M.B.E., tells me you are in residence, and encourages me to hope that I may induce you to take *déjeuner* with me on Thursday, at one o'clock. May I assure you, with all delicacy, that you will not meet here anyone whose presence could cause you the slightest embarrassment?

"Pray excuse this hasty note. Figgis will wait for your answer if you are in.

"Yours very sincerely,

"Algernon Wyse."

Had not Withers been present, who might have misconstrued her action, Miss Mapp would have kissed the note; failing that, she forgave Mrs. Poppit for being an M.B.E.

"The dear woman!" she said. "She has heard, and has told him."

Of course she need not ask Mr. Wyse to tea now . . .

CHAPTER VII

A white frost on three nights running and a terrible blackening of dahlias, whose reputation was quite gone by morning, would probably have convinced the ladies of Tilling that it was time to put summer clothing in camphor and winter clothing in the back-yard to get aired, even if the Padre had not preached that remarkable sermon on Sunday. It was so remarkable that Miss Mapp quite forgot to note grammatical lapses and listened entranced.

The text was, "He made summer and winter," and after repeating the words very impressively, so that there might be no mistake about the origin of the seasons, the Padre began to talk about something quite different — namely, the unhappy divisions which exist in Christian communities. That did not deceive Miss Mapp for a moment: she saw precisely what he was getting at over his oratorical fences. He got at it . . .

Ever since Summer-time had been inaugurated a few years before, it had been one of the chronic dissensions of Tilling. Miss Mapp, Diva and the Padre flatly refused to recognize it, except when they were going by train or tram, when principle must necessarily go to the wall, or they would never have succeeded in getting anywhere, while Miss Mapp, with the halo of martyrdom round her head, had once arrived at a Summer-time party an hour late, in order to bear witness to the truth, and, in consequence, had got only dregs of tea and the last faint strawberry. But the Major and Captain Puffin used the tram so often, that they had fallen into the degrading habit of dislocating their clocks and watches on the first of May, and dislocating them again in the autumn, when they were forced into uniformity with properly-minded people. Irene was flippant on the subject, and said that any old time would do for her. The Poppits followed convention, and Mrs. Poppit, in naming the hour for a party to the stalwarts, wrote "4.30 (your 3.30)." The King, after all, had invited her to be decorated at a particular hour, summer-time, and what was good enough for the King was good enough for Mrs. Poppit.

The sermon was quite uncompromising. There was summer and winter, by Divine ordinance, but there was nothing said about summer-time and winter-time. There was but one Time, and even as Life only stained the white radiance of eternity, as the gifted but, alas! infidel poet remarked, so, too, did Time. But ephemeral as Time was, noon in the Bible clearly meant twelve o'clock, and not one o'clock: towards even, meant towards even, and not the middle of a broiling afternoon. The sixth hour similarly was the Roman way of saying twelve. Winter-time, in fact, was God's time, and though there was nothing wicked (far from it) in adopting strange measures, yet the simple, the childlike, clung to the sacred tradition, which they had received from their fathers and forefathers at their mother's knee. Then followed a long and eloquent passage, which recapitulated the opening about unhappy divisions, and contained several phrases, regarding the lengths to which such divisions might go, which were strikingly applicable to duelling. The peroration recapitulated the recapitulation, in case anyone had missed it, and the coda, the close itself, in the full noon of the winter sun, was full of joy at the healing of all such unhappy divisions. And now . . . The rain rattling against the windows drowned the Doxology.

The doctrine was so much to her mind that Miss Mapp gave a shilling to the offertory instead of her usual sixpence, to be devoted to the organist and choir fund. The Padre, it is true, had changed the hour of services to suit the heresy of the majority, and this for a moment made her hand falter. But the hope, after this convincing sermon, that next year morning service would be at the hour falsely called twelve decided her not to withdraw this handsome contribution.

Frosts and dead dahlias and sermons then were together overwhelmingly convincing, and when Miss Mapp went out on Monday morning to do her shopping, she wore a tweed skirt and jacket, and round her neck a long woollen scarf to mark the end of the summer. Mrs. Poppit, alone in her disgusting ostentation, had seemed to think two days ago that it was cold enough for furs, and she presented a truly ridiculous aspect in an enormous sable coat, under the weight of which she could hardly stagger, and stood rooted to the spot when she stepped out of the Royce. Brisk walking and large woollen scarves saved the others from feeling the cold and from being unable to move, and this morning the High Street was dazzling with the shifting play of bright colours. There was quite a group of scarves at the corner, where Miss Mapp's street debouched into the High Street: Irene was there (for it was probably too cold for Mr. Hopkins that morning), looking quainter than ever in corduroys and mauve stockings with an immense orange scarf bordered with pink. Diva was there, wound up in so delicious a combination of rose-madder and Cambridge blue, that Miss Mapp, remembering the history of the rose-madder, had to remind herself how many things there were in the world more important than worsted. Evie was there in vivid green with a purple border, the Padre had a knitted magenta waistcoat, and Mrs. Poppit that great sable coat which almost prevented movement. They were all talking together in a very animated manner when first Miss Mapp came in sight, and if, on her approach, conversation seemed to wither, they all wore, besides their scarves, very broad, pleasant smiles. Miss Mapp had a smile, too, as good as anybody's.

"Good morning, all you dear things," she said. "How lovely you all look — just like a bed of delicious flowers! Such nice colours! My poor dahlias are all dead."

Quaint Irene uttered a hoarse laugh, and, swinging her basket, went quickly away. She often did abrupt things like that. Miss Mapp turned to the Padre.

"Dear Padre, what a delicious sermon!" she said. "So glad you preached it! Such a warning against all sorts of divisions!"

The Padre had to compose his face before he responded to these compliments.

"I'm reecht glad, fair lady," he replied, "that my bit discourse was to your mind. Come, wee wifie, we must be stepping."

Quite suddenly all the group, with the exception of Mrs. Poppit, melted away. Wee wifie gave a loud squeal, as if to say something, but her husband led her firmly off, while Diva, with rapidly revolving feet, sped like an arrow up the centre of the High Street.

"Such a lovely morning!" said Miss Mapp to Mrs. Poppit, when there was no one else to talk to. "And everyone looks so pleased and happy, and all in such a hurry, busy as bees, to do their little businesses. Yes."

Mrs. Poppit began to move quietly away with the deliberate, tortoise-like progression necessitated by the fur coat. It struck Miss Mapp that she, too, had intended to take part in the general breaking up of the group, but had merely been unable to get under way as fast as the others.

"Such a lovely fur coat," said Miss Mapp sycophantically. "Such beautiful long fur! And what is the news this morning? Has a little bird been whispering anything?"

"Nothing," said Mrs. Poppit very decidedly, and having now sufficient way on to turn, she went up the street down which Miss Mapp had just come. The latter was thus left all alone with her shopping basket and her scarf.

With the unerring divination which was the natural fruit of so many years of ceaseless conjecture, she instantly suspected the worst. All that busy conversation which her appearance had interrupted, all those smiles which her presence had seemed but to render broader and more hilarious, certainly concerned her. They could not still have been talking about that fatal explosion from the cupboard in the garden-room, because the duel had completely silenced the last echoes of that, and she instantly put her finger on the spot. Somebody had been gossiping (and how she hated gossip); somebody had given voice to what she had been so studiously careful not to say. Until that moment, when she had seen the rapid breaking up of the group of her friends all radiant with merriment, she had longed to be aware that somebody had given voice to it, and that everybody (under seal of secrecy) knew the unique queenliness of her position, the overwhelmingly interesting rôle that the violent passions of men had cast her for. She had not believed in the truth of it herself, when that irresistible seizure of coquetry took possession of her as she bent over her sweet chrysanthemums; but the Padre's respectful reception of it had caused her to hope that everybody else might believe in it. The character of the smiles, however, that wreathed the faces of her friends did not quite seem to give fruition to that hope. There were smiles and smiles, respectful smiles, sympathetic smiles, envious and admiring smiles, but there were also smiles of hilarious and mocking incredulity. She concluded that she had to deal with the latter variety.

"Something," thought Miss Mapp, as she stood quite alone in the High Street, with Mrs. Poppit labouring up the hill, and Diva already a rose-madder speck in the distance, "has got to be done," and it only remained to settle what. Fury with the dear Padre for having hinted precisely what she meant, intended and designed that he should hint, was perhaps the paramount emotion in her mind; fury with everybody else for not respectfully believing what she did not believe herself made an important pendant.

"What am I to do?" said Miss Mapp aloud, and had to explain to Mr. Hopkins, who had all his clothes on, that she had not spoken to him. Then she caught sight again of Mrs. Poppit's sable coat hardly further off than it had been when first this thunderclap of an intuition deafened her, and still reeling from the shock, she remembered that it was almost certainly Mrs. Poppit who was the cause of Mr. Wyse writing her that exquisitely delicate note with regard to Thursday. It was a herculean task, no doubt, to plug up all the fountains of talk in Tilling which were spouting so merrily at her expense, but a beginning must be made before she could arrive at the end. A short scurry of nimble steps brought her up to the sables.

"Dear Mrs. Poppit," she said, "if you are walking by my little house, would you give me two minutes' talk? And — so stupid of me to forget just now — will you come in after dinner on Wednesday for a little rubber? The days are closing in now; one wants to make the most of the daylight, and I think it is time to begin our pleasant little winter evenings."

This was a bribe, and Mrs. Poppit instantly pocketed it, with the effect that two minutes later she was in the garden-room, and had deposited her sable coat on the sofa ("Quite shook the room with the weight of it," said Miss Mapp to herself while she arranged her plan).

She stood looking out of the window for a moment, writhing with humiliation at having to be suppliant to the Member of the British Empire. She tried to remember Mrs. Poppit's Christian name, and was even prepared to use that, but this crowning ignominy was saved her, as she could not recollect it.

"Such an annoying thing has happened," she said, though the words seemed to blister her lips. "And you, dear Mrs. Poppit, as a woman of the world, can advise me what to do. The fact is that somehow or other, and I can't think how, people are saying that the duel last week, which was so happily averted, had something to do with poor little me. So absurd! But you know what gossips we have in our dear little Tilling."

Mrs. Poppit turned on her a fallen and disappointed face.

"But hadn't it?" she said. "Why, when they were all laughing about it just now" ("I was right, then," thought Miss Mapp, "and what a tactless woman!"), "I said I believed it. And I told Mr. Wyse."

Miss Mapp cursed herself for her frankness. But she could obliterate that again, and not lose a rare (goodness knew how rare!) believer.

"I am in such a difficult position," she said. "I think I ought to let it be understood that there is no truth whatever in such an idea, however much truth there may be. And did dear Mr. Wyse believe — in fact, I know he must have, for he wrote me, oh, such a delicate, understanding note. He, at any rate, takes no notice of all that is being said and hinted."

Miss Mapp was momentarily conscious that she meant precisely the opposite of this. Dear Mr. Wyse *did* take notice, most respectful notice, of all that was being said and hinted, thank goodness! But a glance at Mrs. Poppit's fat and interested face showed her that the verbal discrepancy had gone unnoticed, and that the luscious flavour of romance drowned the perception of anything else. She drew a handkerchief out, and buried her thoughtful eyes in it a moment, rubbing them with a stealthy motion, which Mrs. Poppit did not perceive, though Diva would have.

"My lips are sealed," she continued, opening them very wide, "and I can say nothing, except that I want this rumour to be contradicted. I daresay those who started it thought it was true, but, true or false, I must say nothing. I have always led a very quiet life in my little house, with my sweet flowers for my companions, and if there is one thing more than another that I dislike, it is that my private affairs should be made matters of public interest. I do no harm to anybody, I wish everybody well, and nothing — nothing will induce me to open my lips upon this subject. I will not," cried Miss Mapp, "say a word to defend or justify myself. What is true will prevail. It comes in the Bible."

Mrs. Poppit was too much interested in what she said to mind where it came from.

"What can I do?" she asked.

"Contradict, dear, the rumour that I have had anything to do with the terrible thing which might have happened last week. Say on my authority that it is so. I tremble to think" — here she trembled very much — "what might happen if the report reached Major Benjy's ears, and he found out who had started it. We must have no more duels in Tilling. I thought I should never survive that morning."

"I will go and tell Mr. Wyse instantly — dear," said Mrs. Poppit.

That would never do. True believers were so scarce that it was wicked to think of unsettling their faith.

"Poor Mr. Wyse!" said Miss Mapp with a magnanimous smile. "Do not think, dear, of troubling him with these little trumpery affairs. He will not take part in these little tittle-tattles. But if you could let dear Diva and quaint Irene and sweet Evie and the good Padre know that I laugh at all such nonsense —"

"But they laugh at it, too," said Mrs. Poppit.

That would have been baffling for anyone who allowed herself to be baffled, but that was not Miss Mapp's way.

"Oh, that bitter laughter!" she said. "It hurt me to hear it. It was envious laughter, dear, scoffing, bitter laughter. I heard! I cannot bear that the dear things should feel like that. Tell them that I say how silly they are to believe anything of the sort. Trust me, I am right about it. I wash my hands of such nonsense."

She made a vivid dumb-show of this, and after drying them on an imaginary towel, let a sunny smile peep out the eyes which she had rubbed.

"All gone!" she said; "and we will have a dear little party on Wednesday to show we are all friends again. And we meet for lunch at dear Mr. Wyse's the next day? Yes? He will get tired of poor little me if he sees me two days running, so I shall not ask him. I will just try to get two tables together, and nobody shall contradict dear Diva, however many shillings she says she has won. I would sooner pay them all myself than have any more of our unhappy divisions. You will have talked to them all before Wednesday, will you not, dear?"

As there were only four to talk to, Mrs. Poppit thought that she could manage it, and spent a most interesting afternoon. For two years now she had tried to unfreeze Miss Mapp, who, when all was said and done, was the centre of the Tilling circle, and who, if any attempt was made to shove her out towards the circumference, always gravitated back again. And now, on these important errands she was Miss Mapp's accredited ambassador, and all the terrible business of the opening of the store-cupboard and her decoration as M.B.E. was quite forgiven and forgotten. There would be so much walking to be done from house to house, that it was impossible to wear her sable coat unless she had the Royce to take her about . . .

The effect of her communications would have surprised anybody who did not know Tilling. A less subtle society, when assured from a first-hand, authoritative source that a report which it had entirely refused to believe was false, would have prided itself on its perspicacity, and said that it had laughed at such an idea, as soon as ever it heard it, as being palpably (look at Miss Mapp!) untrue. Not so Tilling. The very fact that, by the mouth of her ambassador, she so uncompromisingly denied it, was precisely why Tilling began to wonder if there was not something in it, and from wondering if there was not something in it, surged to the conclusion that there certainly was. Diva, for instance, the moment she was told that Elizabeth (for Mrs. Poppit remembered her Christian name perfectly) utterly and scornfully denied the truth of the report, became intensely thoughtful.

"Say there's nothing in it?" she observed. "Can't understand that."

At that moment Diva's telephone bell rang, and she hurried out and in.

"Party at Elizabeth's on Wednesday," she said. "She saw me laughing. Why ask me?"

Mrs. Poppit was full of her sacred mission.

"To show how little she minds your laughing," she suggested.

"As if it wasn't true, then. Seems like that. Wants us to think it's not true."

"She was very earnest about it," said the ambassador.

Diva got up, and tripped over the outlying skirts of Mrs. Poppit's fur coat as she went to ring the bell.

"Sorry," she said. "Take it off and have a chat. Tea's coming.

Muffins!"

"Oh, no, thanks!" said Mrs. Poppit. "I've so many calls to make."

"What? Similar calls?" asked Diva. "Wait ten minutes. Tea, Janet. Quickly."

She whirled round the room once or twice, all corrugated with perplexity, beginning telegraphic sentences, and not finishing them: "Says it's not true — laughs at notion of — And Mr. Wyse believes — The Padre believed. After all, the Major — Little cock-sparrow Captain Puffin — Or t'other way round, do you think? — No other explanation, you know — Might have been blood —"

She buried her teeth in a muffin.

"Believe there's something in it," she summed up.

She observed her guest had neither tea nor muffin.

"Help yourself," she said. "Want to worry this out."

"Elizabeth absolutely denies it," said Mrs. Poppit. "Her eyes were full of —"

"Oh, anything," said Diva. "Rubbed them. Or pepper if it was at lunch. That's no evidence."

"But her solemn assertion —" began Mrs. Poppit, thinking that she was being a complete failure as an ambassador. She was carrying no conviction at all.

"Saccharine!" observed Diva, handing her a small phial. "Haven't got more than enough sugar for myself. I expect Elizabeth's got plenty — well, never mind that. Don't you see? If it wasn't true she would try to convince us that it was. Seemed absurd on the face of it. But if she tries to convince us that it isn't true — well, something in it."

There was the gist of the matter, and Mrs. Poppit proceeding next to the Padre's house, found more muffins and incredulity. Nobody seemed to believe Elizabeth's assertion that there was "nothing in it." Evie ran round the room with excited squeaks, the Padre nodded his head, in confirmation of the opinion which, when he first delivered it, had been received with mocking incredulity over the crab. Quaint Irene, intent on Mr. Hopkins's left knee in the absence of the model, said, "Good old Mapp: better late than never." Utter incredulity, in fact, was the ambassador's welcome ... and all the incredulous were going to Elizabeth's party on Wednesday.

Mrs. Poppit had sent the Royce home for the last of her calls, and staggered up the hill past Elizabeth's house. Oddly enough, just as she passed the garden-room, the window was thrown up.

"Cup of tea, dear Susan?" said Elizabeth. She had found an old note of Mrs. Poppit's among the waste paper for the firing of the kitchen oven fully signed.

"Just two minutes' talk, Elizabeth," she promptly responded.

*****

The news that nobody in Tilling believed her left Miss Mapp more than calm, on the bright side of calm, that is to say. She had a few indulgent phrases that tripped readily off her tongue for the dear things who hated to be deprived of their gossip, but Susan certainly did not receive the impression that this playful magnanimity was attained with an effort. Elizabeth did not seem really to mind: she was very gay. Then, skilfully changing the subject, she mourned over her dead dahlias.

Though Tilling with all its perspicacity could not have known it, the intuitive reader will certainly have perceived that Miss Mapp's party for Wednesday night had, so to speak, further irons in its fire. It had originally been a bribe to Susan Poppit, in order to induce her to spread broadcast that that ridiculous rumour (whoever had launched it) had been promptly denied by the person whom it most immediately concerned. It served a second purpose in showing that Miss Mapp was too high above the mire of scandal, however interesting, to know or care who might happen to be wallowing in it, and for this reason she asked everybody who had done so. Such loftiness of soul had earned her an amazing bonus, for it had induced those who sat in the seat of the scoffers before to come hastily off, and join the thin but unwavering ranks of the true believers, who up till then had consisted only of Susan and Mr. Wyse. Frankly, so blest a conclusion had never occurred to Miss Mapp: it was one of those unexpected rewards that fall like ripe plums into the lap of the upright. By denying a rumour she had got everybody to believe it, and when on Wednesday morning she went out to get the chocolate cakes which were so useful in allaying the appetites of guests, she encountered no broken conversations and gleeful smiles, but sidelong glances of respectful envy.

But what Tilling did not and could not know was that this, the first of the autumn after-dinner bridge-parties, was destined to look on the famous tea-gown of kingfisher-blue, as designed for Mrs. Trout. No doubt other ladies would have hurried up their new gowns, or at least have camouflaged their old ones, in honour of the annual inauguration of evening bridge, but Miss Mapp had no misgivings about being outshone. And once again here she felt that luck waited on merit, for though when she dressed that evening she found she had not anticipated that artificial light would cast a somewhat pale (though not ghastly) reflection from the vibrant blue on to her features, similar in effect to (but not so marked as) the light that shines on the faces of those who lean over the burning brandy and raisins of "snapdragon," this interesting pallor seemed very aptly to bear witness to all that she had gone through. She did not look ill — she was satisfied as to that — she looked gorgeous and a little wan.

The bridge tables were not set out in the garden-room, which entailed a scurry over damp gravel on a black, windy night, but in the little square parlour above her dining-room, where Withers, in the intervals of admitting her guests, was laying out plates of sandwiches and the chocolate cakes, reinforced when the interval for refreshments came with hot soup, whisky and syphons, and a jug of "cup" prepared according to an ancestral and economical recipe, which Miss Mapp had taken a great deal of trouble about. A single bottle of white wine, with suitable additions of ginger, nutmeg, herbs and soda-water, was the mother of a gallon of a drink that seemed aflame with fiery and probably spirituous ingredients. Guests were very careful how they partook of it, so stimulating it seemed.

Miss Mapp was reading a book on gardening upside down (she had taken it up rather hurriedly) when the Poppits arrived, and sprang to her feet with a pretty cry at being so unexpectedly but delightfully disturbed.

"Susan! Isabel!" she said. "Lovely of you to have come! I was reading about flowers, making plans for next year."

She saw the four eyes riveted to her dress. Susan looked quite shabby in comparison, and Isabel did not look anything at all.

"My dear, too lovely!" said Mrs. Poppit slowly.

Miss Mapp looked brightly about, as if wondering what was too lovely: at last she guessed.

"Oh, my new frock?" she said. "Do you like it, dear? How sweet of you. It's just a little nothing that I talked over with that nice Miss Greele in the High Street. We put our heads together, and invented something quite cheap and simple. And here's Evie and the dear Padre. So kind of you to look in."

Four more eyes were riveted on it.

"Enticed you out just once, Padre," went on Miss Mapp. "So sweet of you to spare an evening. And here's Major Benjy and Captain Puffin. Well, that is nice!"

This was really tremendous of Miss Mapp. Here was she meeting without embarrassment or awkwardness the two, who if the duel had not been averted, would have risked their very lives over some dispute concerning her. Everybody else, naturally, was rather taken aback for the moment at this situation, so deeply dyed in the dramatic. Should either of the gladiators have heard that it was the Padre who undoubtedly had spread the rumour concerning their hostess, Mrs. Poppit was afraid that even his cloth might not protect him. But no such deplorable calamity occurred, and only four more eyes were riveted to the kingfisher-blue.

"Upon my word," said the Major, "I never saw anything more beautiful than that gown, Miss Elizabeth. Straight from Paris, eh? Paris in every line of it."

"Oh, Major Benjy," said Elizabeth. "You're all making fun of me and my simple little frock. I'm getting quite shy. Just a bit of old stuff that I had. But so nice of you to like it. I wonder where Diva is. We shall have to scold her for being late. Ah — she shan't be scolded. Diva, darl —"

The endearing word froze on Miss Mapp's lips and she turned deadly white. In the doorway, in equal fury and dismay, stood Diva, dressed in precisely the same staggeringly lovely costume as her hostess. Had Diva and Miss Greele put their heads together too? Had Diva got a bit of old stuff . . . ?

Miss Mapp pulled herself together first and moistened her dry lips.

"So sweet of you to look in, dear," she said. "Shall we cut?"

Naturally the malice of cards decreed that Miss Mapp and Diva should sit next each other as adversaries at the same table, and the combined effect of two lots of kingfisher-blue was blinding. Complete silence on every subject connected, however remotely, with dress was, of course, the only line for correct diplomacy to pursue, but then Major Benjy was not diplomatic, only gallant.

"Never saw such stunning gowns, eh, Padre?" he said. "Dear me, they are very much alike too, aren't they? Pair of exquisite sisters."

It would be hard to say which of the two found this speech the more provocative of rage, for while Diva was four years younger than Miss Mapp, Miss Mapp was four inches taller than Diva. She cut the cards to her sister with a hand that trembled so much that she had to do it again, and Diva could scarcely deal.

*****

Mr. Wyse frankly confessed the next day when, at one o'clock, Elizabeth found herself the first arrival at his house, that he had been very self-indulgent.

"I have given myself a treat, dear Miss Mapp," he said. "I have asked three entrancing ladies to share my humble meal with me, and have provided — is it not shocking of me? — nobody else to meet them. Your pardon, dear lady, for my greediness."

Now this was admirably done. Elizabeth knew very well why two out of the three men in Tilling had not been asked (very gratifying, that reason was), and with the true refinement of which Mr. Wyse was so amply possessed, where he was taking all the blame on himself, and putting it so prettily. She bestowed her widest smile on him.

"Oh, Mr. Wyse," she said. "We shall all quarrel over you."

Not until Miss Mapp had spoken did she perceive how subtle her words were. They seemed to bracket herself and Mr. Wyse together: all the men (two out of the three, at any rate) had been quarrelling over her, and now there seemed a very fair prospect of three of the women quarreling over Mr. Wyse . . .

Without being in the least effeminate, Mr. Wyse this morning looked rather like a modern Troubadour. He had a velveteen coat on, a soft, fluffy, mushy tie which looked as if made of Shirley poppies, very neat knickerbockers, brown stockings with blobs, like the fruit of plane trees, dependent from elaborate "tops," and shoes with a cascade of leather frilling covering the laces. He might almost equally well be about to play golf over putting-holes on the lawn as the guitar. He made a gesture of polished, polite dissent, not contradicting, yet hardly accepting this tribute, remitting it perhaps, just as the King when he enters the City of London touches the sword of the Lord Mayor and tells him to keep it . . .

"So pleasant to be in Tilling again," he said. "We shall have a cosy, busy winter, I hope. You, I know, Miss Mapp, are always busy."

"The day is never long enough for me," said Elizabeth enthusiastically. "What with my household duties in the morning, and my garden, and our pleasant little gatherings, it is always bed-time too soon. I want to read a great deal this winter, too."

Diva (at the sight of whom Elizabeth had to make a strong effort of self-control) here came in, together with Mrs. Poppit, and the party was complete. Elizabeth would have been willing to bet that, in spite of the warmness of the morning, Susan would have on her sable coat, and though, technically, she would have lost, she more than won morally, for Mr. Wyse's repeated speeches about his greediness were hardly out of his mouth when she discovered that she had left her handkerchief in the pocket of her sable coat, which she had put over the back of a conspicuous chair in the hall. Figgis, however, came in at the moment to say that lunch was ready, and she delayed them all very much by a long, ineffectual search for it, during which Figgis, with a visible effort, held up the sable coat, so that it was displayed to the utmost advantage. And then, only fancy,

Susan discovered that it was in her sable muff all the time!

All three ladies were on tenterhooks of anxiety as to who was to be placed on Mr. Wyse's right, who on his left, and who would be given only the place between two other women. But his tact was equal to anything.

"Miss Mapp," he said, "will you honour me by taking the head of my table and be hostess for me? Only I must have that vase of flowers removed, Figgis; I can look at my flowers when Miss Mapp is not here. Now, what have we got for breakfast — lunch, I should say?"

The macaroni which Mr. Wyse had brought back with him from Naples naturally led on to Italian subjects, and the general scepticism about the Contessa di Faraglione had a staggering blow dealt it.

"My sister," began Mr. Wyse (and by a swift sucking motion, Diva drew into her mouth several serpents of dependent macaroni in order to be able to listen better without this agitating distraction), "my sister, I hope, will come to England this winter, and spend several weeks with me." (Sensation.)

"And the Count?" asked Diva, having swallowed the serpents.

"I fear not; Cecco — Francesco, you know — is a great stay-at-home. Amelia is looking forward very much to seeing Tilling. I shall insist on her making a long stay here, before she visits our relations at Whitchurch."

Elizabeth found herself reserving judgment. She would believe in the Contessa Faraglione — no one more firmly — when she saw her, and had reasonable proofs of her identity.

"Delightful!" she said, abandoning with regret the fruitless pursuit with a fork of the few last serpents that writhed on her plate. "What an addition to our society! We shall all do our best to spoil her, Mr. Wyse. When do you expect her?"

"Early in December. You must be very kind to her, dear ladies. She is an insatiable bridge-player. She has heard much of the great players she will meet here."

That decided Mrs. Poppit. She would join the correspondence class conducted by "Little Slam," in "Cosy Corner." Little Slam, for the sum of two guineas, payable in advance, engaged to make first-class players of anyone with normal intelligence. Diva's mind flew off to the subject of dress, and the thought of the awful tragedy concerning the tea-gown of kingfisher-blue, combined with the endive salad, gave a wry twist to her mouth for a moment.

"I, as you know," continued Mr. Wyse, "am no hand at bridge."

"Oh, Mr. Wyse, you play beautifully," interpolated Elizabeth.

"Too flattering of you, Miss Mapp. But Amelia and Cecco do not agree with you. I am never allowed to play when I am at the Villa Faraglione, unless a table cannot be made up without me. But I shall look forward to seeing many well-contested games."

The quails and the figs had come from Capri, and Miss Mapp, greedily devouring each in turn, was so much incensed by the information that she had elicited about them, that, though she joined in the general Lobgesang, she was tempted to inquire whether the ice had not been brought from the South Pole by some Antarctic expedition. Her mind was not, like poor Diva's, taken up with obstinate questionings about the kingfisher-blue tea-gown, for she had already determined what she was going to do about it. Naturally it was impossible to contemplate fresh encounters like that of last night, but another gown, crimson-lake, the colour of Mrs. Trout's toilet for the second evening of the Duke of Hampshire's visit, as Vogue informed her, had completely annihilated Newport with its splendour. She had already consulted Miss Greele about it, who said that if the kingfisher-blue was bleached first the dye of crimson-lake would be brilliant and pure . . . The thought of that, and the fact that Miss Greele's lips were professionally sealed, made her able to take Diva's arm as they strolled about the garden afterwards. The way in which both Diva and Susan had made up to Mr. Wyse during lunch was really very shocking, though it did not surprise Miss Mapp, but she supposed their heads had been turned by the prospect of playing bridge with a countess. Luckily she expected nothing better of either of them, so their conduct was in no way a blow or a disappointment to her.

This companionship with Diva was rather prolonged, for the adhesive Susan, staggering about in her sables, clung close to their host and simulated a clumsy interest in chrysanthemums; and whatever the other two did, manœuvred herself into a strong position between them and Mr. Wyse, from which, operating on interior lines, she could cut off either assailant. More depressing yet (and throwing a sad new light on his character), Mr. Wyse seemed to appreciate rather than resent the appropriation of himself, and instead of making a sortie through the beleaguering sables, would beg Diva and Elizabeth, who were so fond of fuchsias and knew about them so well, to put their heads together over an afflicted bed of these flowers in quite another part of the garden, and tell him what was the best treatment for their anæmic condition. Pleasant and proper though it was to each of them that Mr. Wyse should pay so little attention to the other, it was bitter as the endive salad to both that he should tolerate, if not enjoy, the companionship which the forwardness of Susan forced on him, and while they absently stared at the fuchsias, the fire kindled, and Elizabeth spake with her tongue.

"How very plain poor Susan looks to-day," she said. "Such a colour, though to be sure I attribute that more to what she ate and drank than to anything else. Crimson. Oh, those poor fuchsias! I think I should throw them away."

The common antagonism, Diva felt, had drawn her and Elizabeth into the most cordial of understandings. For the moment she felt nothing but enthusiastic sympathy with Elizabeth, in spite of her kingfisher-blue gown . . . What on earth, in parenthesis, was she to do with hers? She could not give it to Janet: it was impossible to contemplate the idea of Janet walking about the High Street in a tea-gown of kingfisher-blue just in order to thwart Elizabeth . . .

"Mr. Wyse seems taken with her," said Diva. "How he can! Rather a snob. M.B.E. She's always popping in here. Saw her yesterday going round the corner of the street."

"What time, dear?" asked Elizabeth, nosing the scent.

"Middle of the morning."

"And I saw her in the afternoon," said Elizabeth. "That great lumbering Rolls-Royce went tacking and skidding round the corner below my garden-room."

"Was she in it?" asked Diva.

This appeared rather a slur on Elizabeth's reliability in observation.

"No, darling, she was sitting on the top," she said, taking the edge off the sarcasm, in case Diva had not intended to be critical, by a little laugh. Diva drew the conclusion that Elizabeth had actually seen her inside.

"Think it's serious?" she said. "Think he'll marry her?"

The idea of course, repellent and odious as it was, had occurred to Elizabeth, so she instantly denied it.

"Oh, you busy little match-maker," she said brightly. "Such an idea never entered my head. You shouldn't make such fun of dear Susan. Come, dear, I can't look at fuchsias any more. I must be getting home and must say good-bye — au reservoir, rather — to Mr. Wyse, if Susan will allow me to get a word in edgeways."

Susan seemed delighted to let Miss Mapp get this particular word in edgewise, and after a little speech from Mr. Wyse, in which he said that he would not dream of allowing them to go yet, and immediately afterwards shook hands warmly with them both, hoping that the reservoir would be a very small one, the two were forced to leave the artful Susan in possession of the field . . .

It all looked rather black. Miss Mapp's vivid imagination altogether failed to picture what Tilling would be like if Susan succeeded in becoming Mrs. Wyse and the sister-in-law of a countess, and she sat down in her garden-room and closed her eyes for a moment, in order to concentrate her power of figuring the situation. What dreadful people these climbers were! How swiftly they swarmed up the social ladder with their Rolls-Royces and their redcurrant fool, and their sables! A few weeks ago she herself had never asked Susan into her house, while the very first time she came she unloosed the sluices of the store-cupboard, and now, owing to the necessity of getting her aid in stopping that mischievous rumour, which she herself had been so careful to set on foot, regarding the cause of the duel, Miss Mapp had been positively obliged to flatter and to "Susan" her. And if Diva's awful surmise proved to be well-founded, Susan would be in a position to patronize them all, and talk about counts and countesses with the same air of unconcern as Mr. Wyse. She would be bidden to the Villa Faraglione, she would play bridge with Cecco and Amelia, she would visit the Wyses of Whitchurch . . .

What was to be done? She might head another movement to put Mr. Wyse in his proper place; this, if successful, would have the agreeable result of pulling down Susan a rung or two should she carry out her design. But the failure of the last attempt and Mr. Wyse's eminence did not argue well for any further manœuvre of the kind. Or should she poison Mr. Wyse's mind with regard to Susan? . . . Or was she herself causelessly agitated?

Or —

Curiosity rushed like a devastating tornado across Miss Mapp's mind, rooting up all other growths, buffeting her with the necessity of knowing what the two whom she had been forced to leave in the garden were doing now, and snatching up her opera-glasses she glided upstairs, and let herself out through the trap-door on to the roof. She did not remember if it was possible to see Mr. Wyse's garden or any part of it from that watch-tower, but there was a chance . . .

Not a glimpse of it was visible. It lay quite hidden behind the red-brick wall which bounded it, and not a chrysanthemum or a fuchsia could she see. But her blood froze as, without putting the glasses down, she ran her eye over such part of the house-wall as rose above the obstruction. In his drawing-room window on the first floor were seated two figures. Susan had taken her sables off: it was as if she intended remaining there for ever, or at least for tea . . .

CHAPTER VIII

The hippopotamus quarrel over their whisky between Major Flint and Captain Puffin, which culminated in the challenge and all the shining sequel, had had the excellent effect of making the united services more united than ever. They both knew that, had they not severally run away from the encounter, and, so providentially, met at the station, very serious consequences might have ensued. Had not both but only one of them been averse from taking or risking life, the other would surely have remained in Tilling, and spread disastrous reports about the bravery of the refugee; while if neither of them had had scruples on the sacredness of human existence there might have been one if not two corpses lying on the shining sands. Naturally the fact that they both had taken the very earliest opportunity of averting an encounter by flight, made it improbable that any future quarrel would be proceeded with to violent extremes, but it was much safer to run no risks, and not let verbal disagreements rise to hippopotamus-pitch again. Consequently when there was any real danger of such savagery as was implied in sending challenges, they hastened, by mutual concessions, to climb down from these perilous places, where loss of balance might possibly occur. For which of them could be absolutely certain that next time the other of them might not be more courageous? . . .

They were coming up from the tram-station one November evening, both fizzing and fuming a good deal, and the Major was extremely lame, lamer than Puffin. The rattle of the tram had made argument impossible during the transit from the links, but they had both in this enforced silence thought of several smart repartees, supposing that the other made the requisite remarks to call them out, and on arrival at the Tilling station they went on at precisely the same point at which they had broken off on starting from the station by the links.

"Well, I hope I can take a beating in as English a spirit as anybody," said the Major.

This was lucky for Captain Puffin: he had thought it likely that he would say just that, and had got a stinger for him.

"And it worries you to find that your hopes are doomed to disappointment," he swiftly said.

Major Flint stepped in a puddle which cooled his foot but not his temper.

"Most offensive remark," he said. "I wasn't called Sporting Benjy in the regiment for nothing. But never mind that. A worm-cast —"

"It wasn't a worm-cast," said Puffin. "It was sheep's dung!"

Luck had veered here: the Major had felt sure that Puffin would reiterate that utterly untrue contention.

"I can't pretend to be such a specialist as you in those matters," he said, "but you must allow me sufficient power of observation to know a worm-cast when I see it. It was a worm-cast, sir, a cast of a worm, and you had no right to remove it. If you will do me the favour to consult the rules of golf — ?"

"Oh, I grant you that you are more a specialist in the rules of golf, Major, than in the practice of it," said Puffin brightly.

Suddenly it struck Sporting Benjy that the red signals of danger danced before his eyes, and though the odious Puffin had scored twice to his once, he called up all his powers of self-control, for if his friend was anything like as exasperated as himself, the breeze of disagreement might develop into a hurricane. At the moment he was passing through a swing-gate which led to a short cut back to the town, but before he could take hold of himself he had slammed it back in his fury, hitting Puffin, who was following him, on the knee. Then he remembered he was a sporting Christian gentleman, and no duellist.

"I'm sure I beg your pardon, my dear fellow," he said, with the utmost solicitude. "Uncommonly stupid of me. The gate flew out of my hand. I hope I didn't hurt you."

Puffin had just come to the same conclusion as Major Flint: magnanimity was better than early trains, and ever so much better than bullets. Indeed there was no comparison . . .

"Not hurt a bit, thank you, Major," he said, wincing with the shrewdness of the blow, silently cursing his friend for what he felt sure was no accident, and limping with both legs. "It didn't touch me. Ha! What a brilliant sunset. The town looks amazingly picturesque."

"It does indeed," said the Major. "Fine subject for Miss Mapp."

Puffin shuffled alongside.

"There's still a lot of talk going on in the town," he said, "about that duel of ours. Those fairies of yours are all agog to know what it was about. I am sure they all think that there was a lady in the case. Just like the vanity of the sex. If two men have a quarrel, they think it must be because of their silly faces."

Ordinarily the Major's gallantry would have resented this view, but the reconciliation with Puffin was too recent to risk just at present.

"Poor little devils," he said. "It makes an excitement for them. I wonder who they think it is. It would puzzle me to name a woman in Tilling worth catching an early train for."

"There are several who'd be surprised to hear you say that, Major," said Puffin archly.

"Well, well," said the other, strutting and swelling, and walking without a sign of lameness . . .

They had come to where their houses stood opposite each other on the steep cobbled street, fronted at its top end by Miss Mapp's garden-room. She happened to be standing in the window, and the Major made a great flourish of his cap, and laid his hand on his heart.

"And there's one of them," said Puffin, as Miss Mapp acknowledged these florid salutations with a wave of her hand, and tripped away from the window.

"Poking your fun at me," said the Major. "Perhaps she was the cause of our quarrel, hey? Well, I'll step across, shall I, about half-past nine, and bring my diaries with me?"

"I'll expect you. You'll find me at my Roman roads."

The humour of this joke never staled, and they parted with hoots and guffaws of laughter.

It must not be supposed that duelling, puzzles over the portmanteau, or the machinations of Susan had put out of Miss Mapp's head her amiable interest in the hour at which Major Benjy went to bed. For some time she had been content to believe, on direct information from him, that he went to bed early and worked at his diaries on alternate evenings, but maturer consideration had led her to wonder whether he was being quite as truthful as a gallant soldier should be. For though (on alternate evenings) his house would be quite dark by half-past nine, it was not for twelve hours or more afterwards that he could be heard qui-hi-ing for his breakfast, and unless he was in some incipient stage of sleeping-sickness, such hours provided more than ample slumber for a growing child, and might be considered excessive for a middle-aged man. She had a mass of evidence to show that on the other set of alternate nights his diaries (which must, in parenthesis, be of extraordinary fullness) occupied him into the small hours, and to go to bed at half-past nine on one night and after one o'clock on the next implied a complicated kind of regularity which cried aloud for elucidation. If he had only breakfasted early on the mornings after he had gone to bed early, she might have allowed herself to be weakly credulous, but he never qui-hied earlier than half-past nine, and she could not but think that to believe blindly in such habits would be a triumph not for faith but for foolishness. "People," said Miss Mapp to herself, as her attention refused to concentrate on the evening paper, "don't do it. I never heard of a similar case."

She had been spending the evening alone, and even the conviction that her cold apple tart had suffered diminution by at least a slice, since she had so much enjoyed it hot at lunch, failed to occupy her mind for long, for this matter had presented itself with a clamouring insistence that drowned all other voices. She had tried, when, at the conclusion of her supper, she had gone back to the garden-room, to immerse herself in a book, in an evening paper, in the portmanteau problem, in a jig-saw puzzle, and in Patience, but none of these supplied the stimulus to lead her mind away from Major Benjy's evenings, or the narcotic to dull her unslumbering desire to solve a problem that was rapidly becoming one of the greater mysteries.

Her radiator made a seat in the window agreeably warm, and a chink in the curtains gave her a view of the Major's lighted window. Even as she looked, the illumination was extinguished. She had expected this, as he had been at his diaries late — quite naughtily late — the evening before, so this would be a night of infant slumber for twelve hours or so.

Even as she looked, a chink of light came from his front door, which immediately enlarged itself into a full oblong. Then it went completely out. "He has opened the door, and has put out the hall-light," whispered Miss Mapp to herself . . . "He has gone out and shut the door . . . (Perhaps he is going to post a letter.) . . . He has gone into Captain Puffin's house without knocking. So he is expected."

Miss Mapp did not at once guess that she held in her hand the key to the mystery. It was certainly Major Benjy's night for going to bed early . . . Then a fierce illumination beat on her brain. Had she not, so providentially, actually observed the Major cross the road, unmistakable in the lamplight, and had she only looked out of her window after the light in his was quenched, she would surely have told herself that good Major Benjy had gone to bed. But good Major Benjy, on ocular evidence, she now knew to have done nothing of the kind: he had gone across to see Captain Puffin . . . He was not good.

She grasped the situation in its hideous entirety. She had been deceived and hoodwinked. Major Benjy never went to bed early at all: on alternate nights he went and sat with Captain Puffin. And Captain Puffin, she could not but tell herself, sat up on the other set of alternate nights with the Major, for it had not escaped her observation that when the Major seemed to be sitting up, the Captain seemed to have gone to bed. Instantly, with strong conviction, she suspected orgies. It remained to be seen (and she would remain to see it) to what hour these orgies were kept up.

About eleven o'clock a little mist had begun to form in the street, obscuring the complete clarity of her view, but through it there still shone the light from behind Captain Puffin's red blind, and the mist was not so thick as to be able wholly to obscure the figure of Major Flint when he should pass below the gas lamp again into his house. But no such figure passed. Did he then work at his diaries every evening? And what price, to put it vulgarly, Roman roads?

Every moment her sense of being deceived grew blacker, and every moment her curiosity as to what they were doing became more unbearable. After a spasm of tactical thought she glided back into her house from the garden-room, and, taking an envelope in her hand, so that she might, if detected, say that she was going down to the letter-box at the corner to catch the early post, she unbolted her door and let herself out. She crossed the street and tiptoed along the pavement to where the red light from Captain Puffin's window shone like a blurred danger-signal through the mist.

From inside came a loud duet of familiar voices: sometimes they spoke singly, sometimes together. But she could not catch the words: they sounded blurred and indistinct, and she told herself that she was very glad that she could not hear what they said, for that would have seemed like eaves-dropping. The voices sounded angry. Was there another duel pending? And what was it about this time?

Quite suddenly, from so close at hand that she positively leaped off the pavement into the middle of the road, the door was thrown open and the duet, louder than ever, streamed out into the street. Major Benjy bounced out on to the threshold, and stumbled down the two steps that led from the door.

"Tell you it was a worm-cast," he bellowed. "Think I don't know a worm-cast when I see a worm-cast?"

Suddenly his tone changed: this was getting too near a quarrel.

"Well, good-night, old fellow," he said. "Jolly evening."

He turned and saw, veiled and indistinct in the mist, the female figure in the roadway. Undying coquetry, as Mr. Stevenson so finely remarked, awoke, for the topic preceding the worm-cast had been "the sex."

"Bless me," he crowed, "if there isn't an unprotected lady all 'lone here in the dark, and lost in the fog. 'Llow me to 'scort you home, madam. Lemme introduce myself and friend — Major Flint, that's me, and my friend Captain Puffin."

He put up his hand and whispered an aside to Miss Mapp: "Revolutionized the theory of navigation."

Major Benjy was certainly rather gay and rather indistinct, but his polite gallantry could not fail to be attractive. It was naughty of him to have said that he went to bed early on alternate nights, but really . . . Still, it might be better to slip away unrecognized, and, thinking it would be nice to scriggle by him and disappear in the mist, she made a tactical error in her scriggling, for she scriggled full into the light that streamed from the open door where Captain Puffin was standing.

He gave a shrill laugh.

"Why, it's Miss Mapp," he said in his high falsetto. "Blow me, if it isn't our mutual friend Miss Mapp. What a 'strordinary coincidence."

Miss Mapp put on her most winning smile. To be dignified and at the same time pleasant was the proper way to deal with this situation. Gentlemen often had a glass of grog when they thought the ladies had gone upstairs. That was how, for the moment, she summed things up.

"Good evening," she said. "I was just going down to the pillar-box to post a letter," and she exhibited her envelope. But it dropped out of her hand, and the Major picked it up for her.

"I'll post it for you," he said very pleasantly. "Save you the trouble. Insist on it. Why, there's no stamp on it! Why, there's no address on it! I say, Puffie, here's a letter with no address on it. Forgotten the address, Miss Mapp? Think they'll remember it at the post office? Well, that's one of the mos' comic things I ever came across. An, an anonymous letter, eh?"

The night air began to have a most unfortunate effect on Puffin. When he came out it would have been quite unfair to have described him as drunk. He was no more than gay and ready to go to bed. Now he became portentously solemn, as the cold mist began to do its deadly work.

"A letter," he said impressively, "without an address is an uncommonly dangerous thing. Hic! Can't tell into whose hands it may fall. I would sooner go 'bout with a loaded pistol than with a letter without any address. Send it to the bank for safety. Send for the police. Follow my advice and send for the p'lice. Police!"

Miss Mapp's penetrating mind instantly perceived that that dreadful Captain Puffin was drunk, and she promised herself that Tilling should ring with the tale of his excesses to-morrow. But Major Benjy, whom, if she mistook not, Captain Puffin had been trying, with perhaps some small success, to lead astray, was a gallant gentleman still, and she conceived the brilliant but madly mistaken idea of throwing herself on his protection.

"Major Benjy," she said, "I will ask you to take me home. Captain Puffin has had too much to drink —"

"Woz that?" asked Captain Puffin, with an air of great interest.

Miss Mapp abandoned dignity and pleasantness, and lost her temper.

"I said you were drunk," she said with great distinctness. "Major Benjy, will you —"

Captain Puffin came carefully down the two steps from the door on to the pavement.

"Look here," he said, "this all needs 'splanation. You say I'm drunk, do you? Well, I say you're drunk, going out like this in mill' of the night to post letter with no 'dress on it. Shamed of yourself, mill'aged woman going out in the mill' of the night in the mill' of Tilling. Very shocking thing. What do you say, Major?"

Major Benjy drew himself up to his full height, and put on his hat in order to take it off to Miss Mapp.

"My fren' Cap'n Puffin," he said, "is a man of strictly 'stemious habits. Boys together. Very serious thing to call a man of my fren's character drunk. If you call him drunk, why shouldn't he call you drunk? Can't take away man's character like that."

"Abso —" began Captain Puffin. Then he stopped and pulled himself together.

"Absolooly," he said without a hitch.

"Tilling shall hear of this to-morrow," said Miss Mapp, shivering with rage and sea-mist.

Captain Puffin came a step closer.

"Now I'll tell you what it is, Miss Mapp," he said. "If you dare to say that I was drunk, Major and I, my fren' the Major and I will say you were drunk. Perhaps you think my fren' the Major's drunk too. But sure's I live, I'll say we were taking lil' walk in the moonlight and found you trying to post a letter with no 'dress on it, and couldn't find the slit to put it in. But 'slong as you say nothing, I say nothing. Can't say fairer than that. Liberal terms. Mutual Protection Society. Your lips sealed, our lips sealed. Strictly private. All trespassers will be prosecuted. By order. Hic!"

Miss Mapp felt that Major Benjy ought instantly to have challenged his ignoble friend to another duel for this insolent suggestion, but he did nothing of the kind, and his silence, which had some awful quality of consent about it, chilled her mind, even as the sea-mist, now thick and cold, made her certain that her nose was turning red. She still boiled with rage, but her mind grew cold with odious apprehensions: she was like an ice-pudding with scalding sauce . . . There they all stood, veiled in vapours, and outlined by the red light that streamed from the still-open door of the intoxicated Puffin, getting colder every moment.

"Yessorno," said Puffin, with chattering teeth.

Bitter as it was to accept those outrageous terms, there really seemed, without the Major's support, to be no way out of it.

"Yes," said Miss Mapp.

Puffin gave a loud crow.

"The ayes have it, Major," he said. "So we're all frens again. Goonight everybody."

*****

Miss Mapp let herself into her house in an agony of mortification. She could scarcely realize that her little expedition, undertaken with so much ardent and earnest curiosity only a quarter of an hour ago, had ended in so deplorable a surfeit of sensation. She had gone out in obedience to an innocent and, indeed, laudable desire to ascertain how Major Benjy spent those evenings on which he had deceived her into imagining that, owing to her influence, he had gone ever so early to bed, only to find that he sat up ever so late and that she was fettered by a promise not to breathe to a soul a single word about the depravity of Captain Puffin, on pain of being herself accused out of the mouth of two witnesses of being equally depraved herself. More wounding yet was the part played by her Major Benjy in these odious transactions, and it was only possible to conclude that he put a higher value on his fellowship with his degraded friend than on chivalry itself . . . And what did his silence imply? Probably it was a defensive one; he imagined that he, too, would be included in the stories that Miss Mapp proposed to sow broadcast upon the fruitful fields of Tilling, and, indeed, when she called to mind his bellowing about worm-casts, his general instability of speech and equilibrium, she told herself that he had ample cause for such a supposition. He, when his lights were out, was abetting, assisting and perhaps joining Captain Puffin. When his window was alight on alternate nights she made no doubt now that Captain Puffin was performing a similar rôle. This had been going on for weeks under her very nose, without her having the smallest suspicion of it.

Humiliated by all that had happened, and flattened in her own estimation by the sense of her blindness, she penetrated to the kitchen and lit a gas-ring to make herself some hot cocoa, which would at least comfort her physical chatterings. There was a letter for Withers, slipped sideways into its envelope, on the kitchen table, and mechanically she opened and read it by the bluish flame of the burner. She had always suspected Withers of having a young man, and here was proof of it. But that he should be Mr. Hopkins of the fish-shop!

There is known to medical science a pleasant device known as a counter-irritant. If the patient has an aching and rheumatic joint he is counselled to put some hot burning application on the skin, which smarts so agonizingly that the ache is quite extinguished. Metaphorically, Mr. Hopkins was thermogene to Miss Mapp's outraged and aching consciousness, and the smart occasioned by the knowledge that Withers must have encouraged Mr. Hopkins (else he could scarcely have written a letter so familiar and amorous), and thus be contemplating matrimony, relieved the aching humiliation of all that had happened in the sea-mist. It shed a new and lurid light on Withers, it made her mistress feel that she had nourished a serpent in her bosom, to think that Withers was contemplating so odious an act of selfishness as matrimony. It would be necessary to find a new parlour-maid, and all the trouble connected with that would not nearly be compensated for by being able to buy fish at a lower rate. That was the least that Withers could do for her, to insist that Mr. Hopkins should let her have dabs and plaice exceptionally cheap. And ought she to tell Withers that she had seen Mr. Hopkins . . . no, that was impossible: she must write it, if she decided (for Withers' sake) to make this fell communication.

Miss Mapp turned and tossed on her uneasy bed, and her mind went back to the Major and the Captain and that fiasco in the fog. Of course she was perfectly at liberty (having made her promise under practical compulsion) to tell everybody in Tilling what had occurred, trusting to the chivalry of the men not to carry out their counter threat, but looking at the matter quite dispassionately, she did not think it would be wise to trust too much to chivalry. Still, even if they did carry out their unmanly menace, nobody would seriously believe that she had been drunk. But they might make a very disagreeable joke of pretending to do so, and, in a word, the prospect frightened her. Whatever Tilling did or did not believe, a residuum of ridicule would assuredly cling to her, and her reputation of having perhaps been the cause of the quarrel which, so happily did not end in a duel, would be lost for ever. Evie would squeak, quaint Irene would certainly burst into hoarse laughter when she heard the story. It was very inconvenient that honesty should be the best policy.

Her brain still violently active switched off for a moment on to the eternal problem of the portmanteau. Why, so she asked herself for the hundredth time, if the portmanteau contained the fatal apparatus of duelling, did not the combatants accompany it? And if (the only other alternative) it did not — ?

An idea so luminous flashed across her brain that she almost thought the room had leaped into light. The challenge distinctly said that Major Benjy's seconds would wait upon Captain Puffin in the course of the morning. With what object then could the former have gone down to the station to catch the early train? There could be but one object, namely to get away as quickly as possible from the dangerous vicinity of the challenged Captain. And why did Captain Puffin leave that note on his table to say that he was suddenly called away, except in order to escape from the ferocious neighbourhood of his challenger?

"The cowards!" ejaculated Miss Mapp. "They both ran away from each other! How blind I've been!"

The veil was rent. She perceived how, carried away with the notion that a duel was to be fought among the sand-dunes, Tilling had quite overlooked the significance of the early train. She felt sure that she had solved everything now, and gave herself up to a rapturous consideration of what use she would make of the precious solution. All regrets for the impossibility of ruining the character of Captain Puffin with regard to intoxicants were gone, for she had an even deadlier blacking to hand. No faintest hesitation at ruining the reputation of Major Benjy as well crossed her mind; she gloried in it, for he had not only caused her to deceive herself about the early hours on alternate nights, but by his infamous willingness to back up Captain Puffin's bargain, he had shown himself imperviously waterproof to all chivalrous impulses. For weeks now the sorry pair of them had enjoyed the spurious splendours of being men of blood and valour, when all the time they had put themselves to all sorts of inconvenience in catching early trains and packing bags by candle-light in order to escape the hot impulses of quarrel that, as she saw now, were probably derived from drained whisky-bottles. That mysterious holloaing about worm-casts was just such another disagreement. And, crowning rapture of all, her own position as cause of the projected duel was quite unassailed. Owing to her silence about drink, no one would suspect a mere drunken brawl: she would still figure as heroine, though the heroes were terribly dismantled. To be sure, it would have been better if their ardour about her had been such that one of them, at the least, had been prepared to face the ordeal, that they had not both preferred flight, but even without that she had much to be thankful for. "It will serve them both," said Miss Mapp (interrupted by a sneeze, for she had been sitting up in bed for quite a considerable time), "right."

To one of Miss Mapp's experience, the first step of her new and delightful strategic campaign was obvious, and she spent hardly any time at all in the window of her garden-room after breakfast next morning, but set out with her shopping-basket at an unusually early hour. She shuddered as she passed between the front doors of her miscreant neighbours, for the chill of last night's mist and its dreadful memories still lingered there, but her present errand warmed her soul even as the tepid November day comforted her body. No sign of life was at present evident in those bibulous abodes, no qui-his had indicated breakfast, and she put her utmost irony into the reflection that the United Services slept late after their protracted industry last night over diaries and Roman roads. By a natural revulsion, violent in proportion to the depth of her previous regard for Major Benjy, she hugged herself more closely on the prospect of exposing him than on that of exposing the other. She had had daydreams about Major Benjy and the conversion of these into nightmares annealed her softness into the semblance of some red-hot stone, giving vengeance a concentrated sweetness as of saccharine contrasted with ordinary lump sugar. This sweetness was of so powerful a quality that she momentarily forgot all about the contents of Withers's letter on the kitchen table, and tripped across to Mr. Hopkins's with an oblivious smile for him.

"Good morning, Mr. Hopkins," she said. "I wonder if you've got a nice little dab for my dinner to-day? Yes? Will you send it up then, please? What a mild morning, like May!"

The opening move, of course, was to tell Diva about the revelation that had burst on her the night before. Diva was incomparably the best disseminator of news: she walked so fast, and her telegraphic style was so brisk and lucid. Her terse tongue, her revolving feet! Such a gossip!

"Diva darling, I had to look in a moment," said Elizabeth, pecking her affectionately on both cheeks. "Such a bit of news!"

"Oh, Contessa di Faradidleony," said Diva sarcastically. "I heard yesterday. Journey put off."

Miss Mapp just managed to stifle the excitement which would have betrayed that this was news to her.

"No, dear, not that," she said. "I didn't suspect you of not knowing that. Unfortunate though, isn't it, just when we were all beginning to believe that there was a Contessa di Faradidleony! What a sweet name! For my part I shall believe in her when I see her. Poor Mr. Wyse!"

"What's the news then?" asked Diva.

"My dear, it all came upon me in a flash," said Elizabeth. "It explains the portmanteau and the early train and the duel."

Diva looked disappointed. She thought this was to be some solid piece of news, not one of Elizabeth's ideas only.

"Drive ahead," she said.

"They ran away from each other," said Elizabeth, mouthing her words as if speaking to a totally deaf person who understood lip-reading. "Never mind the cause of the duel: that's another affair. But whatever the cause," here she dropped her eyes, "the Major having sent the challenge packed his portmanteau. He ran away, dear Diva, and met Captain Puffin at the station running away too."

"But did —" began Diva.

"Yes, dear, the note on Captain Puffin's table to his house-keeper said he was called away suddenly. What called him away? Cowardice, dear! How ignoble it all is. And we've all been thinking how brave and wonderful they were. They fled from each other, and came back together and played golf. I never thought it was a game for men. The sand-dunes where they were supposed to be fighting! They might lose a ball there, but that would be the utmost. Not a life. Poor Padre! Going out there to stop a duel, and only finding a game of golf. But I understand the nature of men better now. What an eye-opener!"

Diva by this time was trundling away round the room, and longing to be off in order to tell everybody. She could find no hole in Elizabeth's arguments; it was founded as solidly as a Euclidean proposition.

"Ever occurred to you that they drink?" she asked. "Believe in Roman roads and diaries? I don't."

Miss Mapp bounded from her chair. Danger flags flapped and crimsoned in her face. What if Diva went flying round Tilling, suggesting that in addition to being cowards those two men were drunkards? They would, as soon as any hint of the further exposure reached them, conclude that she had set the idea on foot, and then —

"No, Diva darling," she said, "don't dream of imagining such a thing. So dangerous to hint anything of the sort. Cowards they may be, and indeed are, but never have I seen anything that leads me to suppose that they drink. We must give them their due, and stick to what we know; we must not launch accusations wildly about other matters, just because we know they are cowards. A coward need not be a drunkard, thank God! It is all miserable enough, as it is!"

Having averted this danger, Miss Mapp, with her radiant,

excited face, seemed to be bearing all the misery very courageously, and as Diva could no longer be restrained from starting on her morning round they plunged together into the maelstrom of the High Street, riding and whirling in its waters with the solution of the portmanteau and the early train for life-buoy. Very little shopping was done that morning, for every permutation and combination of Tilling society (with the exception, of course, of the cowards) had to be formed on the pavement with a view to the amplest possible discussion. Diva, as might have been expected, gave proof of her accustomed perfidy before long, for she certainly gave the Padre to understand that the chain of inductive reasoning was of her own welding and Elizabeth had to hurry after him to correct this grabbing impression; but the discovery in itself was so great, that small false notes like these could not spoil the glorious harmony. Even Mr. Wyse abandoned his usual neutrality with regard to social politics and left his tall malacca cane in the chemist's, so keen was his gusto, on seeing Miss Mapp on the pavement outside, to glean any fresh detail of evidence.

By eleven o'clock that morning, the two duellists were universally known as "the cowards," the Padre alone demurring, and being swampingly outvoted. He held (sticking up for his sex) that the Major had been brave enough to send a challenge (on whatever subject) to his friend, and had, though he subsequently failed to maintain that high level, shown courage of a high order, since, for all he knew, Captain Puffin might have accepted it. Miss Mapp was spokesman for the mind of Tilling on this too indulgent judgment.

"Dear Padre," she said, "you are too generous altogether. They both ran away: you can't get over that. Besides you must remember that, when the Major sent the challenge, he knew Captain Puffin, oh so well, and quite expected he would run away —"

"Then why did he run away himself?" asked the Padre.

This was rather puzzling for a moment, but Miss Mapp soon thought of the explanation.

"Oh, just to make sure," she said, and Tilling applauded her ready irony.

And then came the climax of sensationalism, when at about ten minutes past eleven the two cowards emerged into the High Street on their way to catch the 11.20 tram out to the links. The day threatened rain, and they both carried bags which contained a change of clothes. Just round the corner of the High Street was the group which had applauded Miss Mapp's quickness, and the cowards were among the breakers. They glanced at each other, seeing that Miss Mapp was the most towering of the breakers, but it was too late to retreat, and they made the usual salutations.

"Good morning," said Diva, with her voice trembling. "Off to catch the early train together — I mean the tram."

"Good morning, Captain Puffin," said Miss Mapp with extreme sweetness. "What a nice little travelling bag! Oh, and the Major's got one too! H'm!"

A certain dismay looked from Major Flint's eyes, Captain Puffin's mouth fell open, and he forgot to shut it.

"Yes; change of clothes," said the Major. "It looks a threatening morning."

"Very threatening," said Miss Mapp. "I hope you will do nothing rash or dangerous."

There was a moment's silence, and the two looked from one face to another of this fell group. They all wore fixed, inexplicable smiles.

"It will be pleasant among the sand-dunes," said the Padre, and his wife gave a loud squeak.

"Well, we shall be missing our tram," said the Major. "Au — au reservoir, ladies."

Nobody responded at all, and they hurried off down the street, their bags bumping together very inconveniently.

"Something's up, Major," said Puffin, with true Tilling perspicacity, as soon as they had got out of hearing . . .

*****

Precisely at the same moment Miss Mapp gave a little cooing laugh.

"Now I must run and do my bittie shopping, Padre," she said, and kissed her hand all round . . . The curtain had to come down for a little while on so dramatic a situation. Any discussion, just then, would be an anti-climax.

CHAPTER IX

Captain Puffin found but a sombre diarist when he came over to study his Roman roads with Major Flint that evening, and indeed he was a sombre antiquarian himself. They had pondered a good deal during the day over their strange reception in the High Street that morning and the recondite allusions to bags, sand-dunes and early trains, and the more they pondered the more probable it became that not only was something up, but, as regards the duel, everything was up. For weeks now they had been regarded by the ladies of Tilling with something approaching veneration, but there seemed singularly little veneration at the back of the comments this morning. Following so closely on the encounter with Miss Mapp last night, this irreverent attitude was probably due to some atheistical manœuvre of hers. Such, at least, was the Major's view, and when he held a view he usually stated it, did Sporting Benjy.

"We've got you to thank for this, Puffin," he said. "Upon my soul, I was ashamed of you for saying what you did to Miss Mapp last night. Utter absence of any chivalrous feeling hinting that if she said you were drunk you would say she was. She was as sober and lucid last night as she was this morning. And she was devilish lucid, to my mind, this morning."

"Pity you didn't take her part last night," said Puffin. "You thought that was a very ingenious idea of mine to make her hold her tongue."

"There are finer things in this world, sir, than ingenuity," said the Major. "What your ingenuity has led to is this public ridicule. You may not mind that yourself — you may be used to it — but a man should regard the consequences of his act on others . . . My status in Tilling is completely changed. Changed for the worse, sir."

Puffin emitted his fluty, disagreeable laugh.

"If your status in Tilling depended on a reputation for blood-thirsty bravery," he said, "the sooner it was changed the better. We're in the same boat: I don't say I like the boat, but there we are. Have a drink, and you'll feel better. Never mind your status."

"I've a good mind never to have a drink again," said the Major, pouring himself out one of his stiff little glasses, "if a drink leads to this sort of thing."

"But it didn't," said Puffin. "How it all got out, I can't say, nor for that matter can you. If it hadn't been for me last night, it would have been all over Tilling that you and I were tipsy as well. That wouldn't have improved our status that I can see."

"It was in consequence of what you said to Mapp —" began the Major.

"But, good Lord, where's the connection?" asked Puffin. "Produce the connection! Let's have a look at the connection! There ain't any connection! Duelling wasn't as much as mentioned last night."

Major Flint pondered this in gloomy, sipping silence.

"Bridge-party at Mrs. Poppit's the day after to-morrow," he said. "I don't feel as if I could face it. Suppose they all go on making allusions to duelling and early trains and that? I shan't be able to keep my mind on the cards for fear of it. More than a sensitive man ought to be asked to bear."

Puffin made a noise that sounded rather like "Fudge!"

"Your pardon?" said the Major haughtily.

"Granted by all means," said Puffin. "But I don't see what you're in such a taking about. We're no worse off than we were before we got a reputation for being such fire-eaters. Being fire-eaters is a wash-out, that's all. Pleasant while it lasted, and now we're as we were."

"But we're not," said the Major. "We're detected frauds! That's not the same as being a fraud; far from it. And who's going to rub it in, my friend? Who's been rubbing away for all she's worth? Miss Mapp, to whom, if I may say so without offence, you behaved like a cur last night."

"And another cur stood by and wagged his tail," retorted Puffin.

This was about as far as it was safe to go, and Puffin hastened to say something pleasant about the hearthrug, to which his friend had a suitable rejoinder. But after the affair last night, and the dark sayings in the High Street this morning, there was little content or cosiness about the session. Puffin's brazen optimism was but a tinkling cymbal, and the Major did not feel like tinkling at all. He but snorted and glowered, revolving in his mind how to square Miss Mapp. Allied with her, if she could but be won over, he felt he could face the rest of Tilling with indifference, for hers would be the most penetrating shafts, the most stinging pleasantries. He had more too, so he reflected, to lose than Puffin, for till the affair of the duel the other had never been credited with deeds of bloodthirsty gallantry, whereas he had enjoyed no end of a reputation in amorous and honourable affairs. Marriage no doubt would settle it satisfactorily, but this bachelor life, with plenty of golf and diaries, was not to be lightly exchanged for the unknown. Short of that . . .

A light broke, and he got to his feet, following the gleam and walking very lame out of general discomfiture.

"Tell you what it is, Puffin," he said. "You and I, particularly you, owe that estimable lady a very profound apology for what happened last night. You ought to withdraw every word you said, and I every word that I didn't say."

"Can't be done," said Puffin. "That would be giving up my hold over your lady friend. We should be known as drunkards all over the shop before you could say winkie. Worse off than before."

"Not a bit of it. If it's Miss Mapp, and I'm sure it is, who has been spreading these — these damaging rumours about our duel, it's because she's outraged and offended, quite rightly, at your conduct to her last night. Mine, too, if you like. Ample apology, sir, that's the ticket."

"Dog-ticket," said Puffin. "No thanks."

"Very objectionable expression," said Major Flint. "But you shall do as you like. And so, with your permission, shall I. I shall apologize for my share in that sorry performance, in which, thank God, I only played a minor rôle. That's my view, and if you don't like it, you may dislike it."

Puffin yawned.

"Mapp's a cat," he said. "Stroke a cat and you'll get scratched. Shy a brick at a cat, and she'll spit at you and skedaddle. You're poor company to-night, Major, with all these qualms."

"Then, sir, you can relieve yourself of my company," said the Major, "by going home."

"Just what I was about to do. Good night, old boy. Same time to-morrow for the tram, if you're not too badly mauled."

Miss Mapp, sitting by the hot-water pipes in the garden-room, looked out not long after to see what the night was like. Though it was not yet half-past ten the cowards' sitting-rooms were both dark, and she wondered what precisely that meant. There was no bridge-party anywhere that night, and apparently there were no diaries or Roman roads either. Why this sober and chastened darkness? . . .

The Major qui-hied for his breakfast at an unusually early hour next morning, for the courage of this resolve to placate, if possible, the hostility of Miss Mapp had not, like that of the challenge, oozed out during the night. He had dressed himself in his frock-coat, seen last on the occasion when the Prince of Wales proved not to have come by the 6.37, and no female breast however furious could fail to recognize the compliment of such a formality. Dressed thus, with top-hat and patent-leather boots, he was clearly observed from the garden-room to emerge into the street just when Captain Puffin's hand thrust the sponge on to the window-sill of his bath-room. Probably he too had observed this apparition, for his fingers prematurely loosed hold of the sponge, and it bounded into the street. Wild surmises flashed into Miss Mapp's active brain, the most likely of which was that Major Benjy was going to propose to Mrs. Poppit, for if he had been going up to London for some ceremonial occasion, he would be walking down the street instead of up it. And then she saw his agitated finger press the electric bell of her own door. So he was not on his way to propose to Mrs. Poppit . . .

She slid from the room and hurried across the few steps of garden to the house just in time to intercept Withers though not with any idea of saying that she was out. Then Withers, according to instructions, waited till Miss Mapp had tiptoed upstairs, and conducted the Major to the garden-room, promising that she would "tell" her mistress. This was unnecessary, as her mistress knew. The Major pressed a half-crown into her astonished hand, thinking it was a florin. He couldn't precisely account for that impulse, but general propitiation was at the bottom of it.

Miss Mapp meantime had sat down on her bed, and firmly rejected the idea that his call had anything to do with marriage. During all these years of friendliness he had not got so far as that, and, whatever the future might hold, it was not likely that he would begin now at this moment when she was so properly punishing him for his unchivalrous behaviour. But what could the frock-coat mean? (There was Captain Puffin's servant picking up the sponge. She hoped it was covered with mud.) It would be a very just continuation of his punishment to tell Withers she would not see him, but the punishment which that would entail on herself would be more than she could bear, for she would not know a moment's peace while she was ignorant of the nature of his errand. Could he be on his way to the Padre's to challenge him for that very stinging allusion to sand-dunes yesterday, and was he come to give her fair warning, so that she might stop a duel? It did not seem likely. Unable to bear the suspense any longer, she adjusted her face in the glass to an expression of frozen dignity and threw over her shoulders the cloak trimmed with blue in which, on the occasion of the Prince's visit, she had sat down in the middle of the road. That matched the Major's frock-coat.

She hummed a little song as she mounted the few steps to the garden-room, and stopped just after she had opened the door. She did not offer to shake hands.

"You wish to see me, Major Flint?" she said, in such a voice as icebergs might be supposed to use when passing each other by night in the Arctic seas.

Major Flint certainly looked as if he hated seeing her, instead of wishing it, for he backed into a corner of the room and dropped his hat.

"Good morning, Miss Mapp," he said. "Very good of you. I — I called."

He clearly had a difficulty in saying what he had come to say, but if he thought that she was proposing to give him the smallest assistance, he was in error.

"Yes, you called," said she. "Pray be seated."

He did so; she stood; he got up again.

"I called," said the Major, "I called to express my very deep regret at my share, or, rather, that I did not take a more active share — I allowed, in fact, a friend of mine to speak to you in a manner that did equal discredit —"

Miss Mapp put her head on one side, as if trying to recollect some trivial and unimportant occurrence.

"Yes?" she said. "What was that?"

"Captain Puffin," began the Major.

Then Miss Mapp remembered it all.

"I hope, Major Flint," she said, "that you will not find it necessary to mention Captain Puffin's name to me. I wish him nothing but well, but he and his are no concern of mine. I have the charity to suppose that he was quite drunk on the occasion to which I imagine you allude. Intoxication alone could excuse what he said. Let us leave Captain Puffin out of whatever you have come to say to me."

This was adroit; it compelled the Major to begin all over again.

"I come entirely on my own account," he began.

"I understand," said Miss Mapp, instantly bringing Captain Puffin in again. "Captain Puffin, now I presume sober, has no regret for what he said when drunk. I quite see, and I expected no more and no less from him. Yes. I am afraid I interrupted you."

Major Flint threw his friend overboard like ballast from a bumping balloon.

"I speak for myself," he said. "I behaved, Miss Mapp, like a — ha — worm. Defenceless lady, insolent fellow drunk — I allude to Captain P — . I'm very sorry for my part in it."

Up till this moment Miss Mapp had not made up her mind whether she intended to forgive him or not; but here she saw how crushing a penalty she might be able to inflict on Puffin if she forgave the erring and possibly truly repentant Major. He had already spoken strongly about his friend's offence, and she could render life supremely nasty for them both — particularly Puffin — if she made the Major agree that he could not, if truly sorry, hold further intercourse with him. There would be no more golf, no more diaries. Besides, if she was observed to be friendly with the Major again and to cut Captain Puffin, a very natural interpretation would be that she had learned that in the original quarrel the Major had been defending her from some odious tongue to the extent of a challenge, even though he subsequently ran away. Tilling was quite clever enough to make that inference without any suggestion from her . . . But if she forgave neither of them, they would probably go on boozing and golfing together, and saying quite dreadful things about her, and not care very much whether she forgave them or not. Her mind was made up, and she gave a wan smile.

"Oh, Major Flint," she said, "it hurt me so dreadfully that you should have stood by and heard that Man — if he is a man — say those awful things to me and not take my side. It made me feel so lonely. I had always been such good friends with you, and then you turned your back on me like that. I didn't know what I had done to deserve it. I lay awake ever so long."

This was affecting, and he violently rubbed the nap of his hat the wrong way . . . Then Miss Mapp broke into her sunniest smile.

"Oh, I'm so glad you came to say you were sorry!" she said. "Dear Major Benjy, we're quite friends again."

She dabbed her handkerchief on her eyes.

"So foolish of me!" she said. "Now sit down in my most comfortable chair and have a cigarette."

Major Flint made a peck at the hand she extended to him, and cleared his throat to indicate emotion. It really was a great relief to think that she would not make awful allusions to duels in the middle of bridge-parties.

"And since you feel as you do about Captain Puffin," she said, "of course, you won't see anything more of him. You and I are quite one, aren't we, about that? You have dissociated yourself from him completely. The fact of your being sorry does that."

It was quite clear to the Major that this condition was involved in his forgiveness, though that fact, so obvious to Miss Mapp, had not occurred to him before. Still, he had to accept it, or go unhoused again. He could explain to Puffin, under cover of night, or perhaps in deaf-and-dumb alphabet from his window . . .

"Infamous, unforgivable behaviour!" he said. "Pah!"

"So glad you feel that," said Miss Mapp, smiling till he saw the entire row of her fine teeth. "And oh, may I say one little thing more? I feel this: I feel that the dreadful shock to me of being insulted like that was quite a lovely little blessing in disguise, now that the effect has been to put an end to your intimacy with him. I never liked it, and I liked it less than ever the other night. He's not a fit friend for you. Oh, I'm so thankful!"

Major Flint saw that for the present he was irrevocably committed to this clause in the treaty of peace. He could not face seeing it torn up again, as it certainly would be, if he failed to accept it in its entirety, nor could he imagine himself leaving the room with a renewal of hostilities. He would lose his game of golf to-day as it was, for apart from the fact that he would scarcely have time to change his clothes (the idea of playing golf in a frock-coat and top-hat was inconceivable) and catch the 11.20 tram, he could not be seen in Puffin's company at all. And, indeed, in the future, unless Puffin could be induced to apologize and Miss Mapp to forgive, he saw, if he was to play golf at all with his friend, that endless deceptions and subterfuges were necessary in order to escape detection. One of them would have to set out ten minutes before the other, and walk to the tram by some unusual and circuitous route; they would have to play in a clandestine and furtive manner, parting company before they got to the club-house; disguises might be needful; there was a peck of difficulties ahead. But he would have to go into these later; at present he must be immersed in the rapture of his forgiveness.

"Most generous of you, Miss Elizabeth," he said. "As for that — well, I won't allude to him again."

Miss Mapp gave a happy little laugh, and having made a further plan, switched away from the subject of captains and insults with alacrity.

"Look!" she said. "I found these little rosebuds in flower still, though it is the end of November. Such brave little darlings, aren't they? One for your button-hole, Major Benjy? And then I must do my little shoppings or Withers will scold me — Withers is so severe with me, keeps me in such order! If you are going into the town, will you take me with you? I will put on my hat."

Requests for the present were certainly commands, and two minutes later they set forth. Luck, as usual, befriended ability, for there was Puffin at his door, itching for the Major's return (else they would miss the tram); and lo! there came stepping along Miss Mapp in her blue-trimmed cloak, and the Major attired as for marriage — top-hat, frock-coat and button-hole. She did not look at Puffin and cut him; she did not seem (with the deceptiveness of appearances) to see him at all, so eager and agreeable was her conversation with her companion. The Major, so Puffin thought, attempted to give him some sort of dazed and hunted glance; but he could not be certain even of that, so swiftly had it to be transformed into a genial interest in what Miss Mapp was saying, and Puffin stared open-mouthed after them, for they were terrible as an army with banners. Then Diva, trundling swiftly out of the fish-shop, came, as well she might, to a dead halt, observing this absolutely inexplicable phenomenon.

"Good morning, Diva darling," said Miss Mapp. "Major Benjy and I are doing our little shopping together. So kind of him, isn't it? and very naughty of me to take up his time. I told him he ought to be playing golf. Such a lovely day! Au reservoir, sweet! Oh, and there's the Padre, Major Benjy! How quickly he walks! Yes, he sees us! And there's Mrs. Poppit; everybody is enjoying the sunshine. What a beautiful fur coat, though I should think she found it very heavy and warm. Good morning, dear Susan! You shopping, too, like Major Benjy and me? How is your dear Isabel?"

Miss Mapp made the most of that morning; the magnanimity of her forgiveness earned her incredible dividends. Up and down the High Street she went, with Major Benjy in attendance, buying grocery, stationery, gloves, eau-de-Cologne, boot-laces, the "Literary Supplement" of *The Times*, dried camomile flowers, and every conceivable thing that she might possibly need in the next week, so that her shopping might be as protracted as possible. She allowed him (such was her firmness in "spoiling" him) to carry her shopping-basket, and when that was full, she decked him like a sacrificial ram with little parcels hung by loops of string. Sometimes she took him into a shop in case there might be someone there who had not seen him yet on her leash; sometimes she left him on the pavement in a prominent position, marking, all the time, just as if she had been a clinical thermometer, the feverish curiosity that was burning in Tilling's veins. Only yesterday she had spread the news of his cowardice broadcast; to-day their comradeship was of the chattiest and most genial kind. There he was, carrying her basket, and wearing frock-coat and top-hat and hung with parcels like a Christmas-tree, spending the entire morning with her instead of golfing with Puffin. Miss Mapp positively shuddered as she tried to realize what her state of mind would have been, if she had seen him thus coupled with Diva. She would have suspected (rightly in all probability) some loathsome intrigue against herself. And the cream of it was that until she chose, nobody could possibly find out what had caused this metamorphosis so paralysing to inquiring intellects, for Major Benjy would assuredly never tell anyone that there was a reconciliation, due to his apology for his rudeness, when he had stood by and permitted an intoxicated Puffin to suggest disgraceful bargains. Tilling — poor Tilling — would go crazy with suspense as to what it all meant.

Never had there been such a shopping! It was nearly lunch-time when, at her front door, Major Flint finally stripped himself of her parcels and her companionship and hobbled home, profusely perspiring, and lame from so much walking on pavements in tight patent-leather shoes. He was weary and footsore; he had had no golf, and, though forgiven, was but a wreck. She had made him ridiculous all the morning with his frock-coat and top-hat and his porterages, and if forgiveness entailed any more of these nightmare sacraments of friendliness, he felt that he would be unable to endure the fatiguing accessories of the regenerate state. He hung up his top-hat and wiped his wet and throbbing head; he kicked off his shoes and shed his frock-coat, and furiously qui-hied for a whisky and soda and lunch.

His physical restoration was accompanied by a quickening of dismay at the general prospect. What (to put it succinctly) was life worth, even when unharassed by allusions to duels, without the solace of golf, quarrels and diaries in the companionship of Puffin? He hated Puffin — no one more so — but he could not possibly get on without him, and it was entirely due to Puffin that he had spent so outrageous a morning, for Puffin, seeking to silence Miss Mapp by his intoxicated bargain, had been the prime cause of all this misery. He could not even, for fear of that all-seeing eye in Miss Mapp's garden-room, go across to the house of the unforgiven sea-captain, and by a judicious recital of his woes induce him to beg Miss Mapp's forgiveness instantly. He would have to wait till the kindly darkness fell . . . "Mere slavery!" he exclaimed with passion.

A tap at his sitting-room door interrupted the chain of these melancholy reflections, and his permission to enter was responded to by Puffin himself. The Major bounced from his seat.

"You mustn't stop here," he said in a low voice, as if afraid that he might be overheard. "Miss Mapp may have seen you come in."

Puffin laughed shrilly.

"Why, of course she did," he gaily assented. "She was at her window all right. Ancient lights, I shall call her. What's this all about now?"

"You must go back," said Major Flint agitatedly. "She must see you go back. I can't explain now. But I'll come across after dinner when it's dark. Go; don't wait."

He positively hustled the mystified Puffin out of the house, and Miss Mapp's face, which had grown sharp and pointed with doubts and suspicions when she observed him enter Major Benjy's house, dimpled, as she saw him return, into her sunniest smiles. "Dear Major Benjy," she said, "he has refused to see him," and she cut the string of the large cardboard box which had just arrived from the dyer's with the most pleasurable anticipations . . .

Well, it was certainly very magnificent, and Miss Greele was quite right, for there was not the faintest tinge to show that it had originally been kingfisher-blue. She had not quite realized how brilliant crimson-lake was in the piece; it seemed almost to cast a ruddy glow on the very ceiling, and the fact that she had caused the orange chiffon with which the neck and sleeves were trimmed to be dyed black (following the exquisite taste of Mrs. Titus Trout) only threw the splendour of the rest into more dazzling radiance. King-fisher-blue would appear quite ghostly and corpse-like in its neigh-bourhood; and painful though that would be for Diva, it would, as all her well-wishers must hope, be a lesson to her not to indulge in such garishness. She should be taught her lesson (D.V.), thought Miss Mapp, at Susan's bridge-party to-morrow evening. Captain Puffin was being taught a lesson, too, for we are never too old to learn, or, for that matter, to teach.

Though the night was dark and moonless, there was an incon-veniently brilliant gas-lamp close to the Major's door, and that strategist, carrying his round roll of diaries, much the shape of a bottle, under his coat, went about half-past nine that evening to look at the rain-gutter which had been weeping into his yard, and let himself out of the back-door round the corner. From there he went down past the fishmonger's, crossed the road, and doubled back again up Puffin's side of the street, which was not so vividly illuminated, though he took the precaution of making himself little with bent knees, and of limping. Puffin was already warming him-self over the fire and imbibing Roman roads, and was disposed to be hilarious over the Major's shopping.

"But why top-hat and frock-coat, Major?" he asked. "Another visit of the Prince of Wales, I asked myself, or the Voice that breathed o'er Eden? Have a drink — one of mine, I mean? I owe you a drink for the good laugh you gave me."

Had it not been for this generosity and the need of getting on the right side of Puffin, Major Flint would certainly have resented such clumsy levity, but this double consideration caused him to take it with unwonted good-humour. His attempt to laugh, indeed, sounded a little hollow, but that is the habit of self-directed merri-ment.

"Well, I allow it must have seemed amusing," he said. "The fact was that I thought she would appreciate my putting a little ceremony into my errand of apology, and then she whisked me off shopping before I could go and change."

"Kiss and friends again, then?" asked Puffin.

The Major grew a little stately over this.

"No such familiarity passed," he said. "But she accepted my regrets with — ha — the most gracious generosity. A fine-spirited woman, sir; you'll find the same."

"I might if I looked for it," said Puffin. "But why should I want to make it up? You've done that, and that prevents her talking about duelling and early trains. She can't mock at me because of you. You might pass me back my bottle, if you've taken your drink."

The Major reluctantly did so.

"You must please yourself, old boy," he said. "It's your business, and no one's ever said that Benjy Flint interfered in another man's affairs. But I trust you will do what good feeling indicates. I hope you value our jolly games of golf and our pleasant evenings sufficiently highly."

"Eh! how's that?" asked Puffin. "You going to cut me too?"

The Major sat down and put his large feet on the fender. "act and diplomacy, Benjy, my boy," he reminded himself.

"Ha! That's what I like," he said, "a good fire and a friend, and the rest of the world may go hang. There's no question of cutting, old man; I needn't tell you that — but we must have one of our good talks. For instance, I very unceremoniously turned you out of my house this afternoon, and I owe you an explanation of that. I'll give it you in one word: Miss Mapp saw you come in. She didn't see me come in here this evening — ha! ha! — and that's why I can sit at my ease. But if she knew —"

Puffin guessed.

"What has happened, Major, is that you've thrown me over for Miss Mapp," he observed.

"No, sir, I have not," said the Major with emphasis. "Should I be sitting here and drinking your whisky if I had? But this morning, after that lady had accepted my regret for my share in what occurred the other night, she assumed that since I condemned my own conduct unreservedly, I must equally condemn yours. It really was like a conjuring trick; the thing was done before I knew anything about it. And before I'd had time to say, 'Hold on a bit,' I was being led up and down the High Street, carrying as much merchandise as a drove of camels. God, sir, I suffered this morning; you don't seem to realize that I suffered; I couldn't stand any more mornings like that: I haven't the stamina."

"A powerful woman," said Puffin reflectively.

"You may well say that," observed Major Flint. "That is finely said. A powerful woman she is, with a powerful tongue, and able to be powerful nasty, and if she sees you and me on friendly terms again, she'll turn the full hose on to us both unless you make it up with her."

"H'm, yes. But as likely as not she'll tell me and my apologies to go hang."

"Have a try, old man," said the Major encouragingly.

Puffin looked at his whisky-bottle.

"Help yourself, Major," he said. "I think you'll have to help me out, you know. Go and interview her: see if there's a chance of my favourable reception."

"No, sir," said the Major firmly, "I will not run the risk of another morning's shopping in the High Street."

"You needn't. Watch till she comes back from her shopping to-morrow."

Major Benjy clearly did not like the prospect at all, but Puffin grew firmer and firmer in his absolute refusal to lay himself open to rebuff, and presently, they came to an agreement that the Major was to go on his ambassadorial errand next morning. That being settled, the still undecided point about the worm-cast gave rise to a good deal of heat, until, it being discovered that the window was open, and that their voices might easily carry as far as the garden-room, they made malignant rejoinders to each other in whispers. But it was impossible to go on quarrelling for long in so confidential a manner, and the disagreement was deferred to a more convenient occasion. It was late when the Major left, and after putting out the light in Puffin's hall, so that he should not be silhouetted against it, he slid into the darkness, and reached his own door by a subtle detour.

Miss Mapp had a good deal of division of her swift mind, when, next morning, she learned the nature of Major Benjy's second errand. If she, like Mr. Wyse, was to encourage Puffin to hope that she would accept his apologies, she would be obliged to remit all further punishment of him, and allow him to consort with his friend again. It was difficult to forgo the pleasure of his chastisement, but, on the other hand, it was just possible that the Major might break away, and, whether she liked it or not (and she would not), refuse permanently to give up Puffin's society. That would be awkward since she had publicly paraded her reconciliation with him. What further inclined her to clemency, was that this very evening the crimson-lake tea-gown would shed its effulgence over Mrs. Poppit's bridge-party, and Diva would never want to hear the word "kingfisher" again. That was enough to put anybody in a good temper. So the diplomatist returned to the miscreant with the glad tidings that Miss Mapp would hear his supplication with a favourable ear, and she took up a stately position in the garden-room, which she selected as audience chamber, near the bell so that she could ring for Withers if necessary.

*****

Miss Mapp's mercy was largely tempered with justice, and she proposed, in spite of the leniency which she would eventually exhibit, to give Puffin "what for," first. She had not for him, as for Major Benjy, that feminine weakness which had made it a positive luxury to forgive him: she never even thought of Puffin as Captain Dicky, far less let the pretty endearment slip off her tongue accidentally, and the luxury which she anticipated from the interview was that of administering a quantity of hard slaps. She had appointed half-past twelve as the hour for his suffering, so that he must go without his golf again.

She put down the book she was reading when he appeared, and gazed at him stonily without speech. He limped into the middle of the room. This might be forgiveness, but it did not look like it, and he wondered whether she had got him here on false pretences.

"Good morning," said he.

Miss Mapp inclined her head. Silence was gold.

"I understood from Major Flint —" began Puffin.

Speech could be gold too.

"If," said Miss Mapp, "you have come to speak about Major Flint you have wasted your time. And mine!"

(How different from Major Benjy, she thought. What a shrimp!)

The shrimp gave a slight gasp. The thing had got to be done, and the sooner he was out of range of this powerful woman the better.

"I am extremely sorry for what I said to you the other night," he said.

"I am glad you are sorry," said Miss Mapp.

"I offer you my apologies for what I said," continued Puffin.

The whip whistled.

"When you spoke to me on the occasion to which you refer," said Miss Mapp, "I saw of course at once that you were not in a condition to speak to anybody. I instantly did you that justice, for I am just to everybody. I paid no more attention to what you said than I should have paid to any tipsy vagabond in the slums. I daresay you hardly remember what you said, so that before I hear your expression of regret, I will remind you of it. You threatened, unless I promised to tell nobody in what a disgusting condition you were, to say that I was tipsy. Elizabeth Mapp tipsy! That was what you said, Captain Puffin."

Captain Puffin turned extremely red. ("Now the shrimp's being boiled," thought Miss Mapp.)

"I can't do more than apologize," said he. He did not know whether he was angrier with his ambassador or her.

"Did you say you couldn't do 'more,'" said Miss Mapp with an air of great interest. "How curious! I should have thought you couldn't have done less."

"Well, what more can I do?" asked he.

"If you think," said Miss Mapp, "that you hurt me by your conduct that night, you are vastly mistaken. And if you think you can do no more than apologize, I will teach you better. You can make an effort, Captain Puffin, to break with your deplorable habits, to try to get back a little of the self-respect, if you ever had any, which you have lost. You can cease trying, oh, so unsuccessfully, to drag Major Benjy down to your level. That's what you can do."

She let these withering observations blight him.

"I accept your apologies," she said. "I hope you will do better in the future, Captain Puffin, and I shall look anxiously for signs of improvement. We will meet with politeness and friendliness when we are brought together and I will do my best to wipe all remembrance of your tipsy impertinence from my mind. And you must do your best too. You are not young, and engrained habits are difficult to get rid of. But do not despair, Captain Puffin. And now I will ring for Withers and she will show you out."

She rang the bell, and gave a sample of her generous oblivion.

"And we meet, do we not, this evening at Mrs. Poppit's?" she said, looking not at him, but about a foot above his head. "Such pleasant evenings one always has there, I hope it will not be a wet evening, but the glass is sadly down. Oh, Withers, Captain Puffin is going. Good morning, Captain Puffin. Such a pleasure!"

Miss Mapp hummed a rollicking little tune as she observed him totter down the street.

"There!" she said, and had a glass of Burgundy for lunch as a treat.

CHAPTER X

The news that Mr. Wyse was to be of the party that evening at Mrs. Poppit's and was to dine there first, *en famille* (as he casually let slip in order to air his French), created a disagreeable impression that afternoon in Tilling. It was not usual to do anything more than "have a tray" for your evening meal, if one of these winter bridge-parties followed, and there was, to Miss Mapp's mind, a deplorable tendency to ostentation in this dinner-giving before a party. Still, if Susan was determined to be extravagant, she might have asked Miss Mapp as well, who resented this want of hospitality. She did not like, either, this hole-and-corner *en famille* work with Mr. Wyse; it indicated a pushing familiarity to which, it was hoped, Mr. Wyse's eyes were open.

There was another point: the party, it had been ascertained, would in all number ten, and if, as was certain, there would be two bridge-tables, that seemed to imply that two people would have to cut out. There were often nine at Mrs. Poppit's bridge-parties (she appeared to be unable to count), but on those occasions Isabel was generally told by her mother that she did not care for bridge, and so there was no cutting out, but only a pleasant book for Isabel. But what would be done with ten? It was idle to hope that Susan would sit out: as hostess she always considered it part of her duties to play solidly the entire evening. Still, if the cutting of cards malignantly ordained that Miss Mapp was ejected, it was only reasonable to expect that after her magnanimity to the United Services, either Major Benjy or Captain Puffin would be so obdurate in his insistence that she must play instead of him, that it would be only ladylike to yield.

She did not, therefore, allow this possibility to dim the pleasure she anticipated from the discomfiture of darling Diva, who would be certain to appear in the kingfisher-blue tea-gown, and find herself ghastly and outshone by the crimson-lake which was the colour of Mrs. Trout's second toilet, and Miss Mapp, after prolonged thought as to her most dramatic moment of entrance in the crimson-lake, determined to arrive when she might expect the rest of the guests to have already assembled. She would risk, it is true, being out of a rubber for a little, since bridge might have already begun, but play would have to stop for a minute of greetings when she came in, and she would beg everybody not to stir, and would seat herself quite, quite close to Diva, and openly admire her pretty frock, "like one I used to have . . . !"

It was, therefore, not much lacking of ten o'clock when, after she had waited a considerable time on Mrs. Poppit's threshold, Boon sulkily allowed her to enter, but gave no answer to her timid inquiry of: "Am I very late, Boon?" The drawing-room door was a little ajar, and as she took off the cloak that masked the splendour of the crimson-lake, her acute ears heard the murmur of talk going on, which indicated that bridge had not yet begun, while her acute nostrils detected the faint but certain smell of roast grouse, which showed what Susan had given Mr. Wyse for dinner, probably telling him that the birds were a present to her from the shooting-lodge where she had stayed in the summer. Then, after she had thrown herself a glance in the mirror, and put on her smile, Boon preceded her, slightly shrugging his shoulders, to the drawing-room door, which he pushed open, and grunted loudly, which was his manner of announcing a guest. Miss Mapp went tripping in, almost at a run, to indicate how vexed she was with herself for being late, and there, just in front of her, stood Diva, dressed not in kingfisher-blue at all, but in the crimson-lake of Mrs. Trout's second toilet. Perfidious Diva had had her dress dyed too . . .

Miss Mapp's courage rose to the occasion. Other people, Majors and tipsy Captains, might be cowards, but not she. Twice now (omitting the matter of the Wars of the Roses) had Diva by some cunning, which it was impossible not to suspect of a diabolical origin, clad her odious little roundabout form in splendours identical with Miss Mapp's, but now, without faltering even when she heard Evie's loud squeak, she turned to her hostess, who wore the Order of M.B.E. on her ample breast, and made her salutations in a perfectly calm voice.

"Dear Susan, don't scold me for being so late," she said, "though I know I deserve it. So sweet of you! Isabel darling and dear Evie! Oh, and Mr. Wyse! Sweet Irene! Major Benjy and Captain Puffin! Had a nice game of golf? And the Padre! . . ."

She hesitated a moment wondering, if she could, without screaming or scratching, seem aware of Diva's presence. Then she soared, lambent as flame.

"Diva darling!" she said, and bent and kissed her, even as St. Stephen in the moment of martyrdom prayed for those who stoned him. Flesh and blood could not manage more, and she turned to Mr. Wyse, remembering that Diva had told her that the Contessa Faradiddleony's arrival was postponed.

"And your dear sister has put off her journey, I understand," she said. "Such a disappointment! Shall we see her at Tilling at all, do you think?"

Mr. Wyse looked surprised.

"Dear lady," he said, "you're the second person who has said that to me. Mrs. Plaistow asked me just now —"

"Yes; it was she who told me," said Miss Mapp in case there was a mistake. "Isn't it true?"

"Certainly not. I told my housekeeper that the Contessa's maid was ill, and would follow her, but that's the only foundation I know of for this rumour. Amelia encourages me to hope that she will be here early next week."

"Oh, no doubt that's it!" said Miss Mapp in an aside so that Diva could hear. "Darling Diva's always getting hold of the most erroneous information. She must have been listening to servants' gossip. So glad she's wrong about it."

Mr. Wyse made one of his stately inclinations of the head.

"Amelia will regret very much not being here to-night," he said, "for I see all the great bridge-players are present."

"Oh, Mr. Wyse!" said she. "We shall all be humble learners compared with the Contessa, I expect."

"Not at all!" said Mr. Wyse. "But what a delightful idea of yours and Mrs. Plaistow's to dress alike in such lovely gowns. Quite like sisters."

Miss Mapp could not trust herself to speak on this subject, and showed all her teeth, not snarling but amazingly smiling. She had no occasion to reply, however, for Captain Puffin joined them, eagerly deferential.

"What a charming surprise you and Mrs. Plaistow have given us, Miss Mapp," he said, "in appearing again in the same beautiful dresses. Quite like —"

Miss Mapp could not bear to hear what she and Diva were like, and wheeled about, passionately regretting that she had forgiven Puffin. This manœuvre brought her face to face with the Major.

"Upon my word, Miss Elizabeth," he said, "you look magnificent to-night."

He saw the light of fury in her eyes, and guessed, mere man as he was, what it was about. He bent to her and spoke low.

"But, by Jove!" he said with supreme diplomacy, "somebody ought to tell our good Mrs. Plaistow that some women can wear a wonderful gown and others — ha!"

"Dear Major Benjy," said she. "Cruel of you to poor Diva."

But instantly her happiness was clouded again, for the Padre had a very ill-inspired notion.

"What ho! fair Madam Plaistow," he humorously observed to Miss Mapp. "Ah! Peccavi! I am in error. It is Mistress Mapp. But let us to the cards! Our hostess craves thy presence at yon table."

Contrary to custom Mrs. Poppit did not sit firmly down at a table, nor was Isabel told that she had an invincible objection to playing bridge. Instead she bade everybody else take their seats, and said that she and Mr. Wyse had settled at dinner that they much preferred looking on and learning to playing. With a view to enjoying this incredible treat as fully as possible, they at once seated themselves on a low sofa at the far end of the room where they could not look or learn at all, and engaged in conversation. Diva and Elizabeth, as might have been expected from the malignant influence which watched over their attire, cut in at the same table and were partners, so that they had, in spite of the deadly antagonism of identical tea-gowns, a financial interest in common, while a further bond between them was the eagerness with which they strained their ears to overhear anything that their hostess and Mr. Wyse were saying to each other.

Miss Mapp and Diva alike were perhaps busier when they were being dummy than when they were playing the cards. Over the background of each mind was spread a hatred of the other, red as their tea-gowns, and shot with black despair as to what on earth they should do now with those ill-fated pieces of pride. Miss Mapp was prepared to make a perfect chameleon of hers, if only she could get away from Diva's hue, but what if, having changed, say, to purple, Diva became purple too? She could not stand a third coincidence, and besides, she much doubted whether any gown that had once been of so pronounced a crimson-lake, could successfully attempt to appear of any other hue except perhaps black. If Diva died, she might perhaps consult Miss Greele as to whether black would be possible, but then if Diva died, there was no reason for not wearing crimson-lake for ever, since it would be an insincerity of which Miss Mapp humbly hoped she was incapable, to go into mourning for Diva just because she died.

In front of this lurid background of despair moved the figures which would have commanded all her attention, have aroused all the feelings of disgust and pity of which she was capable, had only Diva stuck to kingfisher-blue. There they sat on the sofa, talking in voices which it was impossible to overhear, and if ever a woman made up to a man, and if ever a man was taken in by shallow artifices, "they," thought Miss Mapp, "are the ones." There was no longer any question that Susan was doing her utmost to inveigle Mr. Wyse into matrimony, for no other motive, not politeness, not the charm of conversation, not the low, comfortable seat by the fire could possibly have had force enough to keep her for a whole evening from the bridge-table. That dinner *en famille*, so Miss Mapp sarcastically reflected — what if it was the first of hundreds of similar dinners *en famille*? Perhaps, when safely married, Susan would ask her to one of the family dinners, with a glassful of foam which she called champagne, and the leg of a crow which she called game from the shooting-lodge . . . There was no use in denying that Mr. Wyse seemed to be swallowing flattery and any other form of bait as fast as they were supplied him; never had he been so made up to since the day, now two years ago, when Miss Mapp herself wrote him down as uncapturable. But now, on this awful evening of crimson-lake, it seemed only prudent to face the prospect of his falling into the nets which were spread for him . . . Susan the sister-in-law of a Contessa. Susan the wife of the man whose urbanity made all Tilling polite to each other, Susan a Wyse of Whitchurch! It made Miss Mapp feel positively weary of earth . . .

Nor was this the sum of Miss Mapp's mental activities, as she sat being dummy to Diva, for, in addition to the rage, despair and disgust with which these various topics filled her, she had narrowly to watch Diva's play, in order, at the end, to point out to her with lucid firmness all the mistakes she had made, while with snorts and sniffs and muttered exclamations and jerks of the head and pullings-out of cards and puttings of them back with amazing assertions that she had not quitted them, she wrestled with the task she had set herself of getting two no-trumps. It was impossible to count the tricks that Diva made, for she had a habit of putting her elbow on them after she had raked them in, as if in fear that her adversaries would filch them when she was not looking, and Miss Mapp, distracted with other interests, forgot that no-trumps had been declared and thought it was hearts, of which Diva played several after their adversaries' hands were quite denuded of them. She often did that "to make sure."

"Three tricks," she said triumphantly at the conclusion, counting the cards in the cache below her elbow.

Miss Mapp gave a long sigh, but remembered that Mr. Wyse was present.

"You could have got two more," she said, "if you hadn't played those hearts, dear. You would have been able to trump Major Benjy's club and the Padre's diamond, and we should have gone out. Never mind, you played it beautifully otherwise."

"Can't trump when it's no trumps," said Diva, forgetting that Mr. Wyse was there. "That's nonsense. Got three tricks. Did go out. Did you think it was hearts? Wasn't."

Miss Mapp naturally could not demean herself to take any

notice of this.

"Your deal, is it, Major Benjy?" she asked. "Me to cut?"

Diva had remembered just after her sharp speech to her partner that Mr. Wyse was present, and looked towards the sofa to see if there were any indications of pained surprise on his face which might indicate that he had heard. But what she saw there — or, to be more accurate, what she failed to see there — forced her to give an exclamation which caused Miss Mapp to look round in the direction where Diva's bulging eyes were glued . . . There was no doubt whatever about it: Mrs. Poppit and Mr. Wyse were no longer there. Unless they were under the sofa they had certainly left the room together and altogether. Had she gone to put on her sable coat on this hot night? Was Mr. Wyse staggering under its weight as he fitted her into it? Miss Mapp rejected the supposition; they had gone to another room to converse more privately. This looked very black indeed, and she noted the time on the clock in order to ascertain, when they came back, how long they had been absent.

The rubber went on its wild way, relieved from the restraining influence of Mr. Wyse, and when, thirty-nine minutes afterwards, it came to its conclusion and neither the hostess nor Mr. Wyse had returned, Miss Mapp was content to let Diva muddle herself madly, adding up the score with the assistance of her fingers, and went across to the other table till she should be called back to check her partner's figures. They would be certain to need checking.

"Has Mr. Wyse gone away already, dear Isabel?" she said. "How early!"

("And four makes nine," muttered Diva, getting to her little finger.)

Isabel was dummy, and had time for conversation.

"I think he has only gone with Mamma into the conservatory," she said — "no more diamonds, partner? — to advise her about the orchids."

Now the conservatory was what Miss Mapp considered a potting-shed with a glass roof, and the orchids were one anæmic odontoglossum, and there would scarcely be room besides that for Mrs. Poppit and Mr. Wyse. The potting-shed was visible from the drawing-room window, over which curtains were drawn.

"Such a lovely night," said Miss Mapp. "And while Diva is checking the score may I have a peep at the stars, dear? So fond of the sweet stars."

She glided to the window (conscious that Diva was longing to glide too, but was preparing to quarrel with the Major's score) and took her peep at the sweet stars. The light from the hall shone full into the potting-shed, but there was nobody there. She made quite sure of that.

Diva had heard about the sweet stars, and for the first time in her life made no objection to her adversaries' total.

"You're right, Major Flint, eighteen-pence," she said. "Stupid of me: I've left my handkerchief in the pocket of my cloak. I'll pop out and get it. Back in a minute. Cut again for partners."

She trundled to the door and popped out of it before Miss Mapp had the slightest chance of intercepting her progress. This was bitter, because the dining-room opened out of the hall, and so did the book-cupboard with a window which dear Susan called her boudoir. Diva was quite capable of popping into both of these apartments. In fact, if the truants were there, it was no use bothering about the sweet stars any more, and Diva would already have won . . .

There was a sweet moon as well, and just as baffled Miss Mapp was turning away from the window, she saw that which made her positively glue her nose to the cold window-pane, and tuck the curtain in, so that her silhouette should not be visible from outside. Down the middle of the garden path came the two truants, Susan in her sables and Mr. Wyse close beside her with his coat-collar turned up. Her ample form with the small round head on the top looked like a short-funnelled locomotive engine, and he like the driver on the foot-plate. The perfidious things had said they were going to consult over the orchid. Did orchids grow on the lawn? It was news to Miss Mapp if they did.

They stopped, and Mr. Wyse quite clearly pointed to some celestial object, moon or star, and they both gazed at it. The sight of two such middle-aged people behaving like this made Miss Mapp feel quite sick, but she heroically continued a moment more at her post. Her heroism was rewarded, for immediately after the inspection of the celestial object, they turned and inspected each other. And Mr. Wyse kissed her.

Miss Mapp "scriggled" from behind the curtain into the room again.

"Aldebaran!" she said. "So lovely!"

Simultaneously Diva re-entered with her handkerchief, thwarted and disappointed, for she had certainly found nobody either in the boudoir or in the dining-room. But there was going to be a sit-down supper, and as Boon was not there, she had taken a *marron glacé*.

Miss Mapp was flushed with excitement and disgust, and almost forgot about Diva's gown.

"Found your hanky, dear?" she said. "Then shall we cut for partners again? You and me, Major Benjy. Don't scold me if I play wrong."

She managed to get a seat that commanded a full-face view of the door, for the next thing was to see how "the young couple" (as she had already labelled them in her sarcastic mind) "looked" when they returned from their amorous excursion to the orchid that grew on the lawn. They entered, most unfortunately, while she was in the middle of playing a complicated hand, and her brain was so switched off from the play by their entrance that she completely lost the thread of what she was doing, and threw away two tricks that simply required to be gathered up by her, but now lurked below Diva's elbow. What made it worse was that no trace of emotion, no heightened colour, no coy and downcast eye betrayed a hint of what had happened on the lawn. With brazen effrontery Susan informed her daughter that Mr. Wyse thought a little leaf-mould . . .

"What a liar!" thought Miss Mapp, and triumphantly put her remaining trump on to her dummy's best card. Then she prepared to make the best of it.

"We've lost three, I'm afraid, Major Benjy," she said. "Don't you think you overbid your hand just a little wee bit?"

"I don't know about that, Miss Elizabeth," said the Major. "If you hadn't let those two spades go, and hadn't trumped my best heart —"

Miss Mapp interrupted with her famous patter.

"Oh, but if I had taken the spades," she said quickly, "I should have had to lead up to Diva's clubs, and then they would have got the rough in diamonds, and I should have never been able to get back into your hand again. Then at the end if I hadn't trumped your heart, I should have had to lead the losing spade and Diva would have over-trumped; and brought in her club, and we should have gone down two more. If you follow me, I think you'll agree that I was right to do that. But all good players overbid their hands some-times, Major Benjy. Such fun!"

The supper was unusually ostentatious, but Miss Mapp saw the reason for that; it was clear that Susan wanted to impress poor Mr. Wyse with her wealth, and probably when it came to settlements, he would learn some very unpleasant news. But there were agreeable little circumstances to temper her dislike of this extravagant display, for she was hungry, and Diva, always a gross feeder, spilt some hot chocolate sauce on the crimson-lake, which, if indelible, might supply a solution to the problem of what was to be done now about her own frock. She kept an eye, too, on Captain Puffin, to see if he showed any signs of improvement in the direction she had indicated to him in her interview, and was rejoiced to see that one of these glances was clearly the cause of his refusing a second glass of port. He had already taken the stopper out of the decanter when their eyes met . . . and then he put it back again. Improvement already!

Everything else (pending the discovery as to whether chocolate on crimson-lake spelt ruin) now faded into a middle distance, while the affairs of Susan and poor Mr. Wyse occupied the entire foreground of Miss Mapp's consciousness. Mean and cunning as Susan's conduct must have been in entrapping Mr. Wyse when others had failed to gain his affection, Miss Mapp felt that it would be only prudent to continue on the most amicable of terms with her, for as future sister-in-law to a countess, and wife to the man who by the mere exercise of his presence could make Tilling sit up and behave, she would doubtless not hesitate about giving Miss Mapp some nasty ones back if retaliation demanded. It was dreadful to think that this audacious climber was so soon to belong to the Wyses of Whitchurch, but since the moonlight had revealed that such was Mr. Wyse's intention, it was best to be friends with the Mammon of the British Empire. Poppit-cum-Wyse was likely to be a very important centre of social life in Tilling, when not in Scotland or Whitchurch or Capri, and Miss Mapp wisely determined that even the announcement of the engagement should not induce her to give voice to the very proper sentiments which it could not help inspiring.

After all she had done for Susan, in letting the door of high-life in Tilling swing open for her when she could not possibly keep it shut any longer, it seemed only natural that, if she only kept on good terms with her now, Susan would insist that her dear Elizabeth must be the first to be told of the engagement. This made her pause before adopting the obvious course of setting off immediately after breakfast next morning, and telling all her friends, under promise of secrecy, just what she had seen in the moonlight last night. Thrilling to the narrator as such an announcement would be, it would be even more thrilling, provided only that Susan had sufficient sense of decency to tell her of the engagement before anybody else, to hurry off to all the others and inform them that she had known of it ever since the night of the bridge-party.

It was important, therefore, to be at home whenever there was the slightest chance of Susan coming round with her news, and Miss Mapp sat at her window the whole of that first morning, so as not to miss her, and hardly attended at all to the rest of the pageant of life that moved within the radius of her observation. Her heart beat fast when, about the middle of the morning, Mr. Wyse came round the dentist's corner, for it might be that the bashful Susan had sent him to make the announcement, but, if so, he was bashful too, for he walked by her house without pause. He looked rather worried, she thought (as well he might), and passing on he disappeared round the church corner, clearly on his way to his betrothed. He carried a square parcel in his hand, about as big as some jewel-case that might contain a tiara. Half an hour afterwards, however, he came back, still carrying the tiara. It occurred to her that the engagement might have been broken off . . . A little later, again with a quickened pulse, Miss Mapp saw the Royce lumber down from the church corner. It stopped at her house, and she caught a glimpse of sables within. This time she felt certain that Susan had come with her interesting news, and waited till Withers, having answered the door, came to inquire, no doubt, whether she would see Mrs. Poppit. But, alas, a minute later the Royce lumbered on, carrying the additional weight of the Christmas number of *Punch*, which Miss Mapp had borrowed last night and had not, of course, had time to glance at yet.

Anticipation is supposed to be pleasanter than any fulfilment, however agreeable, and if that is the case, Miss Mapp during the next day or two had more enjoyment than the announcement of fifty engagements could have given her, so constantly (when from the garden-room she heard the sound of the knocker on her front door) did she spring up in certainty that this was Susan, which it never was. But however enjoyable it all might be, she appeared to herself at least to be suffering tortures of suspense, through which by degrees an idea, painful and revolting in the extreme, yet strangely exhilarating, began to insinuate itself into her mind. There seemed a deadly probability of the correctness of the conjecture, as the week went by without further confirmation of that kiss, for, after all, who knew anything about the character and anteced-ents of Susan? As for Mr. Wyse, was he not a constant visitor to the fierce and fickle South, where, as everyone knew, morality was wholly extinct? And how, if it was all too true, should Tilling treat this hitherto unprecedented situation? It was terrible to contem-plate this moral upheaval, which might prove to be a social upheaval also. Time and again, as Miss Mapp vainly waited for news, she was within an ace of communicating her suspicions to the Padre. He ought to know, for Christmas (as was usual in December) was daily drawing nearer . . .

There came some half-way through that month a dark and

ominous afternoon, the rain falling sad and thick, and so unusual a density of cloud dwelling in the upper air that by three o'clock Miss Mapp was quite unable, until the street lamp at the corner was lit, to carry out the minor duty of keeping an eye on the houses of Captain Puffin and Major Benjy. The Royce had already lumbered by her door since lunch-time, but so dark was it that, peer as she might, it was lost in the gloom before it came to the dentist's corner, and Miss Mapp had to face the fact that she really did not know whether it had turned into the street where Susan's lover lived or had gone straight on. It was easier to imagine the worst, and she had already pictured to herself a clandestine meeting between those passionate ones, who under cover of this darkness were imperviously concealed from any observation (beneath an umbrella) from her house-roof. Nothing but a powerful searchlight could reveal what was going on in the drawing-room window of Mr. Wyse's house, and apart from the fact that she had not got a powerful searchlight, it was strongly improbable that anything of a very intimate nature was going on there . . . it was not likely that they would choose the drawing-room window. She thought of calling on Mr. Wyse and asking for the loan of a book, so that she would see whether the sables were in the hall, but even then she would not really be much further on. Even as she considered this a sea-mist began to creep through the street outside, and in a few minutes it was blotted from view. Nothing was visible, and nothing audible but the hissing of the shrouded rain.

Suddenly from close outside came the sound of a door-knocker imperiously plied, which could be no other than her own. Only a telegram or some urgent errand could bring anyone out on such a day, and unable to bear the suspense of waiting till Withers had answered it, she hurried into the house to open the door herself. Was the news of the engagement coming to her at last? Late though it was, she would welcome it even now, for it would atone, in part at any rate . . . It was Diva.

"Diva dear!" said Miss Mapp enthusiastically, for Withers was already in the hall. "How sweet of you to come round. Anything special?"

"Yes," said Diva, opening her eyes very wide, and spreading a shower of moisture as she whisked off her mackintosh. "She's come."

This could not refer to Susan . . .

"Who?" asked Miss Mapp.

"Faradiddleony," said Diva.

"No!" said Miss Mapp very loud, so much interested that she

quite forgot to resent Diva's being the first to have the news. "Let's have a comfortable cup of tea in the garden-room. Tea, Withers."

Miss Mapp lit the candles there, for, lost in meditation, she had been sitting in the dark, and with reckless hospitality poked the fire to make it blaze.

"Tell me all about it," she said. That would be a treat for Diva, who was such a gossip.

"Went to the station just now," said Diva. "Wanted a new time-table. Besides the Royce had just gone down. Mr. Wyse and Susan on the platform."

"Sables?" asked Miss Mapp parenthetically, to complete the picture.

"Swaddled. Talked to them. Train came in. Woman got out. Kissed Mr. Wyse. Shook hands with Susan. Both hands. While luggage was got out."

"Much?" asked Miss Mapp quickly.

"Hundreds. Covered with coronets and Fs. Two cabs."

Miss Mapp's mind, on a hot scent, went back to the previous telegraphic utterance.

"Both hands did you say, dear?" she asked. "Perhaps that's the Italian fashion."

"Maybe. Then what else do you think? Faradiddleony kissed Susan! Mr. Wyse and she must be engaged. I can't account for it any other way. He must have written to tell his sister. Couldn't have told her then at the station. Must have been engaged some days and we never knew. They went to look at the orchid. Remember? That was when."

It was bitter, no doubt, but the bitterness could be transmuted into an amazing sweetness.

"Then now I can speak," said Miss Mapp with a sigh of great relief. "Oh, it has been so hard keeping silence, but I felt I ought to. I knew all along, Diva dear, all, all along."

"How?" asked Diva with a fallen crest.

Miss Mapp laughed merrily.

"I looked out of the window, dear, while you went for your hanky and peeped into dining-room and boudoir, didn't you? There they were on the lawn, and they kissed each other. So I said to myself: 'Dear Susan has got him! Perseverance rewarded!'"

"H'm. Only a guess of yours. Or did Susan tell you?"

"No, dear, she said nothing. But Susan was always secretive."

"But they might not have been engaged at all," said Diva with a brightened eye. "Man doesn't always marry a woman he kisses!"

Diva had betrayed the lowness of her mind now by hazarding

that which had for days dwelt in Miss Mapp's mind as almost certain. She drew in her breath with a hissing noise as if in pain.

"Darling, what a dreadful suggestion," she said. "No such idea ever occurred to me. Secretive I thought Susan might be, but immoral, never. I must forget you ever thought that. Let's talk about something less painful. Perhaps you would like to tell me more about the Contessa."

Diva had the grace to look ashamed of herself, and to take refuge in the new topic so thoughtfully suggested.

"Couldn't see clearly," she said. "So dark. But tall and lean. Sneezed."

"That might happen to anybody, dear," said Miss Mapp, "whether tall or short. Nothing more?"

"An eyeglass," said Diva after thought.

"A single one?" asked Miss Mapp. "On a string? How strange for a woman."

That seemed positively the last atom of Diva's knowledge, and though Miss Mapp tried on the principles of psycho-analysis to disinter something she had forgotten, the catechism led to no results whatever. But Diva had evidently something else to say, for after finishing her tea she whizzed backwards and forwards from window to fireplace with little grunts and whistles, as was her habit when she was struggling with utterance. Long before it came out, Miss Mapp had, of course, guessed what it was. No wonder Diva found difficulty in speaking of a matter in which she had behaved so deplorably . . .

"About that wretched dress," she said at length. "Got it stained with chocolate first time I wore it, and neither I nor Janet can get it out."

("Hurrah," thought Miss Mapp.)

"Must have it dyed again," continued Diva. "Thought I'd better tell you. Else you might have yours dyed the same colour as mine again. Kingfisher-blue to crimson-lake. All came out of Vogue and Mrs. Trout. Rather funny, you know, but expensive. You should have seen your face, Elizabeth, when you came in to Susan's the other night."

"Should I, dearest?" said Miss Mapp, trembling violently.

"Yes. Wouldn't have gone home with you in the dark for anything. Murder."

"Diva dear," said Miss Mapp anxiously, "you've got a mind which likes to put the worst construction on everything. If Mr. Wyse kisses his intended you think things too terrible for words; if I look surprised you think I'm full of hatred and malice. Be more generous, dear. Don't put evil constructions on all you see."

"Ho!" said Diva with a world of meaning.

"I don't know what you intend to convey by ho," said Miss Mapp, "and I shan't try to guess. But be kinder, darling, and it will make you happier. Thinketh no evil, you know! Charity!"

Diva felt that the limit of what was tolerable was reached when Elizabeth lectured her on the need of charity, and she would no doubt have explained tersely and unmistakably exactly what she meant by "Ho!" had not Withers opportunely entered to clear away tea. She brought a note with her, which Miss Mapp opened. "Encourage me to hope," were the first words that met her eye: Mrs. Poppit had been encouraging him to hope again.

"To dine at Mr. Wyse's to-morrow," she said. "No doubt the announcement will be made then. He probably wrote it before he went to the station. Yes, a few friends. You going, dear?"

Diva instantly got up.

"Think I'll run home and see," she said. "By the by, Elizabeth, what about the — the tea-gown, if I go? You or I?"

"If yours is all covered with chocolate, I shouldn't think you'd like to wear it," said Miss Mapp.

"Could tuck it away," said Diva, "just for once. Put flowers. Then send it to dyer's. You won't see it again. Not crimson-lake, I mean."

Miss Mapp summoned the whole of her magnanimity. It had been put to a great strain already and was tired out, but it was capable of one more effort.

"Wear it then," she said. "It'll be a treat to you. But let me know if you're not asked. I daresay Mr. Wyse will want to keep it very small. Good-bye, dear; I'm afraid you'll get very wet going home."

CHAPTER XI

The sea-mist and the rain continued without intermission next morning, but shopping with umbrellas and mackintoshes was unusually brisk, for there was naturally a universally felt desire to catch sight of a Contessa with as little delay as possible. The foggy conditions perhaps added to the excitement, for it was not possible to see more than a few yards, and thus at any moment anybody might almost run into her. Diva's impressions, meagre though they were, had been thoroughly circulated, but the morning passed, and the ladies of Tilling went home to change their wet things and take a little ammoniated quinine as a precaution after so long and chilly an exposure, without a single one of them having caught sight of the single eyeglass. It was disappointing, but the disappointment was bearable since Mr. Wyse, so far from wanting his party to be very small, had been encouraged by Mrs. Poppit to hope that it would include all his world of Tilling with one exception. He had hopes with regard to the Major and the Captain, and the Padre and wee wifie, and Irene and Miss Mapp, and of course Isabel. But apparently he despaired of Diva.

She alone therefore was absent from this long, wet shopping, for she waited indoors, almost pen in hand, to answer in the affirmative the invitation which had at present not arrived. Owing to the thickness of the fog, her absence from the street passed unnoticed, for everybody supposed that everybody else had seen her, while she, biting her nails at home, waited and waited and waited. Then she waited. About a quarter past one she gave it up, and duly telephoned, according to promise, viâ Janet and Withers, to Miss Mapp to say that Mr. Wyse had not yet hoped. It was very unpleasant to let them know, but if she had herself rung up and been answered by Elizabeth, who usually rushed to the telephone, she felt that she would sooner have choked than have delivered this message. So Janet telephoned and Withers said she would tell her mistress. And did.

Miss Mapp was steeped in pleasant conjectures. The most likely of all was that the Contessa had seen that roundabout little busybody in the station, and taken an instant dislike to her through her single eyeglass. Or she might have seen poor Diva inquisitively inspecting the luggage with the coronets and the Fs on it, and have learned with pain that this was one of the ladies of Tilling. "Algernon," she would have said (so said Miss Mapp to herself), "who is that queer little woman? Is she going to steal some of my luggage?" And then Algernon would have told her that this was poor Diva, quite a decent sort of little body. But when it came to Algernon asking his guests for the dinner-party in honour of his betrothal and her arrival at Tilling, no doubt the Contessa would have said, "Algernon, I beg . . ." Or if Diva — poor Diva — was right in her conjectures that the notes had been written before the arrival of the train, it was evident that Algernon had torn up the one addressed to Diva, when the Contessa heard whom she was to meet the next evening . . . Or Susan might easily have insinuated that they would have two very pleasant tables of bridge after dinner without including Diva, who was so wrong and quarrelsome over the score. Any of these explanations were quite satisfactory, and since Diva would not be present, Miss Mapp would naturally don the crimson-lake. They would all see what crimson-lake looked like when it decked a suitable wearer and was not parodied on the other side of a card-table. How true, as dear Major Benjy had said, that one woman could wear what another could not . . . And if there was a woman who could not wear crimson-lake it was Diva . . . Or was Mr. Wyse really ashamed to let his sister see Diva in the crimson-lake? It would be just like him to be considerate of Diva, and not permit her to make a guy of herself before the Italian aristocracy. No doubt he would ask her to lunch some day, quite quietly. Or had . . . Miss Mapp bloomed with pretty conjectures, like some Alpine meadow when smitten into flower by the spring, and enjoyed her lunch very much indeed.

The anxiety and suspense of the morning, which, instead of being relieved, had ended in utter gloom, gave Diva a headache, and she adopted her usual strenuous methods of getting rid of it. So, instead of lying down and taking aspirin and dozing, she set out after lunch to walk it off. She sprinted and splashed along the miry roads, indifferent as to whether she stepped in puddles or not, and careless how wet she got. She bit on the bullet of her omission from the dinner-party this evening, determining not to mind one atom about it, but to look forward to a pleasant evening at home instead of going out (like this) in the wet. And never — never under any circumstances would she ask any of the guests what sort of an evening had been spent, how Mr. Wyse announced the news, and how the Faradiddleony played bridge. (She said that satirical word aloud, mouthing it to the puddles and the dripping hedge-rows.) She would not evince the slightest interest in it all; she would cover it with spadefuls of oblivion, and when next she met Mr. Wyse she would, whatever she might feel, behave exactly as usual. She plumed herself on this dignified resolution, and walked so fast that the hedge-rows became quite transparent. That was the proper thing to do; she had been grossly slighted, and, like a true lady, would be unaware of that slight; whereas poor Elizabeth, under such circumstances, would have devised a hundred petty schemes for rendering Mr. Wyse's life a burden to him. But if — if (she only said "if") she found any reason to believe that Susan was at the bottom of this, then probably she would think of something worthy not so much of a true lady but of a true woman. Without asking any questions, she might easily arrive at information which would enable her to identify Susan as the culprit, and she would then act in some way which would astonish Susan. What that way was she need not think yet, and so she devoted her entire mind to the question all the way home.

Feeling better and with her headache quite gone, she arrived in Tilling again drenched to the skin. It was already after tea-time, and she abandoned tea altogether, and prepared to console herself for her exclusion from gaiety with a "good blow-out" in the shape of regular dinner, instead of the usual muffin now and a tray later. To add dignity to her feast, she put on the crimson-lake tea-gown for the last time that it would be crimson-lake (though the same tea-gown still), since to-morrow it would be sent to the dyer's to go into perpetual mourning for its vanished glories. She had meant to send it to-day, but all this misery and anxiety had put it out of her head.

Having dressed thus, to the great astonishment of Janet, she sat down to divert her mind from trouble by Patience. As if to reward her for her stubborn fortitude, the malignity of the cards relented, and she brought out an intricate matter three times running. The clock on her mantelpiece chiming a quarter to eight, surprised her with the lateness of the hour, and recalled to her with a stab of pain that it was dinner-time at Mr. Wyse's, and at this moment some seven pairs of eager feet were approaching the door. Well, she was dining at a quarter to eight, too; Janet would enter presently to tell her that her own banquet was ready, and gathering up her cards, she spent a pleasant though regretful minute in looking at herself and the crimson-lake for the last time in her long glass. The tremendous walk in the rain had given her an almost equally high colour. Janet's foot was heard on the stairs, and she turned away from the glass. Janet entered.

"Dinner?" said Diva.

"No, ma'am, the telephone," said Janet. "Mr. Wyse is on the telephone, and wants to speak to you very particularly."

"Mr. Wyse himself?" asked Diva, hardly believing her ears, for she knew Mr. Wyse's opinion of the telephone.

"Yes, ma'am."

Diva walked slowly, but reflected rapidly. What must have happened was that somebody had been taken ill at the last moment — was it Elizabeth? — and that he now wanted her to fill the gap . . . She was torn in two. Passionately as she longed to dine at Mr. Wyse's, she did not see how such a course was compatible with dignity. He had only asked her to suit his own convenience; it was not out of encouragement to hope that he invited her now. No; Mr. Wyse should want. She would say that she had friends dining with her; that was what the true lady would do.

She took up the ear-piece and said, "Hullo!"

It was certainly Mr. Wyse's voice that spoke to her, and it seemed to tremble with anxiety.

"Dear lady," he began, "a most terrible thing has happened —"

(Wonder if Elizabeth's very ill, thought Diva.)

"Quite terrible," said Mr. Wyse. "Can you hear?"

"Yes," said Diva, hardening her heart.

"By the most calamitous mistake the note which I wrote you yesterday was never delivered. Figgis has just found it in the pocket of his overcoat. I shall certainly dismiss him unless you plead for him. Can you hear?"

"Yes," said Diva excitedly.

"In it I told you that I had been encouraged to hope that you would dine with me to-night. There was such a gratifying response to my other invitations that I most culpably and carelessly, dear lady, thought that everybody had accepted. Can you hear?"

"Of course I can!" shouted Diva.

"Well, I come on my knees to you. Can you possibly forgive the joint stupidity of Figgis and me, and honour me after all? We will put dinner off, of course. At what time, in case you are ever so kind and indulgent as to come, shall we have it? Do not break my heart by refusing. Su — Mrs. Poppit will send her car for you."

"I have already dressed for dinner," said Diva proudly. "Very pleased to come at once."

"You are too kind; you are angelic," said Mr. Wyse. "The car shall start at once; it is at my door now."

"Right," said Diva.

"Too good — too kind," murmured Mr. Wyse. "Figgis, what do I do next?"

Diva clapped the instrument into place.

"Powder," she said to herself, remembering what she had seen in the glass, and whizzed upstairs. Her fish would have to be degraded into kedgeree, though plaice would have done just as well as sole for that; the cutlets could be heated up again, and perhaps the whisking for the apple-meringue had not begun yet, and could still be stopped.

"Janet!" she shouted. "Going out to dinner! Stop the meringue."

She dashed an interesting pallor on to her face as she heard the hooting of the Royce, and coming downstairs, stepped into its warm luxuriousness, for the electric lamp was burning. There were Susan's sables there — it was thoughtful of Susan to put them in, but ostentatious — and there was a carriage rug, which she was convinced was new, and was very likely a present from Mr. Wyse. And soon there was the light streaming out from Mr. Wyse's open door, and Mr. Wyse himself in the hall to meet and greet and thank and bless her. She pleaded for the contrite Figgis, and was conducted in a blaze of triumph into the drawing-room, where all Tilling was awaiting her. She was led up to the Contessa, with whom Miss Mapp, wreathed in sycophantic smiles, was eagerly conversing.

The crimson-lakes . . .

*****

There were embarrassing moments during dinner; the Contessa confused by having so many people introduced to her in a lump, got all their names wrong, and addressed her neighbours as Captain Flint and Major Puffin, and thought that Diva was Mrs. Mapp. She seemed vivacious and good-humoured, dropped her eyeglass into her soup, talked with her mouth full, and drank a good deal of wine, which was a very bad example for Major Puffin. Then there were many sudden and complete pauses in the talk, for Diva's news of the kissing of Mrs. Poppit by the Contessa had spread like wildfire through the fog this morning, owing to Miss Mapp's dissemination of it, and now, whenever Mr. Wyse raised his voice ever so little, everybody else stopped talking, in the expectation that the news was about to be announced. Occasionally, also, the Contessa addressed some remark to her brother in shrill and voluble Italian, which rather confirmed the gloomy estimate of her table-manners in the matter of talking with her mouth full, for to speak in Italian was equivalent to whispering, since the purport of what she said could not be understood by anybody except him . . . Then also, the sensation of dining with a countess produced a slight feeling of strain, which, in addition to the correct behaviour which Mr. Wyse's presence always induced, almost congealed correctness into stiffness. But as dinner went on her evident enjoyment of herself made itself felt, and her eccentricities, though carefully observed and noted by Miss Mapp, were not succeeded by silences and hurried bursts of conversation.

"And is your ladyship making a long stay in Tilling?" asked the (real) Major, to cover the pause which had been caused by Mr. Wyse saying something across the table to Isabel.

She dropped her eyeglass with quite a splash into her gravy, pulled it out again by the string as if landing a fish and sucked it.

"That depends on you gentlemen," she said with greater audacity than was usual in Tilling. "If you and Major Puffin and that sweet little Scotch clergyman all fall in love with me, and fight duels about me, I will stop for ever . . ."

The Major recovered himself before anybody else.

"Your ladyship may take that for granted," he said gallantly, and a perfect hubbub of conversation rose to cover this awful topic.

She laid her hand on his arm.

"You must not call me ladyship, Captain Flint," she said. "Only servants say that. Contessa, if you like. And you must blow away this fog for me. I have seen nothing but bales of cotton-wool out of the window. Tell me this, too: why are those ladies dressed alike? Are they sisters? Mrs. Mapp, the little round one, and her sister, the big round one?"

The Major cast an apprehensive eye on Miss Mapp seated just opposite, whose acuteness of hearing was one of the terrors of Tilling . . . His apprehensions were perfectly well founded, and Miss Mapp hated and despised the Contessa from that hour.

"No, not sisters," said he, "and your la — you've made a little error about the names. The one opposite is Miss Mapp, the other Mrs. Plaistow."

The Contessa moderated her voice.

"I see; she looks vexed, your Miss Mapp. I think she must have heard, and I will be very nice to her afterwards. Why does not one of you gentlemen marry her? I see I shall have to arrange that. The sweet little Scotch clergyman now; little men like big wives. Ah! Married already is he to the mouse? Then it must be you, Captain Flint. We must have more marriages in Tilling."

Miss Mapp could not help glancing at the Contessa, as she made this remarkable observation. It must be the cue, she thought, for the announcement of that which she had known so long . . . In the space of a wink the clever Contessa saw that she had her attention, and spoke rather loudly to the Major.

"I have lost my heart to your Miss Mapp," she said. "I am jealous of you, Captain Flint. She will be my great friend in Tilling, and if you marry her, I shall hate you, for that will mean that she likes you best."

Miss Mapp hated nobody at that moment, not even Diva, off

whose face the hastily-applied powder was crumbling, leaving little red marks peeping out like the stars on a fine evening. Dinner came to an end with roasted chestnuts brought by the Contessa from Capri.

"I always scold Amelia for the luggage she takes with her," said Mr. Wyse to Diva. "Amelia dear, you are my hostess to-night" — everybody saw him look at Mrs. Poppit — "you must catch somebody's eye."

"I will catch Miss Mapp's," said Amelia, and all the ladies rose as if connected with some hidden mechanism which moved them simultaneously . . . There was a great deal of pretty diffidence at the door, but the Contessa put an end to that.

"Eldest first," she said, and marched out, making Miss Mapp, Diva and the mouse feel remarkably young. She might drop her eyeglass and talk with her mouth full, but really such tact . . . They all determined to adopt this pleasing device in the future. The disappointment about the announcement of the engagement was sensibly assuaged, and Miss Mapp and Susan, in their eagerness to be younger than the Contessa, and yet take precedence of all the rest, almost stuck in the doorway. They rebounded from each other, and Diva whizzed out between them. Quaint Irene went in her right place — last. However quaint Irene was, there was no use in pretending that she was not the youngest.

However hopelessly Amelia had lost her heart to Miss Mapp, she did not devote her undivided attention to her in the drawing-room, but swiftly established herself at the card-table, where she proceeded, with a most complicated sort of Patience and a series of cigarettes, to while away the time till the gentlemen joined them. Though the ladies of Tilling had plenty to say to each other, it was all about her, and such comments could not conveniently be made in her presence. Unless, like her, they talked some language unknown to the subject of their conversation, they could not talk at all, and so they gathered round her table, and watched the lightning rapidity with which she piled black knaves on red queens in some packs and red knaves on black queens in others. She had taken off all her rings in order to procure a greater freedom of finger, and her eyeglass continued to crash on to a glittering mass of magnificent gems. The rapidity of her motions was only equalled by the swift and surprising monologue that poured from her mouth.

"There, that odious king gets in my way," she said. "So like a man to poke himself in where he isn't wanted. *Bacco!* No, not that: I have a cigarette. I hear all you ladies are terrific bridge-players: we will have a game presently, and I shall sink into the earth with terror at your Camorra! *Dio!* there's another king, and that's his own queen whom he doesn't want at all. He is *amoroso* for that black queen, who is quite covered up, and he would like to be covered up with her. Susan, my dear" (that was interesting, but they all knew it already), "kindly ring the bell for coffee. I expire if I do not get my coffee at once, and a toothpick. Tell me all the scandal of Tilling, Miss Mapp, while I play — all the dreadful histories of that Major and that Captain. Such a grand air has the Captain — no, it is the Major, the one who does not limp. Which of all you ladies do they love most? It is Miss Mapp, I believe: that is why she does not answer me. Ah! here is the coffee, and the other king: three lumps of sugar, dear Susan, and then stir it up well, and hold it to my mouth, so that I can drink without interruption. Ah, the ace! He is the intervener, or is it the King's Proctor? It would be nice to have a proctor who told you all the love-affairs that were going on. Susan, you must get me a proctor: you shall be my proctor. And here are the men — the wretches, they have been preferring wine to women, and we will have our bridge, and if anybody scolds me, I shall cry, Miss Mapp, and Captain Flint will hold my hand and comfort me."

She gathered up a heap of cards and rings, dropped them on the floor, and cut with the remainder.

Miss Mapp was very lenient with the Contessa, who was her partner, and pointed out the mistakes of her and their adversaries with the most winning smile and eagerness to explain things clearly. Then she revoked heavily herself, and the Contessa, so far from being angry with her, burst into peals of unquenchable merriment. This way of taking a revoke was new to Tilling, for the right thing was for the revoker's partner to sulk and be sarcastic for at least twenty minutes after. The Contessa's laughter continued to spurt out at intervals during the rest of the rubber, and it was all very pleasant; but at the end she said she was not up to Tilling standards at all, and refused to play any more. Miss Mapp, in the highest good-humour, urged her not to despair.

"Indeed, dear Contessa," she said, "you play very well. A little overbidding of your hand, perhaps, do you think? but that is a tendency we are all subject to: I often overbid my hand myself. Not a little wee rubber more? I'm sure I should like to be your partner again. You must come and play at my house some afternoon. We will have tea early, and get a good two hours. Nothing like practice."

The evening came to an end without the great announcement being made, but Miss Mapp, as she reviewed the events of the party, sitting next morning in her observation-window, found the whole evidence so overwhelming that it was no longer worth while to form conjectures, however fruitful, on the subject, and she diverted her mind to pleasing reminiscences and projects for the future. She had certainly been distinguished by the Contessa's marked regard, and her opinion of her charm and ability was of the very highest . . . No doubt her strange remark about duelling at dinner had been humorous in intention, but many a true word is spoken in jest, and the Contessa — perspicacious woman — had seen at once that Major Benjy and Captain Puffin were just the sort of men who might get to duelling (or, at any rate, challenging) about a woman. And her asking which of the ladies the men were most in love with, and her saying that she believed it was Miss Mapp! Miss Mapp had turned nearly as red as poor Diva when that came out, so lightly and yet so acutely . . .

Diva! It had, of course, been a horrid blow to find that Diva had been asked to Mr. Wyse's party in the first instance, and an even shrewder one when Diva entered (with such unnecessary fussing and apology on the part of Mr. Wyse) in the crimson-lake. Luckily, it would be seen no more, for Diva had promised — if you could trust Diva — to send it to the dyer's; but it was a great puzzle to know why Diva had it on at all, if she was preparing to spend a solitary evening at home. By eight o'clock she ought by rights to have already had her tray, dressed in some old thing; but within three minutes of her being telephoned for she had appeared in the crimson-lake, and eaten so heartily that it was impossible to imagine, greedy though she was, that she had already consumed her tray . . . But in spite of Diva's adventitious triumph, the main feeling in Miss Mapp's mind was pity for her. She looked so ridiculous in that dress with the powder peeling off her red face. No wonder the dear Contessa stared when she came in.

There was her bridge-party for the Contessa to consider. The Contessa would be less nervous, perhaps, if there was only one table: that would be more homey and cosy, and it would at the same time give rise to great heart-burnings and indignation in the breasts of those who were left out. Diva would certainly be one of the spurned, and the Contessa would not play with Mr. Wyse . . . Then there was Major Benjy, he must certainly be asked, for it was evident that the Contessa delighted in him . . .

Suddenly Miss Mapp began to feel less sure that Major Benjy must be of the party. The Contessa, charming though she was, had said several very tropical, Italian things to him. She had told him that she would stop here for ever if the men fought duels about her. She had said "you dear darling" to him at bridge when, as adversary, he failed to trump her losing card, and she had asked him to ask her to tea ("with no one else, for I have a great deal to say to you"), when the general macédoine of sables, au reservoirs, and thanks for such a nice evening took place in the hall. Miss Mapp was not, in fact, sure, when she thought it over, that the Contessa was a nice friend for Major Benjy. She did not do him the injustice of imagining that he would ask her to tea alone; the very suggestion proved that it must be a piece of the Contessa's Southern extravagance of expression. But, after all, thought Miss Mapp to herself, as she writhed at the idea, her other extravagant expressions were proved to cover a good deal of truth. In fact, the Major's chance of being asked to the select bridge-party diminished swiftly towards vanishing point.

It was time (and indeed late) to set forth on morning marketings, and Miss Mapp had already determined not to carry her capacious basket with her to-day, in case of meeting the Contessa in the High Street. It would be grander and Wysier and more magnificent to go basket-less, and direct that the goods should be sent up, rather than run the risk of encountering the Contessa with a basket containing a couple of mutton cutlets, a ball of wool and some tooth-powder. So she put on her Prince of Wales's cloak, and, postponing further reflection over the bridge-party till a less busy occasion, set forth in unencumbered gentility for the morning gossip. At the corner of the High Street, she ran into Diva.

"News," said Diva. "Met Mr. Wyse just now. Engaged to Susan. All over the town by now. Everybody knows. Oh, there's the Padre for the first time."

She shot across the street, and Miss Mapp, shaking the dust of Diva off her feet, proceeded on her chagrined way. Annoyed as she was with Diva, she was almost more annoyed with Susan. After all she had done for Susan, Susan ought to have told her long ago, pledging her to secrecy. But to be told like this by that common Diva, without any secrecy at all, was an affront that she would find it hard to forgive Susan for. She mentally reduced by a half the sum that she had determined to squander on Susan's wedding-present. It should be plated, not silver, and if Susan was not careful, it shouldn't be plated at all.

She had just come out of the chemist's, after an indignant interview about precipitated chalk. He had deposited the small packet on the counter, when she asked to have it sent up to her house. He could not undertake to deliver small packages. She left the precipitated chalk lying there. Emerging, she heard a loud, foreign sort of scream from close at hand. There was the Contessa, all by herself, carrying a marketing basket of unusual size and newness. It contained a bloody steak and a crab.

"But where is your basket, Miss Mapp?" she exclaimed. "Algernon told me that all the great ladies of Tilling went marketing in the morning with big baskets, and that if I aspired to be *du monde*, I must have my basket, too. It is the greatest fun, and I have already written to Cecco to say I am just going marketing with my basket. Look, the steak is for Figgis, and the crab is for Algernon and me, if Figgis does not get it. But why are you not *du monde*? Are you *du demi-monde*, Miss Mapp?"

She gave a croak of laughter and tickled the crab . . .

"Will he eat the steak, do you think?" she went on. "Is he not lively? I went to the shop of Mr. Hopkins, who was not there, because he was engaged with Miss Coles. And was that not Miss Coles last night at my brother's? The one who spat in the fire when nobody but I was looking? You are enchanting at Tilling. What is Mr. Hopkins doing with Miss Coles? Do they kiss? But your market basket: that disappoints me, for Algernon said you had the biggest market-basket of all. I bought the biggest I could find: is it as big as yours?"

Miss Mapp's head was in a whirl. The Contessa said in the loudest possible voice all that everybody else only whispered; she displayed (in her basket) all that everybody else covered up with thick layers of paper. If Miss Mapp had only guessed that the Contessa would have a market-basket, she would have paraded the High Street with a leg of mutton protruding from one end and a pair of Wellington boots from the other . . . But who could have suspected that a Contessa . . .

Black thoughts succeeded. Was it possible that Mr. Wyse had been satirical about the affairs of Tilling? If so, she wished him nothing worse than to be married to Susan. But a playful face must be put, for the moment, on the situation.

"Too lovely of you, dear Contessa," she said. "May we go marketing together to-morrow, and we will measure the size of our baskets? Such fun I have, too, laughing at the dear people in Tilling. But what thrilling news this morning about our sweet Susan and your dear brother, though of course I knew it long ago."

"Indeed! how was that?" said the Contessa quite sharply.

Miss Mapp was "nettled" at her tone.

"Oh, you must allow me two eyes," she said, since it was merely tedious to explain how she had seen them from behind a curtain kissing in the garden. "Just two eyes."

"And a nose for scent," remarked the Contessa very genially.

This was certainly coarse, though probably Italian. Miss Mapp's opinion of the Contessa fluctuated violently like a barometer before a storm and indicated "Changeable."

"Dear Susan is such an intimate friend," she said.

The Contessa looked at her very fixedly for a moment, and then appeared to dismiss the matter.

"My crab, my steak," she said. "And where does your nice Captain, no, Major Flint live? I have a note to leave on him, for he has asked me to tea all alone, to see his tiger skins. He is going to be my flirt while I am in Tilling, and when I go he will break his heart, but I will have told him who can mend it again."

"Dear Major Benjy!" said Miss Mapp, at her wits' end to know how to deal with so feather-tongued a lady. "What a treat it will be to him to have you to tea. To-day, is it?"

The Contessa quite distinctly winked behind her eyeglass, which she had put up to look at Diva, who whirled by on the other side of the street.

"And if I said 'To-day,'" she remarked, "you would — what is it that that one says" — and she indicated Diva — "yes, you would pop in, and the good Major would pay no attention to me. So if I tell you I shall go to-day, you will know that is a lie, you clever Miss Mapp, and so you will go to tea with him to-morrow and find me there. *Bene!* Now where is his house?"

This was a sort of scheming that had never entered into Miss Mapp's life, and she saw with pain how shallow she had been all these years. Often and often she had, when inquisitive questions were put her, answered them without any strict subservience to truth, but never had she thought of confusing the issues like this. If she told Diva a lie, Diva probably guessed it was a lie, and acted accordingly, but she had never thought of making it practically impossible to tell whether it was a lie or not. She had no more idea when she walked back along the High Street with the Contessa swinging her basket by her side, whether that lady was going to tea with Major Benjy to-day or to-morrow or when, than she knew whether the crab was going to eat the beefsteak.

"There's his house," she said, as they paused at the dentist's corner, "and there's mine next it, with the little bow-window of my garden-room looking out on to the street. I hope to welcome you there, dear Contessa, for a tiny game of bridge and some tea one of these days very soon. What day do you think? To-morrow?"

(Then she would know if the Contessa was going to tea with Major Benjy to-morrow . . . unfortunately the Contessa appeared to know that she would know it, too.)

"My flirt!" she said. "Perhaps I may be having tea with my flirt to-morrow."

Better anything than that.

"I will ask him, too, to meet you," said Miss Mapp, feeling in some awful and helpless way that she was playing her adversary's game. "Adversary?" did she say to herself? She did. The inscrutable Contessa was "up to" that too.

"I will not amalgamate my treats," she said. "So that is his house! What a charming house! How my heart flutters as I ring the bell!"

Miss Mapp was now quite distraught. There was the possibility that the Contessa might tell Major Benjy that it was time he married, but on the other hand she was making arrangements to go to tea with him on an unknown date, and the hero of amorous adventures in India and elsewhere might lose his heart again to somebody quite different from one whom he could hope to marry. By daylight the dear Contessa was undeniably plain: that was something, but in these short days, tea would be conducted by artificial light, and by artificial light she was not so like a rabbit. What was worse was that by any light she had a liveliness which might be mistaken for wit, and a flattering manner which might be taken for sincerity. She hoped men were not so easily duped as that, and was sadly afraid that they were. Blind fools!

*****

The number of visits that Miss Mapp made about tea-time in this week before Christmas to the post-box at the corner of the High Street, with an envelope in her hand containing Mr. Hopkins's bill for fish (and a postal order enclosed), baffles computation. Naturally, she did not intend, either by day or night, to risk being found again with a blank unstamped envelope in her hand, and the one enclosing Mr. Hopkins's bill and the postal order would have passed scrutiny for correctness, anywhere. But fair and calm as was the exterior of that envelope, none could tell how agitated was the hand that carried it backwards and forwards until the edges got crumpled and the inscription clouded with much fingering. Indeed, of all the tricks that Miss Mapp had compassed for others, none was so sumptuously contrived as that in which she had now entangled herself.

For these December days were dark, and in consequence not only would the Contessa be looking her best (such as it was) at tea-time, but from Miss Mapp's window it was impossible to tell whether she had gone to tea with him on any particular afternoon, for there had been a strike at the gas-works, and the lamp at the corner, which, in happier days, would have told all, told nothing whatever. Miss Mapp must therefore trudge to the letter-box with

Mr. Hopkins's bill in her hand as she went out, and (after a feint of posting it) with it in her pocket as she came back, in order to gather from the light in the windows, from the sound of conversation that would be audible as she passed close beneath them, whether the Major was having tea there or not, and with whom. Should she hear that ringing laugh which had sounded so pleasant when she revoked, but now was so sinister, she had quite determined to go in and borrow a book or a tiger-skin — anything. The Major could scarcely fail to ask her to tea, and, once there, wild horses should not drag her away until she had outstayed the other visitor. Then, as her malady of jealousy grew more feverish, she began to perceive, as by the ray of some dreadful dawn, that lights in the Major's room and sounds of elfin laughter were not completely trustworthy as proofs that the Contessa was there. It was possible, awfully possible, that the two might be sitting in the firelight, that voices might be hushed to amorous whisperings, that pregnant smiles might be taking the place of laughter. On one such afternoon, as she came back from the letter-box with patient Mr. Hopkins's overdue bill in her pocket, a wild certainty seized her, when she saw how closely the curtains were drawn, and how still it seemed inside his room, that firelight dalliance was going on.

She rang the bell, and imagined she heard whisperings inside while it was being answered. Presently the light went up in the hall, and the Major's Mrs. Dominic opened the door.

"The Major is in, I think, isn't he, Mrs. Dominic?" said Miss Mapp, in her most insinuating tones.

"No, miss; out," said Dominic uncompromisingly. (Miss Mapp wondered if Dominic drank.)

"Dear me! How tiresome, when he told me —" said she, with playful annoyance. "Would you be very kind, Mrs. Dominic, and just see for certain that he is not in his room? He may have come in."

"No, miss, he's out," said Dominic, with the parrot-like utterance of the determined liar. "Any message?"

Miss Mapp turned away, more certain than ever that he was in and immersed in dalliance. She would have continued to be quite certain about it, had she not, glancing distractedly down the street, caught sight of him coming up with Captain Puffin.

Meantime she had twice attempted to get up a cosy little party of four (so as not to frighten the Contessa) to play bridge from tea till dinner, and on both occasions the Faradiddleony (for so she had become) was most unfortunately engaged. But the second of these disappointing replies contained the hope that they would meet at their marketings to-morrow morning, and though poor Miss Mapp was really getting very tired with these innumerable visits to the post-box, whether wet or fine, she set forth next morning with the hopes anyhow of finding out whether the Contessa had been to tea with Major Flint, or on what day she was going . . . There she was, just opposite the post office, and there — oh, shame! — was Major Benjy on his way to the tram, in light-hearted conversation with her. It was a slight consolation that Captain Puffin was there too.

Miss Mapp quickened her steps to a little tripping run.

"Dear Contessa, so sorry I am late," she said. "Such a lot of little things to do this morning. (Major Benjy! Captain Puffin!) Oh, how naughty of you to have begun your shopping without me!"

"Only been to the grocer's," said the Contessa. "Major Benjy has been so amusing that I haven't got on with my shopping at all. I have written to Cecco to say that there is no one so witty."

(Major Benjy! thought Miss Mapp bitterly, remembering how long it had taken her to arrive at that. "And witty." She had not arrived at that yet.)

"No, indeed!" said the Major. "It was the Contessa, Miss Mapp, who has been so entertaining."

"I'm sure she would be," said Miss Mapp, with an enormous smile. "And, oh, Major Benjy, you'll miss your tram unless you hurry, and get no golf at all, and then be vexed with us for keeping you. You men always blame us poor women."

"Well, upon my word, what's a game of golf compared with the pleasure of being with the ladies?" asked the Major, with a great fat bow.

"I want to catch that tram," said Puffin quite distinctly, and Miss Mapp found herself more nearly forgetting his inebriated insults than ever before.

"You poor Captain Puffin," said the Contessa, "you shall catch it. Be off, both of you, at once. I will not say another word to either of you. I will never forgive you if you miss it. But to-morrow afternoon, Major Benjy."

He turned round to bow again, and a bicycle luckily (for the rider) going very slowly, butted softly into him behind.

"Not hurt?" called the Contessa. "Good! Ah, Miss Mapp, let us get to our shopping! How well you manage those men! How right you are about them! They want their golf more than they want us, whatever they may say. They would hate us, if we kept them from their golf. So sorry not to have been able to play bridge with you yesterday, but an engagement. What a busy place Tilling is. Let me see! Where is the list of things that Figgis told me to buy? That Figgis! A roller-towel for his pantry, and some blacking for his boots, and some flannel I suppose for his fat stomach. It is all for Figgis. And there is that swift Mrs. Plaistow. She comes like a train with a red light in her face and wheels and whistlings. She talks like a telegram — Good-morning, Mrs. Plaistow."

"Enjoyed my game of bridge, Contessa," panted Diva. "Delightful game of bridge yesterday."

The Contessa seemed in rather a hurry to reply. But long before she could get a word out Miss Mapp felt she knew what had happened . . .

"So pleased," said the Contessa quickly. "And now for Figgis's towels, Miss Mapp. Ten and sixpence apiece, he says. What a price to give for a towel! But I learn housekeeping like this, and Cecco will delight in all the economies I shall make. Quick, to the draper's, lest there should be no towels left."

In spite of Figgis's list, the Contessa's shopping was soon over, and Miss Mapp having seen her as far as the corner, walked on, as if to her own house, in order to give her time to get to Mr. Wyse's, and then fled back to the High Street. The suspense was unbearable: she had to know without delay when and where Diva and the Contessa had played bridge yesterday. Never had her eye so rapidly scanned the movement of passengers in that entrancing thoroughfare in order to pick Diva out, and learn from her precisely what had happened . . . There she was, coming out of the dyer's with her basket completely filled by a bulky package, which it needed no ingenuity to identify as the late crimson-lake. She would have to be pleasant with Diva, for much as that perfidious woman might enjoy telling her where this furtive bridge-party had taken place, she might enjoy even more torturing her with uncertainty. Diva could, if put to it, give no answer whatever to a direct question, but, skilfully changing the subject, talk about something utterly different.

"The crimson-lake," said Miss Mapp, pointing to the basket. "Hope it will turn out well, dear."

There was rather a wicked light in Diva's eyes.

"Not crimson-lake," she said. "Jet-black."

"Sweet of you to have it dyed again, dear Diva," said Miss Mapp. "Not very expensive, I trust?"

"Send the bill in to you, if you like," said Diva.

Miss Mapp laughed very pleasantly.

"That would be a good joke," she said. "How nice it is that the dear Contessa takes so warmly to our Tilling ways. So amusing she was about the commissions Figgis had given her. But a wee bit satirical, do you think?"

This ought to put Diva in a good temper, for there was nothing she liked so much as a few little dabs at somebody else. (Diva was not very good-natured.)

"She is rather satirical," said Diva.

"Oh, tell me some of her amusing little speeches!" said Miss Mapp enthusiastically. "I can't always follow her, but you are so quick! A little coarse too, at times, isn't she? What she said the other night when she was playing Patience, about the queens and kings, wasn't quite — was it? And the toothpick."

"Yes. Toothpick," said Diva.

"Perhaps she has bad teeth," said Miss Mapp; "it runs in families, and Mr. Wyse's, you know — We're lucky, you and I."

Diva maintained a complete silence, and they had now come nearly as far as her door. If she would not give the information that she knew Miss Mapp longed for, she must be asked for it, with the uncertain hope that she would give it then.

"Been playing bridge lately, dear?" asked Miss Mapp.

"Quite lately," said Diva.

"I thought I heard you say something about it to the Contessa. Yesterday, was it? Whom did you play with?"

Diva paused, and, when they had come quite to her door, made up her mind.

"Contessa, Susan, Mr. Wyse, me," she said.

"But I thought she never played with Mr. Wyse," said Miss Mapp.

"Had to get a four," said Diva. "Contessa wanted her bridge. Nobody else."

She popped into her house.

There is no use in describing Miss Mapp's state of mind, except by saying that for the moment she quite forgot that the Contessa was almost certainly going to tea with Major Benjy to-morrow.

CHAPTER XII

"Peace on earth and mercy mild," sang Miss Mapp, holding her head back with her uvula clearly visible. She sat in her usual seat close below the pulpit, and the sun streaming in through a stained glass window opposite made her face of all colours, like Joseph's coat. Not knowing how it looked from outside, she pictured to herself a sort of celestial radiance coming from within, though Diva, sitting opposite, was reminded of the iridescent hues observable on cold boiled beef. But then, Miss Mapp had registered the fact that Diva's notion of singing alto was to follow the trebles at the uniform distance of a minor third below, so that matters were about square between them. She wondered between the verses if she could say something very tactful to Diva, which might before next Christmas induce her not to make that noise . . .

Major Flint came in just before the first hymn was over, and held his top-hat before his face by way of praying in secret, before he opened his hymn-book. A piece of loose holly fell down from the window ledge above him on the exact middle of his head, and the jump that he gave was, considering his baldness, quite justifiable. Captain Puffin, Miss Mapp was sorry to see, was not there at all. But he had been unwell lately with attacks of dizziness, one of which had caused him, in the last game of golf that he had played, to fall down on the eleventh green and groan. If these attacks were not due to his lack of perseverance, no right-minded person could fail to be very sorry for him.

There was a good deal more peace on earth as regards Tilling than might have been expected considering what the week immediately before Christmas had been like. A picture by Miss Coles (who had greatly dropped out of society lately, owing to her odd ways) called "Adam," which was certainly Mr. Hopkins (though no one could have guessed) had appeared for sale in the window of a dealer in pictures and curios, but had been withdrawn from public view at Miss Mapp's personal intercession and her revelation of whom, unlikely as it sounded, the picture represented. The unchivalrous dealer had told the artist the history of its withdrawal, and it had come to Miss Mapp's ears (among many other things) that quaint Irene had imitated the scene of intercession with such piercing fidelity that her servant, Lucy-Eve, had nearly died of laughing. Then there had been clandestine bridge at Mr. Wyse's house on three consecutive days, and on none of these occasions was Miss Mapp asked to continue the instruction which she had professed herself perfectly willing to give to the Contessa. The Contessa, in fact — there seemed to be no doubt about it — had declared that she would sooner not play bridge at all than play with Miss Mapp, because the effort of not laughing would put an un-warrantable strain on those muscles which prevented you from doing so . . . Then the Contessa had gone to tea quite alone with Major Benjy, and though her shrill and senseless monologue was clearly audible in the street as Miss Mapp went by to post her letter again, the Major's Dominic had stoutly denied that he was in, and the notion that the Contessa was haranguing all by herself in his drawing-room was too ridiculous to be entertained for a moment . . . And Diva's dyed dress had turned out so well that Miss Mapp gnashed her teeth at the thought that she had not had hers dyed instead. With some green chiffon round the neck, even Diva looked quite distinguished — for Diva.

Then, quite suddenly, an angel of Peace had descended on the distracted garden-room, for the Poppits, the Contessa and Mr. Wyse all went away to spend Christmas and the New Year with the Wyses of Whitchurch. It was probable that the Contessa would then continue a round of visits with all that coroneted luggage, and leave for Italy again without revisiting Tilling. She had behaved as if that was the case, for taking advantage of a fine afternoon, she had borrowed the Royce and whirled round the town on a series of calls, leaving P.P.C. cards everywhere, and saying only (so Miss Mapp gathered from Withers) "Your mistress not in? So sorry," and had driven away before Withers could get out the information that her mistress was very much in, for she had a bad cold.

But there were the P.P.C. cards, and the Wyses with their future connections were going to Whitchurch, and after a few hours of rage against all that had been going on, without revenge being now possible, and of reaction after the excitement of it, a different reaction set in. Odd and unlikely as it would have appeared a month or two earlier, when Tilling was seething with duels, it was a fact that it was possible to have too much excitement. Ever since the Contessa had arrived, she had been like an active volcano planted down among dangerously inflammable elements, and the removal of it was really a matter of relief. Miss Mapp felt that she would be dealing again with materials whose properties she knew, and since, no doubt, the strain of Susan's marriage would soon follow, it was a merciful dispensation that the removal of the volcano granted Tilling a short restorative pause. The young couple would be back before long, and with Susan's approaching elevation certainly going to her head, and making her talk in a manner wholly intolerable about the grandeur of the Wyses of Whitchurch, it was a boon to be allowed to recuperate for a little, before settling to work afresh to combat Susan's pretensions. There was no fear of being dull: for plenty of things had been going on in Tilling before the Contessa flared on the High Street, and plenty of things would continue to go on after she had taken her explosions elsewhere.

By the time that the second lesson was being read the sun had shifted from Miss Mapp's face, and enabled her to see how ghastly dear Evie looked when focussed under the blue robe of Jonah, who was climbing out of the whale. She had had her disappointments to contend with, for the Contessa had never really grasped at all who she was. Sometimes she mistook her for Irene, sometimes she did not seem to see her, but never had she appeared fully to identify her as Mr. Bartlett's wee wifey. But then, dear Evie was very insignificant even when she squeaked her loudest. Her best friends, among whom was Miss Mapp, would not deny that. She had been wilted by non-recognition; she would recover again, now that they were all left to themselves.

The sermon contained many repetitions and a quantity of split infinitives. The Padre had once openly stated that Shakespeare was good enough for him, and that Shakespeare was guilty of many split infinitives. On that occasion there had nearly been a breach between him and Mistress Mapp, for Mistress Mapp had said, "But then you are not Shakespeare, dear Padre." And he could find nothing better to reply than "Hoots!" . . . There was nothing more of interest about the sermon.

At the end of the service Miss Mapp lingered in the church looking at the lovely decorations of holly and laurel, for which she was so largely responsible, until her instinct assured her that everybody else had shaken hands and was wondering what to say next about Christmas. Then, just then, she hurried out.

They were all there, and she came like the late and honoured guest (Poor Diva).

"Diva, darling," she said. "Merry Christmas! And Evie! And the Padre. Padre dear, thank you for your sermon! And Major Benjy! Merry Christmas, Major Benjy. What a small company we are, but not the less Christmassy. No Mr. Wyse, no Susan, no Isabel. Oh, and no Captain Puffin. Not quite well again, Major Benjy? Tell me about him. Those dreadful fits of dizziness. So hard to understand."

She beautifully succeeded in detaching the Major from the rest. With the peace that had descended on Tilling, she had forgiven him for having been made a fool of by the Contessa.

"I'm anxious about my friend Puffin," he said. "Not at all up to the mark. Most depressed. I told him he had no business to be depressed. It's selfish to be depressed, I said. If we were all depressed it would be a dreary world, Miss Elizabeth. He's sent for the doctor. I was to have had a round of golf with Puffin this afternoon, but he doesn't feel up to it. It would have done him much more good than a host of doctors."

"Oh, I wish I could play golf, and not disappoint you of your round, Major Benjy," said she.

Major Benjy seemed rather to recoil from the thought. He did not profess, at any rate, any sympathetic regret.

"And we were going to have had our Christmas dinner together to-night," he said, "and spend a jolly evening afterwards."

"I'm sure quiet is the best thing for Captain Puffin with his dizziness," said Miss Mapp firmly.

A sudden audacity seized her. Here was the Major feeling lonely as regards his Christmas evening: here was she delighted that he should not spend it "jollily" with Captain Puffin . . . and there was plenty of plum-pudding.

"Come and have your dinner with me," she said. "I'm alone too."

He shook his head.

"Very kind of you, I'm sure, Miss Elizabeth," he said, "but I think I'll hold myself in readiness to go across to poor old Puffin, if he feels up to it. I feel lost without my friend Puffin."

"But you must have no jolly evening, Major Benjy," she said. "So bad for him. A little soup and a good night's rest. That's the best thing. Perhaps he would like me to go in and read to him. I will gladly. Tell him so from me. And if you find he doesn't want anybody, not even you, well, there's a slice of plum-pudding at your neighbour's, and such a warm welcome."

She stood on the steps of her house, which in summer were so crowded with sketchers, and would have kissed her hand to him had not Diva been following close behind, for even on Christmas Day poor Diva was capable of finding something ill-natured to say about the most tender and womanly action . . . and Miss Mapp let herself into her house with only a little wave of her hand . . .

Somehow the idea that Major Benjy was feeling lonely and missing the quarrelsome society of his debauched friend was not entirely unpleasing to her. It was odd that there should be anybody who missed Captain Puffin. Who would not sooner play golf all alone (if that was possible) than with him, or spend an evening alone rather than with his companionship? But if Captain Puffin had to be missed, she would certainly have chosen Major Benjy to be the person who missed him. Without wishing Captain Puffin any unpleasant experience, she would have borne with equanimity the news of his settled melancholia, or his permanent dizziness, for Major Benjy with his bright robustness was not the sort of man to prove a willing comrade to a chronically dizzy or melancholic friend. Nor would it be right that he should be so. Men in the prime of life were not meant for that. Nor were they meant to be the victims of designing women, even though Wyses of Whitchurch . . . He was saved from that by their most opportune departure.

In spite of her readiness to be interrupted at any moment, Miss Mapp spent a solitary evening. She had pulled a cracker with Withers, and severely jarred a tooth over a threepenny-piece in the plum-pudding, but there had been no other events. Once or twice, in order to see what the night was like, she had gone to the window of the garden-room, and been aware that there was a light in Major Benjy's house, but when half-past ten struck, she had despaired of company and gone to bed. A little carol-singing in the streets gave her a Christmas feeling, and she hoped that the singers got a nice supper somewhere.

Miss Mapp did not feel as genial as usual when she came down to breakfast next day, and omitted to say good-morning to her rainbow of piggies. She had run short of wool for her knitting, and Boxing Day appeared to her a very ill-advised institution. You would have imagined, thought Miss Mapp, as she began cracking her egg, that the tradespeople had had enough relaxation on Christmas Day, especially when, as on this occasion, it was immediately preceded by Sunday, and would have been all the better for getting to work again. She never relaxed her efforts for a single day in the year, and why —

An overpowering knocking on her front-door caused her to stop cracking her egg. That imperious summons was succeeded by but a moment of silence, and then it began again. She heard the hurried step of Withers across the hall, and almost before she could have been supposed to reach the front door, Diva burst into the room.

"Dead!" she said. "In his soup. Captain Puffin. Can't wait!"

She whirled out again and the front door banged.

Miss Mapp ate her egg in three mouthfuls, had no marmalade at all, and putting on the Prince of Wales's cloak tripped down into the High Street. Though all shops were shut, Evie was there with her market-basket, eagerly listening to what Mrs. Brace, the doctor's wife, was communicating. Though Mrs. Brace was not, strictly speaking, "in society," Miss Mapp waived all social distinctions, and pressed her hand with a mournful smile.

"Is it all too terribly true?" she asked.

Mrs. Brace did not take the smallest notice of her, and, dropping her voice, spoke to Evie in tones so low that Miss Mapp could not catch a single syllable except the word soup, which seemed to imply that Diva had got hold of some correct news at last. Evie gave a shrill little scream at the concluding words, whatever they were, as Mrs. Brace hurried away.

Miss Mapp firmly cornered Evie, and heard what had happened. Captain Puffin had gone up to bed last night, not feeling well, without having any dinner. But he had told Mrs. Gashly to make him some soup, and he would not want anything else. His parlour-maid had brought it to him, and had soon afterwards opened the door to Major Flint, who, learning that his friend had gone to bed, went away. She called her master in the morning, and found him sitting, still dressed, with his face in the soup which he had poured out into a deep soup-plate. This was very odd, and she had called Mrs. Gashly. They settled that he was dead, and rang up the doctor, who agreed with them. It was clear that Captain Puffin had had a stroke of some sort, and had fallen forward into the soup which he had just poured out . . .

"But he didn't die of his stroke," said Evie in a strangled whisper. "He was drowned."

"Drowned, dear?" said Miss Mapp.

"Yes. Lungs were full of ox-tail, oh, dear me! A stroke first, and he fell forward with his face in his soup-plate and got his nose and mouth quite covered with the soup. He was drowned. All on dry land and in his bedroom. Too terrible. What dangers we are all in!"

She gave a loud squeak and escaped, to tell her husband.

*****

Diva had finished calling on everybody, and approached rapidly.

"He must have died of a stroke," said Diva. "Very much depressed lately. That precedes a stroke."

"Oh, then, haven't you heard, dear?" said Miss Mapp. "It is all too terrible! On Christmas Day, too!"

"Suicide?" asked Diva. "Oh, how shocking!"

"No, dear. It was like this . . ."

*****

Miss Mapp got back to her house long before she usually left it. Her cook came up with the proposed bill of fare for the day.

"That will do for lunch," said Miss Mapp. "But not soup in the evening. A little fish from what was left over yesterday, and some toasted cheese. That will be plenty. Just a tray."

Miss Mapp went to the garden-room and sat at her window.

"All so sudden," she said to herself.

She sighed.

"I daresay there may have been much that was good in Captain Puffin," she thought, "that we knew nothing about."

She wore a wintry smile.

"Major Benjy will feel very lonely," she said.

EPILOGUE

Miss Mapp went to the garden-room and sat at her window . . .

It was a warm, bright day of February, and a butterfly was enjoying itself in the pale sunshine on the other window, and perhaps (so Miss Mapp sympathetically interpreted its feelings) was rather annoyed that it could not fly away through the pane. It was not a white butterfly, but a tortoise-shell, very pretty, and in order to let it enjoy itself more, she opened the window and it fluttered out into the garden. Before it had flown many yards, a starling ate most of it up, so the starling enjoyed itself too.

Miss Mapp fully shared in the pleasure first of the tortoise-shell and then of the starling, for she was enjoying herself very much too, though her left wrist was terribly stiff. But Major Benjy was so cruel: he insisted on her learning that turn of the wrist which was so important in golf.

"Upon my word, you've got it now, Miss Elizabeth," he had said to her yesterday, and then made her do it all over again fifty times more. ("Such a bully!") Sometimes she struck the ground, sometimes she struck the ball, sometimes she struck the air. But he had been very much pleased with her. And she was very much pleased with him. She forgot about the butterfly and remembered the starling.

It was idle to deny that the last six weeks had been a terrific strain, and the strain on her left wrist was nothing to them. The worst tension of all, perhaps, was when Diva had bounced in with the news that the Contessa was coming back. That was so like Diva: the only foundation for the report proved to be that Figgis had said to her Janet that Mr. Wyse was coming back, and either Janet had misunderstood Figgis, or Diva (far more probably) had misunderstood Janet, and Miss Mapp only hoped that Diva had not done so on purpose, though it looked like it. Stupid as poor Diva undoubtedly was, it was hard for Charity itself to believe that she had thought that Janet really said that. But when this report proved to be totally unfounded, Miss Mapp rose to the occasion, and said that Diva had spoken out of stupidity and not out of malice towards her . . .

Then in due course Mr. Wyse had come back and the two Poppits had come back, and only three days ago one Poppit had become a Wyse, and they had all three gone for a motor-tour on the Continent in the Royce. Very likely they would go as far south as Capri, and Susan would stay with her new grand Italian connections. What she would be like when she got back Miss Mapp forbore to conjecture, since it was no use anticipating trouble; but Susan had been so grandiose about the Wyses, multiplying their incomes and their acreage by fifteen or twenty, so Miss Mapp conjectured, and talking so much about county families, that the liveliest imagination failed to picture what she would make of the Faragliones. She already alluded to the Count as "My brother-in-law Cecco Faraglione," but had luckily heard Diva say "Faradiddleony" in a loud aside, which had made her a little more reticent. Susan had taken the insignia of the Member of the British Empire with her, as she at once conceived the idea of being presented to the Queen of Italy by Amelia, and going to a court ball, and Isabel had taken her manuscript book of Malaprops and Spoonerisms. If she put down all the Italian malaprops that Mrs. Wyse would commit, it was likely that she would bring back two volumes instead of one.

Though all these grandeurs were so rightly irritating, the departure of the "young couple" and Isabel had left Tilling, already shocked and shattered by the death of Captain Puffin, rather flat and purposeless. Miss Mapp alone refused to be flat, and had never been so full of purpose. She felt that it would be unpardonably selfish of her if she regarded for a moment her own loss, when there was one in Tilling who suffered so much more keenly, and she set herself with admirable singleness of purpose to restore Major Benjy's zest in life, and fill the gap. She wanted no assistance from others in this: Diva, for instance, with her jerky ways would be only too apt to jar on him, and her black dress might remind him of his loss if Miss Mapp had asked her to go shares in the task of making the Major's evenings less lonely. Also the weather, during the whole of January, was particularly inclement, and it would have been too much to expect of Diva to come all the way up the hill in the wet, while it was but a step from the Major's door to her own. So there was little or nothing in the way of winter-bridge as far as Miss Mapp and the Major were concerned. Piquet with a single sympathetic companion who did not mind being rubiconned at threepence a hundred was as much as he was up to at present.

With the end of the month a balmy foretaste of spring (such as had encouraged the tortoise-shell butterfly to hope) set in, and the Major used to drop in after breakfast and stroll round the garden with her, smoking his pipe. Miss Mapp's sweet snowdrops had begun to appear, and green spikes of crocuses pricked the black earth, and the sparrows were having such fun in the creepers. Then one day the Major, who was going out to catch the 11.20 tram, had a "golf-stick," as Miss Mapp so foolishly called it, with him, and a golf-ball, and after making a dreadful hole in her lawn, she had hit the ball so hard that it rebounded from the brick-wall, which was quite a long way off, and came back to her very feet, as if asking to be hit again by the golf-stick — no, golf-club. She learned to keep her wonderfully observant eye on the ball and bought one of her own. The Major lent her a mashie — and before anyone would have thought it possible, she had learned to propel her ball right over the bed where the snowdrops grew, without beheading any of them in its passage. It was the turn of the wrist that did that, and Withers cleaned the dear little mashie afterwards, and put it safely in the corner of the garden-room.

To-day was to be epoch-making. They were to go out to the real links by the 11.20 tram (consecrated by so many memories), and he was to call for her at eleven. He had qui-hied for porridge fully an hour ago.

After letting out the tortoise-shell butterfly from the window looking into the garden, she moved across to the post of observation on the street, and arranged snowdrops in a little glass vase. There were a few over when that was full, and she saw that a reel of cotton was close at hand, in case she had an idea of what to do with the remainder. Eleven o'clock chimed from the church, and on the stroke she saw him coming up the few yards of street that separated his door from hers. So punctual! So manly!

Diva was careering about the High Street as they walked along it, and Miss Mapp kissed her hand to her.

"Off to play golf, darling," she said. "Is that not grand? Au reservoir."

Diva had not missed seeing the snowdrops in the Major's button-hole, and stood stupefied for a moment at this news. Then she caught sight of Evie, and shot across the street to communicate her suspicions. Quaint Irene joined then and the Padre.

"Snowdrops, i'fegs!" said he . . .

THE END

CPSIA information can be obtained at www.ICGtesting.com
Printed in the USA
BVOW010053170212

283160BV00001B/18/P